D0842806

THE DEAD GIRLS OF HYSTERIA HALL

Also by
KATIE ALENDER

Bad Girls Don't Die
From Bad to Cursed
As Dead as It Gets
Marie Antoinette, Serial Killer
Famous Last Words

THE
DEAD GIRLS
OF
HYSTERIA HALL

KATIE ALENDER

Point

For Eve, a true friend

Copyright © 2015 by Katie Alender

All rights reserved. Published by Point, an imprint of Scholastic Inc., *Publishers since 1920.* SCHOLASTIC, POINT, and associated logos are trademarks and/or registered trademarks of Scholastic Inc.

The publisher does not have any control over and does not assume any responsibility for author or third-party websites or their content.

No part of this publication may be reproduced, stored in a retrieval system, or transmitted in any form or by any means, electronic, mechanical, photocopying, recording, or otherwise, without written permission of the publisher. For information regarding permission, write to Scholastic Inc., Attention: Permissions Department, 557 Broadway, New York, NY 10012.

This book is a work of fiction. Names, characters, places, and incidents are either the product of the author's imagination or are used fictitiously, and any resemblance to actual persons, living or dead, business establishments, events, or locales is entirely coincidental.

Library of Congress Cataloging-in-Publication Data

Alender, Katie, author.
The dead girls of Hysteria Hall / Katie Alender.—First edition.
pages cm
Summary: Sixteen-year-old Cordelia and her family move into the house they just inherited in Pennsylvania, a former insane asylum the locals call Hysteria Hall—unfortunately the house does not want defiant girls like Delia, so it kills her, and as she wanders the house, meeting the other ghosts and learning the dark secrets of the Hall, she realizes that she has to find a way to save her sister, parents, and perhaps herself.
ISBN 978-0-545-63999-6 (jacketed hardcover) 1. Asylums—Juvenile fiction. 2. Haunted houses—Juvenile fiction. 3. Secrecy—Juvenile fiction. 4. Sisters—Juvenile fiction. 5. Families—Pennsylvania—Juvenile fiction. 6. Horror tales. 7. Ghost stories. [1. Haunted houses—Fiction. 2. Psychiatric hospitals—Fiction. 3. Ghosts—Fiction. 4. Secrets—Fiction. 5. Sisters—Fiction. 6. Family life—Fiction. 7. Horror stories.] I. Title.
PZ7.A3747De 2015
813.6—dc23
[Fic]
2014046681

10 9 8 7 6 5 4 3 2 1   15 16 17 18 19

Printed in the U.S.A.   23
First edition, September 2015
Book design by Yaffa Jaskoll

PART ONE

(Before the Fact)

OBSERVATIONS MADE AFTER THE FACT

Every fairy tale starts the same: *Once upon a time.*

Maybe that's why we love them so much. We all get to be part of that story. Just by existing, you get your once upon a time. It's part of the deal.

What's not part of the deal, it turns out, is the happily ever after.

CHAPTER 1

You know that feeling when someone's eyes are on you—watching you, studying your movement, your breathing? And how it gives you this whole new awareness of how much effort it takes to just stand there like a normal person?

Well, that's basically how I'd felt for the past three months. Like I was being watched. Stalked . . .

By my own parents.

Even at a gas station in the middle of nowhere, Pennsylvania, Mom hovered about three feet away from me, her eyes constantly darting in my direction, as if at any second I might decide to run for the hills. But every time I glanced up, she whipped her gaze to something else—a can of Spam, a magazine about crocheting, a package of tropical-fruit-flavored candies.

It was almost like a game. Could I catch her? *Tag! I got you! You're it!* I never caught her. But I still knew she was looking.

A sinking, suffocating feeling came over my chest.

They were never going to trust me again.

I hunched over my phone and typed *SAVE ME*, then held my breath as the "sending" bar made an agonizing crawl across the top of the screen. Finally, the text went through, and a few seconds later, my best friend Nic's reply popped up: <:(

A clown-hat sad face. The saddest kind of sad face there is.

EXACTLY, I replied, but this time the message failed. I felt a shock of anxiety. I was *intellectually* prepared to be entering a cellular dead zone, but I hadn't prepared myself emotionally to be cut off from society for two whole months.

Mom leaned toward me, holding up a can of bean dip. "Does that say partially hydrogenated corn oil?" she asked. "I left my reading glasses in the car."

"Mom," I said. "You're a million miles from Whole Foods. Everything here is made of toxic waste. Get used to it. Embrace it."

She suppressed a shudder, then reluctantly tucked the bean dip into the crook of her elbow.

"You wanted to do this," I said, an edge of accusation in my voice. I wasn't going to let her class herself in my category—in the *victim* column.

Unintentionally, her eyes flicked over to my father in the next aisle. "I guess just get whatever you want," she said. "We're not going to make it to the grocery store tonight."

I gave her an aloof shrug and went to troll the aisles, where I passed my little sister, Janie, jittering around with a month's supply of sugary cereals in her arms. Perfect. Just what she needed, more unnecessary energy. In a family of academics, Janie stood alone. My parents were professors, and I hoped to major in some Romance language (I just hadn't decided which one yet) and become a scholar of obscure European literature.

Janie's dream? To someday have her own reality show.

Even her looks set her apart—willowy, with white-blond hair and crystal-blue eyes, where the rest of us were average height, with dirty-blond hair and eyes ranging from gray-blue (Mom) to blue-gray (Dad), with me in between, sporting a color you could probably call "dishwater," if dishwater had a few redeeming qualities.

Janie was a performer. She was the prettiest, wittiest, most sparkling complete twerp of a human being you ever wanted to backhand on a daily basis. And with all that sugar to fuel her, she'd be insufferable. But what else was new?

Continuing through the aisles, I came across my father, studying a can of chicken. He shook his head. "How can they legally call this food?"

"Spare me," I said, grabbing a bag of Doritos and a jar of bright-orange queso dip.

My parents were welcome to pretend this was some grand family adventure, but I knew better. We *all* knew better. I was the only one of us willing to admit it.

Mom, Janie, and I converged on the register, Mom's cheeks flushing pink as the clerk, whose name tag read TOM, surveyed our purchases.

"We just drove up from Atlanta," she said. "That's why we have all this junk."

The clerk looked up at her, blank incomprehension on his face.

"Mom, Tom doesn't care," I said. "As long as you don't try to steal anything."

He grunted gratefully in my direction.

For some reason, my mother assumes strangers are interested in our lives. Maybe because her students spend all their free time kissing up to her and pretending to care about insignificant details of her existence. Mom never met a situation she couldn't kablooey into an awkward overshare.

"We're actually going to be staying the whole summer near here," she went on. "In Rotburg."

Tom looked up—not at Mom, but at me. "Rotburg, huh? You got family there?"

"Kind of," my mother said. "My husband's great-aunt recently passed away, and we're going to her house."

"Cordelia Piven," I put in. "I was named after her."

Abruptly, Tom stopped messing with the cash drawer. "Her *house*?"

"Yeah," Janie said, picking a Ring Pop out of a box on the counter and adding it to the pile. "She died and left it to *Delia*. It's so unfair. She didn't leave me anything."

Tom seemed to know that I was Delia, and he set his gaze squarely on me. "You been up there before?"

"To the house?" Mom answered. "No."

"We couldn't even see it online," I said. "The satellite image was all cloudy."

Pretty frustrating, actually. To inherit a house from one's old great-great-aunt and not even be able to see what it looked like. The picture in my head had come to resemble a little cottage full of overstuffed floral chairs and ceramic cats (or possibly actual cats).

I'd never met Aunt Cordelia in person, but still, her death

had made me a little sad. Back when I was in the sixth grade, she and I had exchanged a series of pen-pal letters for one of my school assignments. We'd long since fallen out of touch, but our brief correspondence had given me a sense of connection with her.

When Mom and Dad had shared the news that she'd passed away and left me everything she owned, I had gone back and looked over her letters. She seemed like a nice old lady, always overflowing with excitement about the tidbits of my life I'd sent her (of course, that could have been nice-old-lady manners). But there was nothing that indicated she felt some deep bond— certainly nothing to suggest that she might someday blow right by my dad's possible claim to his family's property and bestow the entire cat-and-crocheted-blanket-filled house on me, a sixteen-year-old.

I suggested we all go to the funeral, but Mom and Dad said there wasn't going to be one. Which was pretty sad in itself, I guess.

"Oh," Tom said now. "There's plenty to see. Where are you all staying?"

Mom and I exchanged a glance. "At the house," she said.

Tom's jaw dropped. "You're staying at Hysteria Hall?"

"Where?" I asked.

Just then, Dad plopped his bags of cashews and roasted almonds on the counter.

"Did you say *Hysteria Hall?*" Mom asked.

"I don't mean any disrespect," Tom said. "But that's what folks call it, on account of the . . . ah . . . the women."

"The women? Brad, have you heard this?" Mom asked.

I sensed a change in my father's energy—a sudden rigidity in his posture. "We should get back on the road, Lisa," he said. Dad, for his part, had a way of making authoritative pronouncements as if we were all his royal subjects. Probably from being treated like a minor god-figure by his eager-beaver students. (Sadly, when your parents are professors, college loses a lot of its mystique.)

"But what does it mean?" Mom stared at the counter, as if the answer might lie in the Pick Six lotto tickets displayed under the glass.

"Well, people kind of forgot about the place for a long time," Tom said, sounding apologetic. "But now they're all talking about it again because of how she died."

"And what does *that* mean?" my mother asked Tom. "How did she die?"

"It's starting to get dark," Dad announced. "There's supposed to be a storm this evening."

"Wouldn't you like to know, Brad?" Mom turned to him. "I just assumed she passed away peacefully in bed or something. The lawyers never said anything, come to think about it."

"I'd definitely like to know," I said.

When I spoke, my parents realized that Janie and I were listening to every word of the conversation.

Dad glanced from my little sister to me and then handed his credit card over the counter. Tom swiped it and passed it back.

"They *did*, actually," Dad said to Mom, a tight smile on his lips. "And we can talk about it later." He grabbed all the bags and started for the door.

"Have a nice day," Tom called as the door closed behind us.

As we settled back into the car, I sent what I figured might be my last text to Nic in a long time:

HEADING INTO ROTBURG. PARENTS ACTING WEIRD AS USUAL. JANIE WON'T STOP SINGING BOY BAND SONGS.

I watched it send, and then I added one final message:

JUST KILL ME NOW.

OBSERVATIONS MADE AFTER THE FACT

Things weren't always bad with my parents. For a lot of my life, we actually got along great. I was a huge nerd, they were huge nerds . . . I was the daughter they could relate to, whereas Janie was this beautiful blond creature who moved among us like a Barbie doll among Star Trek figurines.

We used to talk. And laugh. And just . . . be people, without all the tension that comes from not understanding, not trusting, not bothering to try to know who someone really is.

If I could go back, I know I'd do things differently, but I don't even know exactly what that means. I'd still get annoyed by my parents' overbearing watchfulness. I'd still find Janie about the most irritating person on the planet. Maybe we'd have a couple of idyllic days, but before long, I'm sure we'd be back to our old ways.

But maybe all that doesn't even matter—the day-to-day stuff. The important thing is that you know, at your core, that you love someone and are loved.

Not getting along perfectly isn't a huge flaw.

It's just . . . life.

But maybe I'm getting ahead of myself.

CHAPTER 2

It was the longest driveway I'd ever been on—practically a road all by itself.

And it's mine, I marveled, watching the trees go by in a blur.

All of it—the ten-foot brick wall, the rusted metal entry gate, the untended brush and the unending ribbon of bumpy, decaying asphalt. My head spun at the thought of actually owning something so real, so significant. My own house. What would it look like? Would it be cute and well kept, or falling apart, in disrepair? Seeing as we planned to spend the whole summer getting it ready to sell, my hopes were pretty realistically in the "glass half-empty" range.

We rounded a corner and the structure came into view.

Janie was the first one to speak. "Delia gets *that*?!" she spat, her long-simmering jealousy boiling over. "Are you kidding me? That's not a house! It's a hotel or something!"

Our parents didn't answer. They were staring (we all were) at an immense gray building that resembled a giant stone monster that had perched on a hill to rest.

It was easily a hundred feet wide and three stories tall—four, if you counted the space under the roof gables, which must have been an attic. Wings extended off each side, and each floor was lined with a dozen windows. The entrance was an imposing pair of double doors under a stone overhang.

It was so big that I had to duck down in my seat to see all the way to the faded gray roof tiles that blurred into the misty late afternoon sky.

"Nice house, *Deedee*," Janie said darkly, using what had been her nickname for me when she was little, and which she now used to drive me to the brink of sisterly homicide. "It's probably haunted."

"Your face is haunted," I said.

My sister let out a warning squeal, but before we could get into it, Mom cleared her throat. "There's a storm coming. Let's get everything inside, please."

Dad parked underneath the overhang and we all climbed out of the car. Mom opened the trunk and loaded my sister up with air mattresses and pillows, then grabbed a pair of suitcases. They disappeared through the front doors together.

When Dad and I were alone outside, he looked up at the building. "I must say, Delia, this is not what I expected."

Yeah, join the club. "How'd Aunt Cordelia die, Dad?" I asked. "For real."

My father sighed as he began handing me duffel bags. "She killed herself," he said. "But *please* don't tell Janie. Hysterics are the last thing we need."

I was surprised that I wasn't very surprised. In a way I felt like I'd known it. Poor Aunt Cordelia. "Why do you think she did it?"

He thought for a second. "She was old . . . and probably

very lonely. And sick. Apparently, there was some dementia toward the end."

Very lonely. There was a sad weight in my stomach. If I hadn't stopped writing to her, would she have been a happier person? Would she have stayed alive?

"Where did she do it?" I asked.

My father brightened. "That's the good news. She wasn't even on the property. She swallowed a bunch of pills and went for a walk along the highway. They actually thought she'd died of natural causes until they found the empty bottles and did a postmortem."

The good news? "God," I said, imagining an old lady limping down that endless driveway, growing dizzy and weak. "That's terrible."

"I appreciate your compassion, but you didn't even know her. Don't resort to melodrama." Typical Dad—nothing was worth caring about unless it affected him directly.

"I *did* know her," I said, scowling out at the decrepit fountain in the center of the driveway. "I still have her letters. And I'm not being melodramatic. Did she leave a note?"

My father ran his hand over his chin. "Not that I know of," he said. "But look around . . . maybe you'll find something."

I nodded and started for the doors, intending to do just that. In fact, I'd already decided to make learning more about Aunt Cordelia my number one priority. She'd cared enough about me to leave me her house—not just her house, her *mansion*. How long had it been since somebody had cared about *her*?

Besides, what else was I going to do with the endless days that stretched before me? Clean toilets? Repair the plumbing?

Play Yahtzee with Janie? Scroll through old pictures of me and my ex-boyfriend Landon on my phone?

As I crossed the threshold into the house, my father called to me. "Delia," he said.

I turned, one foot in, one foot out, to look back at him.

"Don't get too attached to this place, okay?" he said. "It's not like you can stay here forever."

OBSERVATIONS MADE AFTER THE FACT

Can't stay forever, eh?

Wanna bet?

CHAPTER 3

A sweet scent filled my nose the moment I crossed the threshold. I couldn't place it right away, but it clouded the back of my mind with memories of sunny summer walks with Mom when I was younger—the bright blue sky overhead, the two of us picking tiny wildflowers . . .

Buttercups. That was the smell. Little yellow buttercup flowers.

After I figured that out, I could focus on looking around. The foyer was spacious, with a high ceiling, an elaborate chandelier, dark red wallpaper, and an antique couch off to the side. It didn't resemble any foyer I'd ever seen, actually. It looked more like . . . a lobby.

To my left was a door. I looked at the metal plaque, darkened with grime, screwed into the wall next to it.

HEAD WARDRESS

Hmm. I had no idea what a *wardress* was.

"Delia?" Mom's voice startled me. She and Janie stood oddly still on the far side of the room, staring at the wall.

"What's going on?" I asked. "What's a wardress?"

Mom let out a bitter half laugh, half sniff. "You'll find out in a minute. Come here."

I walked over.

On the wall before them was a large wooden plaque caked in a layer of dust. Hanging above it was the portrait of a handsome, severe-looking man in a suit and bowler hat.

Embossed on the panel, in old-fashioned block letters, were the words:

THE PIVEN INSTITUTE

FOR THE CARE AND CORRECTION OF TROUBLED FEMALES

FOUNDED 1866 BY MAXWELL G. PIVEN

"Hysteria Hall," Mom said, her gaze locked on the writing. "The word *hysteria* originated from the Greek *hystera*, meaning 'womb.' Female hysteria was a blanket diagnosis applied to women for everything from schizophrenia to having too many opinions."

Mom had a PhD in women's studies. To put it mildly, she didn't find stuff like this amusing. Janie and I heard the danger in her tone and didn't comment.

"That's Maxwell?" Janie asked, standing on tiptoe and reaching a finger up to touch the dried swirls of oil paint. "He looks mean."

I batted her finger away. "He's the founder of an insane asylum," I said. "Not Mr. Rogers."

The silence was broken by artificially cheerful whistling as Dad entered the room behind us. We all spun to face him at once.

"What's up?" he asked.

"What's up," I said, "is that I'm the only sixteen-year-old I know who owns a mental hospital."

He didn't answer right away.

"Brad," Mom said, a trace of sharpness in her voice, "you don't seem surprised."

"Oh no, I am," he said. "I am. A mental hospital? That's . . . not what I imagined."

My mother folded her arms over her chest. "What did you imagine?"

Now Dad was starting to look a little uncomfortable. "A school, maybe? I mean, I didn't know details. The lawyer told me it was some kind of institute, and that there was a recovery center interested in the property, once the structure was retrofitted . . ."

"Wow," I said. "Way to keep all the important stuff to yourself."

"What's a recovery center?" Janie asked.

"Same thing," I said. "A place for crazy people." I crouched to pick up the bags I'd dropped, then started back for the front doors.

"Where are you going?" Dad asked.

"To the car," I said. "We can't stay here."

"Of course we can. Where else would we stay?"

I stared at him in blank disbelief. "Um . . . how about anywhere that *isn't* an abandoned mental hospital?"

Dad shook his head. "Don't be overdramatic. Cordelia lived here her whole life, and—"

"And look what happened to her!" I said. "Exactly. I'm not staying."

"If we don't get this place to at least a basic level of safety and cleanliness, we can't sell it," Dad said. "And if we can't do that as a family, then someday it will be all your responsibility. And you'll have to do it alone."

"Okay," I said. "Sounds perfect. I'll deal with it when I'm older."

Not the answer my father had hoped to hear. He sighed. "We've already decided that this is what we're going to do this summer. It's a family project, and—"

"Some project. We do all the work, and Delia gets all the money," Janie said, tossing her long blond hair haughtily over her shoulder. (I'd caught her practicing that move once in the mirror and thought it was a little too sad even to make fun of.)

"No more debate," Dad said. "We're staying. Cordelia had a small apartment, separate from the rest of the institute, and that's where we'll be living. No more discussion. Right, Lisa?"

Mom took a few long seconds to think before she spoke. "Okay," she finally said, turning away. Her usually sleek hair was starting to fuzz out from its perfect ponytail.

I hate to admit it, because it highlights a certain amount of adolescent self-absorption, but that was the first time it occurred to me that maybe this wasn't my mother's ideal way to pass the summer—that maybe she'd been roped into it, just like I had. Ordinarily, Mom's idea of a good time was an evening spent in the air-conditioned den of our house, eating takeout Chinese and following obscure threads of Internet research on her laptop. Maybe being locked away in the middle of nowhere was almost as much of a punishment to her as it was to me.

I caught my mother's eye. The briefest hint of mutual understanding passed between us, but then she turned away, smoothing her hair. A dim light of hope began to glow in my heart. Maybe

Mom would be my ticket out of this place. But I knew her better than to press the issue when she was exhausted and irritated.

Finding out what a wardress was would just have to wait, because Dad opened another door on the far side of the room and held it open for us. *"Mesdames,"* he said grandly, "I present the main hall."

Janie screwed up her face. "How do you know that?"

"There's a sign on the door, *madame*," Dad said.

"I'm a *mademoiselle*," my sister said, rolling her eyes.

"I should hope so." My father gave me a goofy wink.

I wanted to roll my eyes at him, too, but his dumb sense of humor always made me feel a stab of tenderness. He couldn't help it if all his jokes were dad jokes.

The "main hall" wasn't quite as grand as its name implied. It was a long, low-ceilinged passageway with several doors leading off of it. Even the lush wallpaper and hanging brass lamps didn't dampen the claustrophobic feeling, and I was relieved when Dad opened the first door on the right.

"The superintendent's apartment," he said. "I guess that makes us the new superintendents."

We stepped into a good-sized living room. There was also a dining area, a tiny kitchen, a bathroom, and a single bedroom. Once upon a time it had been a luxurious space, with gilded wallpaper and checkerboard floors, but now it felt old and worn—basically, like an old lady had been living there alone for decades. There were deep ruts in the floor from Aunt Cordelia's walker, which was still stashed in the corner of the bedroom, a medical-looking metal tray on the kitchen counter, and a lavender couch in the living room. A table in the corner held a small, old-fashioned TV set, but for all her frantic channel flipping, Janie couldn't get a signal.

"Not as bad as you thought, is it?" Dad asked, looking from Mom to me. "It's pretty clean, considering. Toward the end there was a home-care nurse who cleaned up even though Cordelia ordered her not to. The place was a wreck. She'd poured *salt* everywhere and scratched up the wood floors pretty badly."

"Like this?" Janie asked, looking down at her feet. We all walked over to see the word *DON'T* carved into the wood in letters about a foot tall.

"Wow," Mom said. "That's not going to buff out."

"Don't what?" Janie asked.

"Don't worry about it," Dad said. "We'll sand it down. You'll never even know it was there."

"Sounds super fun," I said. "Can't wait to get started on that. Anyhoo, I'm going to go look around. I'll see you guys later."

"Whoa, whoa, whoa," Mom said. "You can't just wander off."

"I'm not wandering," I protested. "I just want to see what's here."

My mother's glance at Dad was clearly an appeal for backup, but Dad shrugged. "I don't see how it can hurt. It's probably just a bunch of empty rooms."

"Maybe Janie can go with you," Mom suggested.

"No way!" Janie shrieked. She'd already retreated to the couch to play games on her phone.

"Well . . ." My mother peered out the window at the line of dark gray clouds that had appeared on the horizon. "Just don't go outside."

"I'm not looking to get struck by lightning," I said, grabbing the key ring off the stained wood dining table. I slung my army-green messenger bag over my shoulder and pushed through the door to the hallway.

Maybe I was more annoyed than I had any right to be, but I was sick of being treated like a flight risk.

Okay, yes, I'd messed up.

Yes, I'd messed up in a really big way.

But no, I was not a delinquent. No, I was not a liar. No, I was not looking, at every turn, for a chance to run off and end up living on the streets, picking pockets and sleeping in bus stops.

I just made *one* bad call.

It started back in January. I was hanging out at Nic's house, along with my then boyfriend, Landon (more on that particular disaster in a moment). It had been cold and rainy for about two weeks straight, and we were going stir-crazy from being inside.

"Where would you go right now, if you could go anywhere?" Nic asked.

"Hawaii," Landon said.

"Hogwarts," I said.

Landon poked me in the ribs. "Dork."

"I'd go to the beach," Nic said. "Any beach where it's warm. I haven't seen the ocean in like three years."

"Me neither," I said. And that was fine with me. I'm not the beach-going type. The thought of being crowded into an endless

23

sea of sun worshippers was the opposite of tempting—give me wizard school any day.

"You know what we should do?" Landon said. "We should go someplace for spring break."

"To the beach!" Nic said, sitting up.

"Or to Orlando . . . ?" I said. "You know there's an entire theme park—"

"Yes, Delia," Nic said. "We know."

"Not Orlando," Landon said. *"Daytona."*

"Okay, and which one of our moms is going to be willing to come with us to Daytona?" I asked.

Landon flipped his floppy blond hair to the other side of his head. "Um . . . why would we invite someone's mom?"

I was puzzled by his lack of understanding. I mean, a lot of my geekiness went over his head, but I thought this was pretty cut-and-dried. "Maybe . . . so we'd be allowed to go?"

Nic was sitting on the edge of the bed in deep contemplation. Then she brightened. "Hey! My church does a youth group trip every spring break. We could tell our parents we're going on that, and then just fly down to Daytona. They don't have to know about it."

Oh. So I was the one who hadn't understood. This trip was supposed to be *sans* parental units. My stomach lurched. As far as child-rearing styles went, my mother and father leaned pretty far into the "over-watchfulness" category. If I snuck off to another state—without so much as a grown-up in the group—and they found out . . . ? I'd be grounded until forever.

"I know what you're thinking," Nic said, leveling me with her dark-lashed gaze. "You're thinking about Brad and Lisa."

"Specifically, about the heart attacks they'd have if they found out," I said.

"But they don't have to find out!" Nic said. "The youth group goes to the Bahamas. They don't have cell service. So we send an e-mail every couple of days and say we stopped in at an Internet café. You'll come back with sand in your shoes and a sunburn. They'll never even know."

I closed my eyes for a moment to think about it—about the epicness of it—and as I did, I felt Landon's warm hand on my forearm. A straining sensation pulled at my heart.

"Just consider it, Delia," he said softly.

Landon McKay wasn't the quarterback of the football team or anything, but I'd never quite gotten past feeling like I was the lucky one in the relationship and he was doing me some sort of undeserved favor. Because of this, he held the upper hand in negotiations of every sort.

"Yeah, but why do we have to go to Daytona?" I asked.

Nic shrugged. "Because that's where cool people go. And we're nothing if not incredibly cool."

I was silent.

"All right, we can spend *one* day in Orlando at your Hogwarts theme park," Nic said. "Deal?"

"Deal, deal, deal," Landon urged, smiling at me.

He flopped his floppy hair again, and I knew resistance was futile.

"Deal," I said, the sound of the word settling uncomfortably in my ears as Landon's hand closed tightly around mine.

It's definitely fair to say I had a bad feeling about the whole thing from the beginning. When the time came to siphon money from my savings account to pay for the plane ticket and my share of our fleabag motel room, even Nic seemed to be having second thoughts. The problem was, neither one of us was willing to admit it.

The morning of March 8, I hugged my parents good-bye, commanded Janie to stay out of my room, and ran out to Nic's waiting car with a suitcase full of sunscreen and bathing suits, reminding myself that statistically, 99 percent of the things we worry about never occur.

Except two things happened.

One, I accidentally left my cell phone on the kitchen counter.

Two, Landon texted said cell phone three minutes after I'd left for the airport to say he changed his mind and thought maybe it wasn't an awesome idea so he wasn't going to go. And OH, by the way, last night he ran into a girl he'd gone to summer camp with and realized he had feelings for her and thought it was fair that we take this week apart to explore the idea of not being a couple anymore. And OH, double by the way, he still loved me and cared for me and wanted me and Nic to be super careful in Daytona because he'd heard it could get a little wild.

So after five months of being a couple, the boy I kind of in the back of my head could picture myself eventually marrying (I know, I know, but I couldn't help myself) not only sold me out but also dumped me . . . over text.

Too bad I wasn't there to see it.

But Janie was.

So my parents showed up at the airport, demanded to be let through security and practically caused a national security crisis, and then accosted Nic and me in the waiting area, where we were drinking Starbucks and keeping watch for Landon.

It was a *super* fun day.

Dumped, caught, and yeah—grounded until graduation.

Later that night, as I lay on my bed, I reached for the framed photo of Landon that smiled at me from the nightstand and flipped it facedown.

Next time I get a bad feeling about something, I thought, *I'm going to run so fast in the other direction all that'll be left is dust.*

OBSERVATIONS MADE AFTER THE FACT

Ashes to ashes, dust to dust.

In a way, I was right.

All that's left of any of us is dust.

Living people can be so arrogant sometimes.

(And I can say that, because I was one.)

CHAPTER 4

My exploration had two main objectives: One, to see more of the building, because (creepy or not) it was by far the most impressive thing I had ever been able to claim as my own, and that provoked in me a burning curiosity to see every nook and cranny.

Two, I wanted to unearth more about Aunt Cordelia. The letters she'd written me were rubber-banded together in my messenger bag. I'd reread them on the car ride and noticed repeated mentions of a room that she loved—her own little office, where she felt free and peaceful. If there *was* some secret worth learning about Aunt Cordelia's death, about what she'd done and why, it had to be in that room. She'd listed a few details about it: blue-painted walls, an antique lamp, and a little desk by a window where the sunlight came slanting in. So I knew that the room wasn't in the superintendent's apartment.

I decided to start in the wardress's office, which was dim and smelled like stale library books, with wood-paneled walls and a large, fancy desk. Everything was old-fashioned and covered in a quarter inch of dust.

The desk was in immaculate order, not an item out of place except for a folder labeled DISCHARGE PAPERWORK—1943.

In that moment, it fully sank in that the charming cottage of my daydreams was an honest-to-goodness *mental institution*. An incredulous laugh bubbled out of me at the sheer preposterousness of it.

But when I picked up the envelope, revealing a perfectly dust-free rectangle on the desk's surface, an uncomfortable tingle made its way down my neck. In more than seventy years, *no one* had come into this room and moved this folder?

A dozen yellow slips of paper spilled out when I tipped the envelope. I picked up the closest one. There was a name typed at the top: VICTORIA FOWLER, and below that, a date: JULY 18, 1943.

I wondered what Victoria had done, and whether being here had helped her at all. Just how troubled did a female have to be to be sent to a place with the word *institute* in its name, anyway? Were the patients criminals, murderers, completely insane? Or were they just headstrong women whose families decided things would be easier if they were locked away?

Having recently been categorized as moderately "troubled" myself, I was a little sensitive to the idea.

I shook off the uneasy feeling. Back to business. There was no way this was the room Aunt Cordelia had talked about in her letters.

A second door, labeled NO UNAUTHORIZED ADMITTANCE, opened into a little nurses' office that contained a bed, a desk, and two chairs. On one of the chairs was a metal surgical tray, identical to the one in Cordelia's kitchen.

I paused on my way through to glance at a newspaper clipping that had been left on the corner of the desk. The headline read: ROTBURG SANITARIUM TO CLOSE DOORS AFTER 77 YEARS. I scanned the first few paragraphs, which quoted a man from the Pennsylvania State Board of Medicine as saying that there had been numerous problems at the Piven Institute over the years, and the decision to close was "strongly supported" by the state.

The imposing stone institution has remained in the care of the Piven family since its founding, even after the 1885 disappearance of founder Maxwell Piven. Local legend speculates that Maxwell, tired of the day-to-day burdens of his role, went west to California in search of a new life.

Hmm. Maybe we Pivens have always been the type to sneak off without permission.

Next I found myself in a small back hallway. The closest door had a sign that read NURSES' DORMITORY, and the other signs were for the kitchen, janitorial closet, basement, and patient stairway.

I hesitated, thinking how nice it would be to explore somewhere light and tidy, like a dormitory for efficient, white-frocked nurses. But by now I had a sense, down to my core, that what I was searching for wasn't contained in any cheerful, well-kept rooms.

The kitchen, janitorial closet, and basement seemed too creepy for solo exploration. So I passed by them and started to climb the stairwell.

On the second floor, I came to a small landing with a cork bulletin board on the wall. A yellowed paper sign was pinned to it with rusted thumbtacks:

IF THOU BE HUMBLED AND RENOUNCE THY SIN,
THY PITEOUS SOUL MAY FIND MERCY WITHIN.
—LORD P. LINDLEY

Golly. How inspirational.

The door next to the bulletin board was marked DAY ROOM. I entered to find a large, airy space. The walls were papered in yellowing ivory decorated with trailing, flowery vines. There was a plush Persian rug on the floor, a stone fireplace, an upright piano, and a row of rocking chairs. It could have been a parlor at a college or nursing home . . . except for the wire screens bolted in front of the windows.

The June sunshine had been trapped in the room all afternoon, and the air was stuffy and warm. I slipped off my cardigan and set it on a small table, then walked over to look more closely at a small writing desk by the window. Could *this* room have been Cordelia's refuge? From her letters, I didn't get the impression that the place I was searching for was so . . . roomy. She'd made it sound like she had a little corner, tucked away by itself. Besides, the walls weren't blue.

I set my bag down on one of the chairs next to the piano and reached inside it for the bundle of letters, unfolding one to see if I could find any useful information.

Dear Little Namesake, (that was what she always called me)

I was so pleased to hear about your third-place finish in the Holiday Fun Run. I was never very athletic myself. Of course such qualities weren't valued in my family, especially in the girls . . .

It continued on in that way—small talk about her childhood (although she never mentioned spending that childhood at a mental institution), compliments on my penmanship, lots of little bits of advice, and a word of hello to my teacher.

At the end, I found a paragraph that seemed to offer a bit of insight:

Well, the light is beginning to fade in my little sanctuary—do you have a sanctuary in your home? Someplace you can go to be with your thoughts? Whenever I need something, I seem to be able to find it here. But, as dear as mine is to me, the sun sets on the other side of the house, so it gets dark early here. I don't like to be alone in the dark. So I will pack up my work for the day and say farewell for now. I look forward to your next letter, and hearing about the results of the spelling test you were worried about . . .

The sun sets in the west, so her room had to be on the east side of the house. That narrowed things down a bit.

I was about to open the next letter when something across the room danced into my peripheral vision—a difference in the light on the wall. I looked up, but whatever it was—if, in fact, it had been anything at all—was gone.

But when I glanced back at the letters, I immediately saw the same thing at the outer edge of my eyesight. I cut my gaze to the right, without moving my head, and saw what it really was: a reflection dancing on the wall, like a sparkling spiderweb. It was about four feet in diameter, and it was in constant motion.

It reminded me of the way the sun bounces off the unsettled surface of a swimming pool.

It had to be coming from some body of water somewhere— but where?

I set the letters on the top shelf of the piano. Then I went to the window and stared down over the grounds, looking for the source of the reflection . . . but there was no water in sight. Only the line of trees in the distance, hills so small you couldn't even really call them hills, and one shallow, dry ditch a hundred feet away.

Then what could be causing the dancing pattern of light?

As soon as I turned my head to study it, it was gone again.

Awash in equal amounts of wariness and embarrassment, I went back to looking around the day room. On the far side of the room was another door, this one marked WARD, but it was locked, and having made it this far without having to use the keys, I wasn't eager to begin now.

Then there came a sound from behind me—a faint, clear ringing, like jingle bells.

I nearly jumped out of my skin. Then I spun around. "Hello? Mom? Dad?"

No one answered.

"Who's there? Janie?"

I listened for a reply. No sound—not a word, a breath, not even more jingling.

It was nothing. Nothing.

But I didn't really believe myself.

It seemed like everywhere my eyes landed—the piano, the floral-cushioned chairs—I caught a hint of a movement just finished, a moment of sudden, expectant stillness, like the space between an inhale and an exhale—as if some wily trespasser was lurking in the shadows, slipping around just out of my sight.

Time to go. Aunt Cordelia's office was clearly on the other side of the building. What was to be gained by poking around in here?

That's why I'm going, I thought, starting for the door. Not because of the hairs standing up on the back of my neck, but because I was on a mission.

I stopped by the door to pick my cardigan up off the table, and froze when I realized that the table was completely bare.

My sweater was gone.

I blinked as my brain tried to catch up to my eyes. I almost freaked out, but managed to hold it together long enough to kneel and look under the table. Sure enough, my gray cardigan lay in a crumpled heap. I grabbed it and shook out the dust bunnies.

That was when I noticed what was strange about the table where I'd set it—

The polished wood tabletop gleamed in the low light, bare and lustrous.

Unlike every other surface in the entire building, there wasn't so much as a single speck of dust on it.

My footsteps echoed off the narrow stairway walls as if someone else was right behind me.

Once I was in the hall, I went through the door I assumed would lead me back to the nurses' office, from which I'd find my way out to the lobby and then back to my parents. But by the time I'd stepped inside, reached for the light switch, and realized there *was* no light switch, the door had closed behind me—and locked.

I had the key ring in my pocket, but in the pitch-dark there was no way to know which key was the correct one. I fumbled for my phone, turned on the flashlight, and surveyed my surroundings. Shadows of the ornate hanging lamps leapt erratically in the motion of my flashlight. This wasn't the nurses' office. I'd found a shortcut back to the main hall.

The door to the superintendent's apartment was the farthest one to my right, and I had no trouble finding it. But the knob wouldn't turn—it was locked. I knocked a couple of times and then hung back, waiting for someone to come let me in.

Out of nowhere came the sound of bells ringing loudly, not two feet away from me.

I swung around, looking for its source.

Don't jump to crazy conclusions, I told myself. Maybe Aunt Cordelia had a cat. That was possible, right? If she'd had a cat, and the cat had been alone since April, it would probably be eager to find someone new to feed it. It could be following me around—

Jingle jingle jingle.

Before I knew it, I was up against the wall, the line of the wood molding pressing into my lower back.

Jingle jingle.

There was no cat. There was no one but me.

In some of Aunt Cordelia's letters, she'd said that even though she lived alone, she never felt truly alone. At the time I thought that was because she maybe had a lot of nice friends who came visiting.

Now I was starting to think she'd meant something else entirely.

Why were my parents not opening the door?

My hands shaking, I raised the key chain to my face and squinted at each key, scanning the peeling labels frantically. Finally, I found one that read SUPE-APT and stuck it in the keyhole.

Before I could turn it, though, the bells turned shrill—an unpleasant jangle rather than a gentle ringing. And still, no one—nothing—was there.

Then I heard a sound to my right—the sound of something being dragged.

I couldn't even will myself to turn my body, so instead I just turned my head and my flashlight, fully prepared for the sight of some ancient, forgotten old mental patient who'd been hiding in the shadows, surviving all these years by eating rats.

I didn't see an emaciated old woman.

But someone *had* been in the hall with me. The rug had been rolled back on itself, revealing a six-inch-tall letter scratched into the hardwood floor beneath it. More of Aunt Cordelia's dementia-induced vandalism.

It was an *E*.

Driven by curiosity, I went to the far end of the rug and pulled the whole thing out of the way.

In the narrow spill of light from my phone, I read the first letter: a deeply gouged *D*.

I walked down the hall, piecing the words together as I saw each new letter.

O...N...T...

SELL THE HOUSE.

Then I noticed smaller letters, under the *E* in *HOUSE*. One last word. I held my phone closer.

DELIA.

The message was for me.

My dead great-aunt had gouged messages into the floor for me.

The light on my phone blinked out.

Adrenaline propelling me forward, I rushed back to the door, forcing the key to turn in the lock. I followed the sounds of my parents' voices back to the dimly lit bedroom, where three silhouettes stood in the corner over a pile of luggage.

One of the silhouettes turned around.

"Honey?" Mom said.

I was too out of breath for a lengthy explanation. The words came out of my mouth in a puff.

"I can't stay here," I said. "I'm leaving. Tonight."

CHAPTER 5

As my eyes adjusted to the light, the first things I could make out were Dad's raised eyebrows. "Excuse me?"

"I'm not staying here," I said, gulping in another breath. "I can't. I refuse."

Mom's face wrinkled in concern. "Delia, what happened? You look pale."

"You look *crazy*," Janie added, her eyes like little moons on her face.

I dodged my mother's arm as she reached out for me. Then I took a moment to figure out how exactly one might go about telling one's parents that one would rather scoop one's eyeball out with a plastic spork than spend one more minute in this place, where something sinister oozed beneath every door, down the walls, up from the floorboards . . .

"I think I know why Aunt Cordelia ran away and killed herself."

"*Delia.*" My father looked annoyed. "I thought we agreed—"

"Did she really, Brad? Your aunt killed herself?" Mom interrupted.

Dad sighed and shot me a look that plainly said, *Sellout.*

39

"Delia," he said, "I'd really appreciate it if you would sit down, take some deep breaths, and think this over like a rational person."

"There's nothing to rationalize," I said stiffly, wrapping my arms around myself. "Unless you see what I saw—unless you feel that thing watching you, following you, stalking you . . ."

"That's enough," my father said. "You're scaring Janie."

That much was perfectly true. My sister looked like a statue, her lips slightly parted.

Mom eased her arm around Janie's shoulders, but Janie jumped away. "I'm not staying here!" she said. "If Delia's leaving, I am, too."

Normally, her copycatting would have irritated me, but in this case I was relieved. Janie might have been a total pain, but at the end of the day she was my sister. And I didn't want her in this house.

"Tell us what happened," Mom said. "You're frightening me."

I wove my fingers together and took a deep breath. "Something chased me around. With bells. And there's this light on the wall upstairs, and a table that won't let you put things on it. And Cordelia left a message *for me* on the floor in the main hall—*Don't sell the house, Delia.*"

"Oh, you're kidding. Did she carve up the hall floor, too?" Dad asked, sighing into his hand.

Really? *That* was the part that concerned him? A massive chill went up my spine, contracting every muscle in my back. I turned toward my mother. "Mom, please," I said. "We have to leave. This place . . . I think it's haunted."

For a beat, we all stared at each other.

Then Dad crossed his arms. "No," he said. "I'm sorry, but no. We came here for the summer, as a family, and we're staying for the summer—as a family. I don't know what you think you saw, Delia, but one old lady's senile ramblings aren't—"

He blathered on, but I wasn't hearing his words.

No more discussing for me. I'd moved on to planning. I had to get my things and go, as fast as I could. They'd never drive me, so I'd walk myself back to town, or as far back as I needed to go to get cell service, at which point I would call Nic. She would do whatever it took to help.

I spied the pile of suitcases in the corner and moved to grab mine, an old scraped-up red bag that had been Mom's in college.

"What do you think you're doing?" my father asked.

I turned to face him. "Leaving."

Dad's slow-burning sigh seethed with frustration. "You're not leaving."

Our eyes met.

"Brad, maybe—" Mom said.

"Lisa, I've got this, thank you," Dad said.

"*I* don't want to leave, Daddy," Janie said, with a golden-girl smile. Traitor.

"Janie," he snapped, "find something else to do for a little while."

My sister scowled and slipped out of the room.

"No one's going anywhere," Mom said, exasperated. "There's a huge downpour practically on top of us. We'll talk it over first thing tomorrow morning."

Even more reason to get out. The thought of being stuck here on a dark and stormy night . . . "No way," I said.

"*Yes* way," Dad said.

My parents looked as determined as I'd ever seen them. I knew that no matter how hard I pressed, I'd lose this argument. I had a choice: try to leave now, and deal with the potentially nuclear-level fallout, or leave later, when they weren't looking. Once they noticed I was missing, they might call the police to pick me up, but that was fine. I'd much rather spend the night in jail than in this house.

Time to re-strategize.

So I shrugged and attempted to act resigned. "Whatever."

"First thing tomorrow," Mom promised, her shoulders rounding with relief.

Dad nodded sharply, forced to play nice but obviously furious that I had the nerve to defy them.

I turned away, nursing more than a little fury of my own.

In the sticky silence that followed, we realized that Janie had taken my father's instructions seriously and left the apartment altogether. Dad talked Mom out of going to look for her, but I was on edge, picturing the words on the floor, the light dancing on the walls, and my oblivious little sister in the middle of it all.

A few minutes later, she showed up, dusty but unharmed. The keys clanked as she dropped them on the table. On her face was a wide-eyed expression I couldn't decipher. She'd always been delicate, like a ballerina. Now I had the urge to stand in front of her like some sort of bodyguard.

I went over to her. "Did anything happen?"

"Yeah," she said, her voice hushed.

"What?" I asked.

She glanced around. "Come closer," she said. "I'll whisper it."

I leaned toward her, my heart pounding, as she stood on her tiptoes and raised her mouth to my ear.

"It was . . ." Her voice trailed off.

"It's okay," I said. "Don't be afraid to tell me."

"It was . . . *BOO!*" she shouted directly into my eardrum, deafening me. Then she (wisely) rushed away as I stood frozen with rage. Her gleeful laughter bounced off the walls.

I couldn't *believe* I'd been worried about her.

"You are such a jerk," I hissed.

"At least I'm not a scaredy-cat!" She danced farther away. "You're just mad because I'm braver than you."

Then she (very wisely) ducked out of my reach and ran for the kitchen, just as Mom stuck her head out and said, "Time to eat. Has anyone seen that tray that was in here before?"

After our tense dinner of gas-station gourmet, I stood up. "So where are we sleeping?"

"We can put the air mattresses over in the corner by the TV, I guess," Mom said.

"No, not there!" Janie said. "I found someplace better!"

She was wiggling like a delighted puppy.

"Upstairs," she said. "I found a place called Ward. It has bedrooms. And real beds!"

I thought of the door in the day room marked WARD—the one I'd been too afraid to go through. Maybe Janie *was* actually braver than me (but that didn't make her any less of a jerk).

"If there are beds up there, they're a hundred years old," I said. "They're probably full of maggots and bedbugs."

"No," she protested. "I sat on one. It was nice."

Mom and Dad exchanged a dubious look.

"You can't seriously be thinking of letting her sleep up there," I said.

"Oh, Janie, I don't know," Mom said to my sister. "If Delia would go, then maybe . . . but the rooms must be so . . . *old*. And dusty."

Not *Delia doesn't like it up there*. Just a general distaste for dust and oldness.

"We brought clean sheets," Janie said. Then her eyes cut over to me, and in them I saw expectant curiosity, like she was waiting for my reaction.

Thirty minutes earlier she'd been scared enough to want to run away with me. Now she wanted to spend the night in some weird part of the house. This was just a bratty dare, designed to get a rise out of me, and I refused to give her the satisfaction. What difference did it make? I wasn't planning to sleep there, anyway.

So I shrugged. "I'm beyond caring at this point."

Maybe we'd get lucky and the ghost would eat my sister.

The ward hall, which I'd expected to be starkly institutional, with concrete and metal and straitjackets, appeared to be a perfectly normal hallway—the kind you might find at a posh boarding school. There was a communal bathroom and six individual patient rooms, which Janie had actually been right about—they seemed pretty nice, furnished with matching dark wood nightstands, dressers, and vanity tables. The closest one to the bathroom—Room 1—had a pastel-pink bedspread and a dresser with a missing drawer.

"I'll take this one." The words left my mouth before I knew they were coming.

"I thought you hated pink," Dad said, moving past me with my suitcase.

That was true. And the broken dresser reminded me of a sinister, toothless smile.

"I like the view," I said. "Plus, it's as far from Janie as I can get."

And as close to the exit.

"I heard you!" Janie shouted from the room she'd chosen— Room 6, the one at the very end of the hall.

After Mom and Dad headed back downstairs, I loaded up my messenger bag with everything I'd need to hit the road. It might be a long, rainy walk to town, and a suitcase would just slow me down. I wished I'd thought to bring an umbrella.

Down the hall, Janie was singing softly to herself.

In spite of my sister's many (many, many) shortcomings, she had perfect pitch and a natural talent for singing. I certainly wasn't looking forward to the day she realized just *how* good she was. With my luck, she'd win one of those TV talent shows and end up a millionaire, and I'd be the talentless reject sister, forgotten in the shadows. Sometimes I felt like our whole family was waiting for that to happen.

Her voice, clear and lovely, drifted down the hall while I waited on the bed with my packed bag, watching the minutes tick by on my phone. I'd changed from my jeans and T-shirt into an old baggy burgundy sweater of Dad's and gray leggings dotted with white hearts. On my feet were a pair of knockoff Ugg boots, and my hair was pulled up into a messy bun. It was basically a half step up from pajamas, but I figured that if I was going to spend the night in a bus station (or juvie lockup), I might as well be comfortable.

My feet rested on the little round stool I'd pulled away from the vanity, rocking it back and forth on its uneven legs in time with my sister's song. Her flawless rhythm and the gentle knock of the wood against the floor lulled me into a bit of a trance. I found myself following the words of her song. It was one I'd never heard before, and it was old-fashioned—a complete departure from her usual repertoire of pop songs about breakups.

"Beautiful dreamer, wake unto me . . . Starlight and dewdrops are waiting for thee . . ."

Her voice drifted off, like she'd fallen asleep. Excellent. This would be my best chance to sneak out. I got up off the bed, accidentally knocking over the little wooden footstool with a clatter. I hurriedly set it upright. But as soon as my fingers let go of the smooth, round edge, it knocked itself over again . . .

And rolled toward me.

I watched in silence, unable to believe my eyes.

Then it bumped up against my foot.

My heart racing, I scrambled backward, running into the bed and knocking something loose behind me. I turned around to see that I had dislodged a leather strap, complete with buckles, bolted to the bed frame. Lifting the bedspread, I found more straps—one for each wrist and ankle, and a big one that would fit perfectly across a torso.

Don't freak out, I told myself. *Just go. Get your things and go.*

I grabbed my messenger bag and purse, double-checked to make sure I had my phone and charger, and started into the hall. The bathroom door gaped open, and I caught a flash of lightning through the window.

A high-pitched scream filled the air.

It was the kind of sound that overloads your brain, leaving you blank except for the sudden, all-consuming awareness of a person in horrible distress.

Janie!

I dropped my stuff and ran back to her room, gasping at the sight that greeted me—

My sister was strapped into the bed, her thin wrists and ankles caught fast in the leather buckles. The big one was cinched tightly around her chest, although she was doing an admirable job of fighting against it, writhing and struggling like a fish in a net.

"Janie!" I said, racing to the bed. "Are you okay?"

"Delia!!!" she shrieked. *"Get me out, get me out, get me out!"*

"I'm trying!" I said, fumbling with the buckle on her right ankle.

"No, my hands," she panted, wild-eyed. "Please. Do my hands first."

My parents' footsteps thundered down the hall. They rushed in just as I was starting to undo my sister's right hand.

"What on *earth*?" Mom cried.

Without waiting for an explanation, my parents each grabbed a strap and went to work. The leather was so dried with age that it cracked wherever it was bent, leaving a pattern of fine lines in the dull brown surface.

"What happened here?" Mom asked. "What were you girls doing?"

"Now hold on," I said, so surprised that I let go of my sister's wrist. "*We girls* weren't doing anything. *She, Janie* somehow got herself strapped down."

"I did not!" Janie snapped, shaking her bound wrist at me. Mom reached across to finish what I'd started.

The thing was, I actually believed my sister. How would she have gotten herself strapped in? Even if she'd been able to buckle her own ankles and torso, how could she do *both* of her hands?

"You have to be more careful," Mom said. "What if we hadn't been around?"

My sister's jaw set. "*I didn't do it.* I was *asleep.*"

Fear started to rise inside me like an approaching tsunami. The house was closing in on us.

Mom gave Janie a dubious look. "Sweetheart, how else would you have gotten stuck in the restraints?"

"Janie," Dad said, "you need to tell us the truth. How did this happen?"

Janie's eyes narrowed. Her mouth began to open.

The air in my lungs turned dry and heavy and hot.

I knew what she was going to say before she said it. The impact of her words was as inevitable as two cars skidding toward each other across an icy intersection.

"Delia did it."

OBSERVATIONS MADE AFTER THE FACT

Despite this incident, and despite everything she went on to tell herself in the coming years, what happened to me that night was not my sister's fault.

CHAPTER 6

She's lying," I said.

"Delia," my father said, his words coming slowly at first, and then gaining speed, "the drama queen act has to stop. You have done everything in your power to ruin this for the whole family, and I for one am sick of it."

"Ruin it?" I asked. "It *came* ruined!"

"Brad," Mom said, clucking her tongue. "You know I hate the phrase *drama queen*."

"Yes, and I'm sorry, but it applies." Dad took a deep breath and turned to face me. "I know you feel like you're some sort of victim in all this, but here's the fact: You did something wrong. And you got caught. And now you can accept the consequences like a man."

Mom hmmphed.

"Like a *grown-up*, then," Dad said. "You only think about yourself. And that needs to change."

I turned away.

"Where do you think you're going?" he asked.

Did they seriously not understand?

"Leaving," I said. "So go ahead and start cooking up some new consequences."

"Cordelia," Dad said. His voice was as serious as death. "You're *not* leaving."

I didn't even bother looking back. I threw the words over my shoulder.

"Watch me," I said.

My messenger bag was right where I'd left it, but my purse was gone, and I couldn't leave without my wallet and phone. I paused, imagining for a moment that I'd heard shrill laughter— then shook it off and went back to my room. My purse was lying limply on the floor, its contents spread out as if a wild animal had rifled through them.

I heard my parents coming down the hall, their low, tense voices punctuated by Janie's excited outbursts. Then there was murmuring, and Janie cried out indignantly, which I took to mean that our parents were telling her, yet again, to mind her own beeswax. Loud stomping and the muffled slam of a door confirmed my suspicions.

I picked up my purse, braced myself, and looked up to see Mom and Dad standing just outside my door.

"Look," I said. "I understand why this whole summer project thing is important to you. But I can't spend another minute in this house."

They exchanged a long, exhausted look, which seemed like a good sign. Like I was wearing them down—never underestimate the power of wearing your parents down.

"You're overwrought," Dad said.

"I'm not, though." I set my purse on the bed and forced my voice to sound reasonable. "I'm of perfectly sound mind and body. But I don't know how long that will last, if you make me stay here."

Mom pinched the bridge of her nose. Her sinuses were probably going crazy from all the dust, which meant it wouldn't be long before she ended up with a migraine. I considered inviting her to come with me. Let Dad and Janie get their weird kicks out of this twisted place. My mother and I had standards.

Then Mom reached out. I thought she was going to, I don't know, try to take my hand or something. I made up my mind not to let her.

But instead, she ever so gently took hold of the doorknob . . . and ever so gently closed the door.

I stared for a second, not quite comprehending. But when I heard the jangling of the key ring, I got it. I mean, I seriously *Got It*.

They had locked me in.

"What?!" I yelled. "What are you *doing*?"

"Honey, it's only temporary. Until we can figure this out." My mother's voice was thin and brittle.

I tried to yank open the door, but it didn't budge. Of course it didn't—it was bolted shut. It was doing what it was designed to do. "You're locking me up in here? Like a crazy person? Just another hysterical troubled female?"

I could practically picture Mom flinching.

"Of course you're not crazy," Dad said. The unhappiness

in his voice was palpable. "But you need to take a little time to relax."

"I don't *want* time! I'm not going to relax!" I got louder and louder, until I was basically shouting my lungs out. *"I need to get out of this awful place, now!"*

"Delia," Dad said softly. "We simply can't allow you to run off again."

Again. The word scraped the inside of my brain like a piece of balled-up tinfoil.

Of course they would connect two completely unrelated incidents into a pattern, as if I were a serial killer from some criminal profiling TV show.

"This isn't like Daytona." I managed to lower my voice but couldn't keep my teeth from gritting. "I'm not trying to run off somewhere. I'm just trying to get out of this place."

"But . . . why?" Mom asked.

"I don't know," I said. "I just *need to*." And when I said it, I realized how true it was—how desperately I had to get away from whatever was in this house. My skin began to feel like it was crawling with insects. I rubbed my hands on my arms, trying to push the sensation away.

"Please," I said. "Please just let me out."

"We will," Dad said.

"When?"

I could feel their helplessness radiating through the door.

"We're not sure," Mom said lamely.

I tugged on the seam of my sweater, my rage and indignation rising, until the pent-up energy propelled me toward the door. I slammed into it with my shoulder.

Mom let out a little surprised yelp, and I bashed into the door again.

Not for the first time (or the last, it may be worth noting), my emotions were starting to get the better of me.

"Now hang on, sweetheart," Dad said, and I could tell by the *sweetheart* and the note of anxiety behind his words that he was heartily wishing the situation had progressed differently.

Smash. When I hit the door for a third time, a shooting pain went down my left arm. I clutched my elbow and backed away, my breath coming in heavy huffs.

"You have to understand," Dad said. "After what happened with spring break—"

"Go away." My voice was low, but I knew they heard me.

Mom spoke in her most conciliatory tone. "Honey, we're going to go call Carol, and then we'll come back and work this out."

Carol was the family therapist my parents had insisted we start seeing after the spring-break incident. She was nice enough, but mostly I just sat in her office staring at her collection of exotic conch shells while my parents tried to goad me into sharing my feelings.

"Yeah, do that," I said. "Tell her you locked me up in an insane asylum. She'll love it. Very empowering."

There was an uncomfortable, shuffling pause. Then Mom's voice piped up, faint and hesitantly hopeful. "Delia, if we opened the door now, what would you do?"

"Run," I said. "As far from you people as I can get."

I should have just lied. But seriously—what no one seemed

to believe anymore was that, at heart, I'm actually an honest person.

My parents sighed in unison.

Then I spoke the last words they would ever hear from my earthly person.

"I hate you," I said. "And by the way, tell Janie I hate her, too."

After a moment of wounded silence, their reluctant footsteps led away.

OBSERVATIONS MADE AFTER THE FACT

I hate you. And by the way, tell Janie I hate her, too.

Let me tell you something.

On a cold and loveless night, when the silver moonlight drinks the color from the earth and the grass tumbles in the wind like waves tossed on an endless, angry sea . . .

That is not the kind of memory that keeps you warm.

CHAPTER 7

I frothed and fumed by the door for a few minutes, but that kind of anger really saps your energy. It wasn't long before exhaustion set in.

I walked over to the window to take a look at the storm. Clouds boiled on the horizon, gray upon gray piling together into a churning darkness. Rain had begun to advance across the vastness of the property—you could see it pulsing its way over the hills. Sharp, sudden bursts of wind shook the old glass panes in their frames.

Just at the crest of the hill, a dozen spidery tendrils of electricity emerged from the cloud like writhing fingers. Then thunder struck, so loud that my ears went momentarily numb. It came in rolls, constant and deafening, rumbling all the way into the center of my chest.

I stepped away from the window.

I started to have the odd feeling that this was, on some level, weirdly personal.

No, Delia. It's just a storm. An act of nature.

But the room around me grew darker.

And it wasn't the kind of darkness that comes with nightfall.

Something caught my eye at the seam where the ceiling and wall met above the window. A dark, oily-looking fog crawled along the plaster, winding its way down the vines on the wallpaper—as if it were part of the design.

Slowly, I turned around.

A pulsing layer of black smoke filled the room.

I watched as the smoke descended the walls, its movements hypnotic. It seemed to breathe, somehow—pausing with each inhale, going a little faster with each exhale . . .

I lost myself in watching it slide down toward me.

Then I became vaguely aware of a horrible creaking noise, like the building was going to collapse. Thumping footsteps in the hall outside. Shouting.

But all I could focus on was the smoke.

It reached the floor and sinewed along the grains of the floorboards and through the intricate weave of the carpet toward my feet. It began to coat my skin. I could feel it on my legs, even through my leggings—an irresistible velvety softness.

Though my thoughts had grown swirling and vague, some part of me knew this wasn't good. I tried to back away, away, away from the grasping mist.

From a far-off place: banging on the door. Voices raised in panic.

But I wasn't panicking. I wasn't thinking at all.

Somehow the smoke found its way between the bricks and through the invisible seams in the plaster. It worked its way under the floorboards and baseboards, rippling beneath the wallpaper. The bed gave a short, sharp jerk, and the little stool fell to its side and rolled wildly around the room. Bells rang, and rang, and rang, and then cut off suddenly.

Everything was centered on me. The rug began to crawl inward, dragging its tassels against the dusty floor. The dresser, bolted in place, stretched and strained in an effort to break free. The room was alive—or something was alive in there with me.

I inched back as far as I could, until I was standing against the wire barrier that covered the window.

Behind me, the window flew open, filling the room with a miniature tempest.

Faintly, from across an endless distance, there was more shouting.

As if my shoulders were being gently guided . . . I turned around.

The wire barrier between the window and myself had been torn away.

I looked wonderingly down at my hands, which were crisscrossed in cuts and soaked in blood.

The slippery smoke was now up to my neck. It squeezed lightly on my throat, and then the warmth of it stroked my chin before slipping, sweet and smoky, down my throat. It seemed as if the fingers of a gentle hand softly shut my eyelids for me and coaxed the breath out of my lungs.

I tried to open my mouth.

I tried to call for my mother.

But there was only silence.

And deep, deep darkness.

PART TWO

(After the Fact)

CHAPTER 8

I jolted awake. The storm had quieted, leaving behind only a strange glowing quality in the evening light.

Mom and Dad were arguing outside the door. "Where were they?!" Dad demanded. I heard clumsy fumbling with a set of keys.

"In the day room!" Mom's voice was an octave higher than normal. "On the floor next to one of the tables! I don't know how they got all the way out there!"

"You guys, relax," I called, backing away from the window. "I'm fine."

I watched the door because (sue me) I wanted to enjoy their expressions of fear and regret. They *should* feel regret. They'd locked me in here and then apparently lost the keys—during a huge, scary storm, no less.

I had my line all ready to say. *Parents of the Year, guys.*

So when the door flew open, I spread my arms wide. But in the moment, I couldn't bring myself to taunt them. Instead, I said, "Are you ready to listen to reason now?"

But they didn't speak. Mom stared to my left, mouth agape.

"The window . . ." she said. Her voice was soft and strained.

"Okay, sure, don't worry about me," I said. "Worry about the window. I'm just your daughter."

Neither of them answered me. Their arms hung limply at their sides like a pair of broken puppets. They were fixated on the window, and I wondered if there was more damage than I'd realized. Repairing old windows like this would probably cost a fortune. But when I turned around, I saw the window swinging open, perfectly intact.

I felt a little wave of relief.

But something was still wrong with my parents. Very wrong.

"Oh no," my mother said as she approached the open window. "Oh no, *oh no, oh no.*"

She dropped to her knees, still repeating *no, no, no.* Dad stayed frozen, standing above her.

Not gonna lie, I was getting a little freaked out. "You guys, it's okay. It was only a storm. I'm not even that mad."

They didn't look up.

"Just . . . answer me." I was suddenly so cold I couldn't stand it. "Why won't you *answer* me?"

And then my mother made this sound that I wish I could scrub out of my brain, this strangled half cry, half moan that meandered and twisted and turned to a wail, and then to a scream, and the scream just went on and on.

Then, in one swift motion, Dad grabbed my mother by the arm and pulled her out of the room. I heard their footsteps galloping down the hall.

In the silence, I stepped closer and looked out the window.

On the ground twenty feet below, sprawled and broken like a doll, was a body.

The eyes were open, but there was no spark of life in them.

I know that person, I thought.

But from where? The answer was buried in my head somewhere, like the lyrics to a song you haven't heard in years. I just had to catch the answer, the way you catch one word in your memory and then the whole song comes flooding back.

I know that sweater.

Burgundy. Baggy. It was my father's sweater. I remembered a Christmas card photo of him wearing it.

My thoughts slid together in a confused mush. I knew I should know who that was down there, but I couldn't put my finger on it. I rubbed my face with my hands, feeling dizzy.

Janie? Oh God. Could that be my sister? Could it—

No. I squeezed my eyes shut and tried to remember.

Dad handing me a folded burgundy bundle after I borrowed it for the bazillionth time. Telling me to wear it with pride and restore it to its former coolness. Mom laughing and saying it was never cool, but it might have a chance now . . .

Now that Delia will be wearing it.

So . . . wait. That was *my* sweater? And was that my *face?* But why was my face down there?

Why was *my face* attached to a dead body?

It hit me with a *pop!*—the instant, horrible, irrefutable truth:

That wasn't some random dead body.

That was *my* dead body.

CHAPTER 9

I stared down at my dead self.

From behind me came the sound of bells, more clearly than I'd ever heard it before.

I turned around. A girl about my age stood a few feet away, wearing a pair of long, silky ivory pants and a matching tunic top. Her black hair was cut in a sleek bob that barely grazed her chin. She had a striking look—a thin uniformity to her eyebrows, a distinctive pink glow on the apples of her cheeks.

Around each of her wrists was a thin leather strap with a pair of jingle bells attached to it.

She folded her arms, sending a fresh peal of ringing through the air while she grimly surveyed the room. Then she stepped closer to the window and peeked out. Seeing the body below, she bit her lower lip and glanced at me.

"I see we both died in our pajamas." Her voice was crisp, with a lilting British accent. Her large brown eyes were keenly intelligent as they flicked from my booted feet to my face. "I tried to get you to leave. Guess I didn't try hard enough."

I didn't answer. I was mesmerized by the light coming off her alabaster skin, and the way her body seemed to flicker slightly . . . as if she was constantly having to catch herself to stop from fading away.

"Eliza Duncombe," she said, stepping toward me with her hand extended. "Welcome to Hysteria Hall."

When I didn't reach out and shake her hand, she smoothly drew it back and gave me a cool smile. "Just a little joke we have among ourselves here. Obviously, it's quite a rude nickname for the place. What year is it now? Is it the nineteen eighties yet? The last time I asked someone, it was nineteen forty-three. It could be the eighties by now, right? I died in twenty-two. Very difficult to keep it all straight, you know. Well, you *wouldn't* know, would you?"

I took a step back.

Now she considered me as if I might be a little slow. "Aren't you going to talk to me?"

No. I was not, in fact, going to talk to her.

What I was going to do was scream.

I screamed until Eliza Duncombe turned away and vanished into thin air. I screamed until the body on the ground became a blur. I screamed until I collapsed in on myself.

Until the whole universe collapsed around me.

At some point, I stopped screaming and fell to vacantly staring around the room. The ceiling looked like a normal ceiling. The walls looked like normal walls.

I can't be dead. This is only a dream.

But there was nothing dreamlike about the flurry of activity that soon took over my room. Police officers and paramedics crawled all over the place. My mother's sobs carried in from the hallway. A woman in a suit stood at the open window, taking pictures of the body.

Yes, *the* body. It was no longer me—*my* body—but just a thing, separate from me.

Of course the fact that there was a dead body on the ground, one that looked exactly like me, was intensely, soul-shakingly disturbing. But that body wasn't mine anymore. I didn't feel the urge to link back up with the pitiful corpse lying on the ground any more than you would throw yourself onto an old sofa you've hauled out to the curb.

I wasn't ready to let go of my life—at that point I hadn't even contemplated the remotest possibility of doing so—but my body was a different story. I could watch the guys in the COUNTY CORONER shirts load it onto a stretcher without breaking down.

My parents, however, could not. Mom gripped her hair in her fists, twisting and pulling as if she were trying to scalp herself. Dad's chest rose and sank so quickly that one of the paramedics finally told him to sit down and take deep breaths or he was going to pass out.

Seeing their reactions, a very un-dreamlike stab of pain pierced right through the center of my chest. So I turned away and watched the body below being loaded into a van. Then I followed a pair of detectives as they made their way downstairs, pretending as best I could that I was just another onlooker, a member of the team.

But as I moved through the house, it began to sink in that things were capital-*D Different* now.

Walking, for instance—I could walk on the floor, no problem. It felt solid under my feet, just like it always had. But going down the hallway, I could actually feel the air go *through* me. It was almost like walking in the rain and feeling the water against your skin, except I felt it on the inside of my skin, too.

As I wove between all the people gathered in the lobby, the shock began to set in. I caught sight of Janie hunched on the couch, looking impossibly frail and thin, wrapped tightly in the arms of a female police officer. The woman spoke quietly into my sister's ear, but Janie didn't seem to hear her. Her face was red and puffy, her eyes glazed. I'd never realized how much life had been in my sister's face until it was replaced by this dull, depthless sorrow.

I drifted by a group of paramedics talking about how "Hysteria Hall" gave them the creeps.

"You kidding me?" one of the guys said. He was short and wiry with mahogany skin. "Who would bring their kids to a place like this?"

For a split second, I felt oddly vindicated. Then I remembered that my parents had just had their lives ruined, and I felt guilty.

"I heard the house is cursed," said a female paramedic with a long red braid.

"Yeah," the first guy said. "My granddad was part of the government team that came here to scout for copper during the Depression. His twin brother got sucked into a ditch and drowned . . . only there was no water in the ditch. They never figured out how it happened."

"Well, clearly," the redhead said, forming her hands into creepy claws, "it was a *haunted* ditch. *Boogedy boogedy.*"

From behind me came the authoritative clearing of a throat, and the paramedics jumped to attention at the appearance of a man in a dark suit who walked past them and over to my parents, seated on one of the sofas. He introduced himself as Detective Kinsella, then began to ask them questions—like why I'd been alone in the room, what they'd observed in the house, and then more and more small questions that grew from the big ones like branches. He was after every detail.

And then he went for it. "So you say you were angry with your daughter," he said slowly. "Did you . . . strike her?"

Mom looked up, agape. "*Strike* her? You mean . . . hit her?"

"We've never touched our daughters in anger in their entire lives!" My father's voice was almost a roar, and he started to get to his feet. "And for you to suggest otherwise is inviting a lawsuit—"

Detective Kinsella remained totally unruffled. He held up his hand. "Mr. Piven—"

"*Dr.* Piven," my father seethed, apparently not too grief-stricken to be all high and mighty about his PhD.

"Dr. Piven," Kinsella said. "Please understand that these are standard questions that must be asked. Because your daughter's condition is somewhat alarming."

"Of course it is." Mom broke into fresh sobs. "She's *dead.*"

Dad exhaled through his teeth. "She fell out a window—"

"Fell," the detective repeated. "Forgive me, I know this is difficult. But . . . did you happen to see her hands?"

"What are you saying?" my father asked.

The officer sighed. "That she seemed to have worked quite hard to detach the wire screen from the window. Did your daughter seem upset to you at all? Had she been in treatment for any mental disorders, had any traumatic breakups—"

Dad leapt to his feet. "My daughter did *not* kill herself!"

"She was in therapy, but we all were," Mom said. "Not for any specific disorder. Lately, we've just had some . . . communication issues within the family."

The officer nodded and made another note.

"I'm telling you," Dad said. "Delia didn't jump from that window. Maybe she wanted some fresh air and lost her balance—"

"But her hands were covered in blood," my mother whispered. "I saw them. She opened that screen herself."

Then she just sort of—I don't know, melted. Her shoulders rolled inward and her head hung low on her neck. She seemed to shrink to the size of a child. "Why did she do it?" Mom asked softly. "Why didn't she come to us?"

"This is ridiculous!" And then my father made a fist, hauled back, and punched the wall so hard he made an actual indentation in the wallpaper.

"Excuse me, Mr.—*Dr.* Piven," the detective said, standing up and grabbing him by the elbow. "Why don't we all go get some fresh air?"

I'd never seen my parents like this—Mom totally unhinged, Dad aggressive and belligerent. It made me feel a little jittery, so I walked away, toward the door that led to the wardress's office. A few minutes of peace and quiet would do me good.

Part of what bothered me was that I didn't actually remember what had happened. *Did* I pull that protective screen away from the window? It seemed unlikely that they'd be wrong about something that evident.

Did I really . . .

I shied away from the question, trying to suppress it under a bushel of other, marginally less troubling thoughts, but it popped back up anyway.

Did I really jump?

I couldn't stop myself from asking, but I could refuse to answer. I was at the door to the wardress's office. Instinctively, I reached for the doorknob, but my hand went right through it.

I tried again, but the same thing happened.

"Sorry, sugar, that's not how you do it."

Startled, I looked up and saw a girl watching me. She was a few years older than me and so breathtakingly beautiful that for a second I forgot to think about being dead.

She wasn't even wearing makeup. Her only ornamentation was ash-blond hair that flowed in graceful waves almost to her waist. Her brown eyes glittered, framed by thick, dark lashes. Her smile was sympathetic, her lips a perfect cupid's bow. The dress she wore was pale blue cotton, floor length, with a high neck and a white ribbon tied around her slender waist. There was nothing especially fancy about it, but its simple loveliness made me feel like a toad.

And she smelled overwhelmingly of buttercups.

She was a ghost, of course. Another ghost. They were *everywhere*. I was surrounded by them. I'd been surrounded by them from the moment I stepped inside the stupid building.

"I mean, I suppose you *could* do it that way," the ghost said to me. "Well, *I* could, *you* couldn't, not yet—but it's not worth the trouble." She had a Southern accent, with soft, rolled *R*s and drawn-out vowels.

I stared at the doorknob.

"Shall I show you how?" she asked in her sweetest charm-school voice. "Oh, and how rude of me to not introduce myself. I'm Florence Beauregard." She pronounced it *bo-re-gahhhd*, with an airy manner that suggested a refined upbringing.

Florence watched me expectantly, clearly willing to help. But I wanted nothing to do with any ghosts at all, and prettiness and polite manners weren't enough to change that.

I ignored her and plunged straight ahead, planning to walk right through the door. But instead I ran right into it. My head radiated pain as if it were a real head that had just made contact with a real door. I reached up and tried to rub the ache away.

Florence stood to the side, looking slightly amused, her eyebrows raised. "I told you, that's not going to work. Let me—"

She came closer, and I jerked away.

"No," I said. "Just go away. Leave me alone."

She cocked her head to the side, and her smile evaporated. "All right, sugar. Enjoy yourself."

She disappeared through the wardress door as if it weren't even there.

I turned around. The activity level in the lobby had gradually descended from a buzz to a low murmur. While the police officers held little meetings among themselves, my parents now sat on the sofa with Janie, who was asleep with her head in Mom's lap.

Dad and Mom didn't look like they were going to be able to sleep. Maybe ever again.

I sat on the floor at their feet. I wanted to lean against Mom's knees, but I went right through them, which gave me a sick, spinning sensation. So I leaned against the sofa instead.

I didn't think about being dead, in the larger sense. There was time for that later. For now, I just needed to feel like a member of the family. Oh, the irony—what I wanted most in the whole world was to stay right there with my parents. Safe. Loved. Overprotected. One of the group. Suddenly, nothing else seemed important at all. For the life of me, I couldn't understand why I'd ever been so eager to distance myself from them.

My mother shifted. Her eyes slowly came into focus, and then they trained on the double doors that led out to the front yard. "She'll walk in," she said faintly, dazed. "Any minute."

Dad, who had been zoned out, snapped to attention.

Mom's free hand drifted over and grabbed his wrist. He tensed and almost pulled away, then sat deathly still, like he was within striking distance of a rattlesnake.

"This isn't real," Mom said, her gaze never wavering, her voice growing eerily clear. "This isn't happening. Watch—I'm going to say her name, and she's going to walk through those doors."

"Lisa—"

"*Don't say a word*," Mom said, her voice thick with despair. "We just need to wait a minute. We just need to sit here. And then she'll come back. I'll say her name, and she'll come back."

Dad closed his eyes. "She won't come back. She can't."

"Yes, she will. She has to. She's my baby, and *she has to come back.*"

My father glanced over at Mom, dread on his face. He was about to speak when she cried out in a horrid, jagged voice.

"Delia!" she yelled. "Delia!"

Janie snapped awake and sat up, her eyes wild with fear.

"Stop it!" Dad hissed. "You're scaring Janie."

"Why are you saying her name?" my sister asked, struggling to get to her feet. "Is Delia alive? Was this a joke? I *knew* it was a joke!"

"Delia!" Mom said again. She leapt to her feet and ran to the front door, pulling it open and shouting hoarsely into the morning air. "Delia! Delia! *Come back!*"

Janie stared at my father, her mouth open. "Daddy? Is Delia really alive?"

"Oh God. Oh God, *no.*" My father's face suddenly seemed to crack into a thousand pieces, and Janie collapsed against him. They were both sobbing. I'd never seen my father cry before. *Never in my whole life,* I realized. My whole life. Which was now over.

The room was in sudden, bewildering chaos. Despite the paramedics who hurried over to try to calm her down, Mom went on calling my name.

"Delia!" My mother's voice broke. And something inside me broke, too.

"Mom, I'm here!" I yelled, running toward her. "Mom! I'm right here! I can see you! I can hear you!"

She paused.

"I'm here!" I wailed. I couldn't stop myself. "Look at me, Mom. Just turn and look at me!"

She turned. And I swear—*I swear*—she looked right at me.

Hope blossomed in my heart. I could take being dead, I could take being a ghost, if my mother could see and hear me. If I just had someone I loved to hold on to, to anchor me and love me and make me feel real.

But the bright, expectant look in my mother's eyes went out like a candle on a pitch-black night.

"She's not coming," she said, like it had just occurred to her. Her eyes traveled across the room. "She's not coming . . . because she's dead."

My heart cracked in two. The strength went out of me. I sank to the floor, buried my head in my arms, and wept. Over and over the pain in my chest expanded and crested, like a wave hitting the shore, while the tears burned my eyes like acid.

When I was drained of tears, I raised my head to find that the lobby was nearly empty. The detectives were herding my parents out the front doors.

I ran to follow them, but the bolt latched with a decisive *clank* before I could get out. Without thinking, I went to open it.

My hand went right through the doorknob.

I didn't try a second time. I slid to the floor, my back against the wall.

Silence settled around me like ashes.

"It's because a door is a barrier. Like a wall or a floor."

Jingle jingle.

I looked up. Eliza, the ghost in the silk pajamas, stood a few feet away, leaning against the stairway railing.

When she saw that I was listening, she went on. "Unless you *want* to pass through one, barriers will stop you, just like they did when you were alive."

"But I did want to pass through it," I said. My voice was hoarse and mumbly. "My parents are out there."

She took a few steps toward me. "There are different ways of wanting something. I suppose what I mean is that you have to believe you can do it."

I curled deeper into myself, my arms wrapped around my knees. I felt worn out, used up.

"Sorry, but I'm not going to talk to you." My voice hardened. "I want you to leave me alone. All of you."

"All of us? Like I'm the head of a committee?" She frowned. "You should try to be more friendly. It can get very lonely here."

"Yeah?" I said, and felt a sudden spark of suspicion. "Is that why you pushed me out a window? Because you're lonely?"

Eliza suddenly seemed brighter somehow—like her intensity had been dialed up. "Look at your hands," she said coldly. "I suppose *I* pulled the metal screen out of the wall?"

I really looked at them, for the first time. They were covered in scratches and cuts—there was no blood, but there were definite signs of damage.

"Like I said before," Eliza said. "I did my best. It's not my fault if you couldn't take a hint. Do you know how lucky you were even to have the chance to leave? The rest of us couldn't. *We* were truly stuck here. You had the option to open the door and walk out, so don't blame me if you didn't take it."

Then she pivoted in place and grandly walked away,

straight through the wall, her silk pajamas billowing gracefully behind her.

Whatever. I was glad she was gone. I closed my eyes, determined to forget all about her. And the other one—Florence. I didn't need some old-timey, know-it-all ghosts following me around dead-shaming me.

Besides, it wouldn't be long before my family was going to pack up and leave this place, probably forever. And one thing about my plans definitely hadn't changed: living or dead, I wasn't planning to stay here a minute longer than I had to.

I was going home if it killed me.

CHAPTER 10

Hours later, a pair of police officers came back inside, and I followed them to the superintendent's apartment.

My family's bags were still piled in the corner, so they had to come back. Even if they couldn't bring themselves to sleep here, surely they would return to get their things. And through the window, I could see that the car was still parked outside.

All I had to do was wait. With a sigh of relief, I sank onto the sofa, half expecting to crash to the floor, but the cushions caught me. I found a good spot to sit and stare at the car.

The police officers left. When the sky began to darken, I realized I'd been in the same spot for probably ten hours. But I wasn't hungry, sore, or cramped. I didn't even have to pee. I found these revelations terrifying. Without the minor needs of day-to-day life, was I even real anymore?

Even though I understood on some level that I was dead, that hadn't stopped me from also thinking of myself as somehow alive. After all, I could still walk, and talk, and think . . .

But I *wasn't* alive, was I?

I could sit there, unchanged, for a hundred years, during which time every single person I knew and cared about would grow old and die. Even if I went home to live with my parents, I'd still have to watch the passing years suck the life out of their bodies.

Not only that, but I'd have to see them living every day in complete misery. I'd probably end up going to my own funeral, which would be weird and horrible. Would Landon even come? I pictured him sitting in the front row, sobbing remorsefully, then swearing off other women forever and joining a monastery, where he would spend the rest of his life pining for me.

Yeah, right. He would probably just bring his new girl-friend. The camp counselor, whose arms were probably weighed down by all the friendship bracelets she got for being tanned and athletic and pretty. No. Landon was, pardon the expression, dead to me.

But my best friend, Nic . . . Nic would be heartbroken.

For a while, anyway. But even she would forget about me eventually. There would come a time when she'd get through a whole day without even a fleeting thought of me or the amazing times we had together. Some other girl—maybe her college roommate (who, by the way, was supposed to be *me*) would be the maid of honor at her wedding. Nic would bring me up in conversation sometimes, and I would be this mysterious, tragic part of her past.

I didn't want to be a dim anecdote from someone's childhood. I wanted to be a *person*.

And what about my parents? Would they forget me, too?

I was wallowing in my own thoughts, melancholy and unfocused, when I suddenly noticed that everything around me seemed slightly . . . off. And not just the kind of "off" that happens when you're dead. *Off*-er than that.

I snapped back to awareness.

The light in the room had brightened. The hills outside were washed in pale morning sun.

And my family's belongings had disappeared.

My heart in my throat, I raced to the window, where I could see them in various stages of getting into the car: Janie fastening her seat belt in the backseat; Dad in the passenger seat; Mom standing just outside the car talking to a police officer; and my mom's brother, my uncle James, lowering himself into the driver's side.

I felt dizzy with confusion. What happened? How did I miss their return?

I ran to the door and spent a few seconds pawing uselessly at the knob before I remembered that I wasn't going to be able to open it. I balled my hands into fists and banged on the door. It didn't make a sound, and the door remained solid.

No. This couldn't be happening. I wasn't going to have to stay trapped in the house like an animal in a cage and watch my family drive off and leave me. That would be too brutal, too unfair. I had to get in that car.

I tried the door again. Nothing.

"Please!" I yelled, my voice rising in panic. "Please! Let me out! I need to get out!"

My chest ached, and tears sprang to my eyes. I covered my face with my hands.

I couldn't do it.

Jingle, jingle.

"Eliza?" I snapped my head up to look around, but there was no sign of her . . .

Except that someone had opened the door.

"Thank you, *thank you*, wherever you are!" I called over my shoulder. "Good-bye!"

I reached the car just as Mom was getting into the backseat next to Janie.

Not willing to chance being left behind, I threw myself in next to them.

I landed hard, at first not sure what was happening—all I could make out was darkness. But when I stood up, I realized that I had somehow gone *through* the car. I was partly inside it with my family, but my feet were still on the ground, and my head was up above the roof.

I tried to sit. I couldn't. I fell to the ground, landing painfully on a tailbone I didn't even have.

Uncle James turned to the backseat and said, "Ready?"

Mom nodded, then started to weep into her hands. Janie buried her head in Mom's sleeve as the engine started up.

The car moved away, first filling my body with a strange scraping sensation and then leaving me seated on the driveway.

"What?" I said. "No, wait! Wait for me!"

The car jolted down the gravel path, and I started to run, thinking I'd never catch up—but after a moment, I felt the same lost, slippery sensation that had come over me when I'd been waiting for my parents on the couch. And then, suddenly—

The car stopped.

Relief overwhelmed me, as well as the comforting idea that they must have sensed their daughter's ghost running behind them like a crazy person. I still didn't know exactly how to get myself into the car, but if I had a couple of minutes, I was sure I would figure it out.

Then I noticed a new sensation—a weird, almost *dragging* pressure against my legs. When I looked down, a dirty fog seemed to hover off the ground. I could feel it like sandpaper, going through my body.

No, the fog wasn't just hovering; there was a kind of slow movement *within* it. I saw a larger particle on a downward course and knelt to study it. Up close, I realized that it wasn't fog at all. The large particles were gravel from the driveway, and the grit against my skin was dust and dirt kicked up in the car's wake. Speaking of the car, when I turned back to it, I found that it had moved away from me—not very far, maybe a foot—but definitely out of my reach, where before it had been an easy arm's length.

For a second, I was totally flummoxed by the fact that the car and gravel both seemed to be moving in ultraslow motion. Then I sort of understood.

Now that I was dead, time was unpredictable. Sometimes it would slide ahead and leave me stuck in a distant moment—like when I had completely missed my family coming back into the house to get their things. And sometimes it would skid to a halt and send me pitching forward in fast motion when the rest of the world was practically at a standstill. Like now.

I glanced back at the house, cursing myself for rejecting Eliza's offer to teach me more about interacting with the world. Should I risk going back to find her and begging for help? What if time sped up again and I came back outside to find the dust settled, the driveway empty, and my family gone?

I couldn't chance it. I walked back to the car, tried to step inside, and walked right through the metal frame. Then I stepped out and tried again.

But over and over, I got the same results. Finally, I walked back to stand in the shade of a leafy tree and watched the car. They'd gone about fifty feet in what felt to me like an hour. At this rate, they wouldn't reach the end of the driveway for at least another day, so it seemed safe to take a little break.

And then a guy materialized beside me.

I was so shocked I almost screamed—and he didn't look any less surprised to see me.

He backed a few feet away, his posture formal. He must have been near my age—probably a year or two older—and his skin was dark brown, his hair neatly cut close to his head. His eyes had the golden-flecked luster of rain on a bed of fallen autumn leaves.

He was obviously a ghost.

"Who are you?" I demanded, too flustered to attempt a polite introduction.

"Theo Hawkins," the boy said, watching me warily. "Who are *you*?"

Theo was tall and thin, wearing a blue button-down shirt with the sleeves rolled up, and an untied bow tie that hung loose from his collar. His pants were dark gray trousers, held up by a pair of suspenders attached to their high waist, and on his feet he wore polished black boots with leather laces.

In spite of everything, I still had enough mental real estate to feel a little embarrassed about the comparative shabbiness of my appearance. If I'd known I was going to be stuck for all eternity with a bunch of ghosts off the best-dressed list, I would have opted for a pair of ballet flats and maybe done something else with my hair.

"I'm Delia Piven," I said.

His eyebrows went up. "You're not the Cordelia Piven who lives here."

"Well, technically," I said, "I am now. I'm her great-great-niece. I was named after her, but I just go by Delia."

Theo frowned down at me. "And . . . how did you end up here?"

I didn't know whether he meant "here at the house" or "here among the dearly departed," so I started at the beginning. "Aunt Cordelia died and left this place to me. My family came for the summer to fix it up. We didn't know what it was until we got here."

"It's not a good place." Theo gazed back at the house, looking concerned, and then turned back to me. "But how did you get *out here*?"

"What do you mean?" I asked, my patience wearing thin. "First I died, then I walked out the door."

He stared at me.

"Why is that a problem?"

"It's not a problem," he said. "But you're the only one who's ever come outside."

I stared at the looming stone facade of the institute, trying to figure out what he meant. "I don't understand."

"There are others," he said. "Many others. But they can't come outside."

"They can't?" I thought of Eliza and Florence. "What about you?"

"I died out here. I'm free to roam." He glanced down at his shoes. "I worked for the government. Surveying the land. Ever heard of the Strategic Minerals Act?"

I shook my head.

He didn't seem surprised. "We were scouting for land that might be worth mining. I was here, working, and I had an accident."

"What kind of accident?" I asked, though I suspected I already knew the answer. "Unless that's too personal."

I got the feeling it kind of was, but he did his best to be polite. "I was coming across the property over to the west of the house—through the graveyard—and I fell," he explained. "Ended up underwater somehow. Don't remember much after that."

My granddad's twin brother got sucked into a ditch and drowned, the paramedic had said.

So that had been Theo.

"There's a graveyard?" I asked.

Theo pointed off to the part of the grounds that would be visible from the day room window. "It's well populated."

"So's the house," I said.

He gave me a half smile. His still, quiet nature was like soothing balm on an itchy bug bite. I realized that by fraternizing with another ghost, I was breaking the pledge I'd made to myself. But Theo didn't seem particularly ghostlike. He was just a normal person. And the opportunity to talk to a normal person was too tempting to pass up.

"I'm really the first one who's come out here?" I asked. "Then who do you talk to?"

"I don't," he said. "Sometimes I see them through the windows, but we never meet."

"Could you go inside the house?"

"I wouldn't, even if I could." He shot me a sharp look. "I have no interest in what lies there."

"What?" I asked. "What lies in the house?"

"Many things," he said. "None of them good."

Even with my limited experience, that sounded like a fair description.

I glanced over at the car. While Theo and I had been making our introductions, Janie had turned to look out the window. The sight of her grief-stained face was like a thousand tiny pickaxes chopping at my heart. Feeling drained, I sat down on the grass with my chin on my knees.

Theo eased himself to the ground next to me. "You're not from around here?"

"No," I said. "We live in Georgia. What about you?"

"Born in Philly," he said. "But since I started with the Geological Survey, I rent a place in Faust, about ten miles from here . . . I mean, I *did* rent a place." He shook his head.

I wondered if ghosts ever got used to using the past tense. "I guess I'd be surprised if it even exists anymore."

"When were you born?" I asked him.

"Nineteen twenty-one," he said, which sounded crazy to me. So, so far away. "Died in nineteen forty."

I thought back to history class, to what I knew of that time period. "So right before the war," I said.

His brow furrowed. "There was a war going on in Europe when I died. Did we get into that?"

"In a big way." I leaned back on my hands. "And there have been a lot more wars since then."

"Too bad." Theo hesitated, then leaned back, too. "The living don't know what they have. They waste it. I know I did."

His words hit a little too close to home. I glanced at the car again. It still hadn't moved. If only I could get in there with them, if I could stay with them and be part of their lives. It might somehow make up for the things I said before I died— things that were too painful and horrid for me even to remember.

"Did you ever get to see your family . . . after?" I asked Theo.

"After I died? My twin brother came," he said. "Once. But it didn't go well. And he never came back. Dead now, I suppose."

"Didn't go well?" I asked.

"Long story." He might as well have said, *The end*.

After that, silence grew like a wall between us. So I got up, brushed off my hands—out of pure habit, because they didn't have a speck of dirt on them—and studied the side of the car, trying to reason out what could be the trick. It *should* work. A car was an object, not a barrier.

I turned to Theo. "Can you touch things? Make them move?"

In answer, he ran his hand over the grass, flattening it out. Because of the time slip, it didn't spring right back up—it would rise gradually over the next several minutes, a fraction of a millimeter at a time.

"Teach me how to do it," I said. Something about Theo made me feel more at ease than I had with Eliza or Florence. His spirit was calm and down-to-earth. I actually enjoyed being around him, I realized. If I weren't leaving, maybe we could have been friends. "Teach me how to interact with things, so I can get in the car and go home."

Up to that point, Theo's face had been haltingly, politely curious, but when I stated my intention flat out, his features hardened. He broke our eye contact and reached over to set the flattened grass upright again.

I'd said something wrong.

"Theo?" I asked.

"No," he said, abruptly standing up. "I can't."

I was too shocked to reply.

He looked at me with a mixture of pity and impatience. "It's not going to work, Delia. Even if you could get in the car—which you aren't powerful enough to do, not yet—you can't leave."

"But—" I cut myself off, taken aback by the expression on his face. He looked almost offended.

"If we could leave," he said, "do you think any one of us would still be here?"

I shook my head. No. We couldn't leave? I refused to believe it. He was wrong, wrong, wrong. He had to be wrong.

And then I understood why Aunt Cordelia had dragged herself out to the road before committing suicide. Why she hadn't let herself die on the property.

Because then she would have been stuck forever.

Like me.

CHAPTER 11

My voice turned to granite. "No," I said. "Maybe the rest of you couldn't do it, but I can. I will."

Theo shrugged. "Maybe you can. Best of luck to you."

Then he disappeared.

I felt a beat of sadness and then turned to check on the car. It was nearing the trees—which meant the gate.

Which meant the exit.

I ran ahead. Between the rusted metal gates, I could see the line where the rubble of the asphalt met with the smooth gray ribbon of highway.

Theo's wrong, I thought again. *I want this more than they all do. They just never wanted it enough.*

And then I plunged forward, toward the road. Best-case scenario, I'd go right through the gate. Then I could just walk home to Atlanta. Who cared, right? I had all the time in the world. Worst-case, I'd be bounced back like when I tried to cross the walls inside the house.

What I hadn't counted on was an absolute rock-bottom scenario—

—In which a stunning electric shock went through me, tensing every nonexistent muscle in my nonbody, sending my upper and lower jaws slamming into each other, setting my ears ringing, and landing me flat on my back, stunned. Possibly paralyzed.

I lay on the ground staring up at the trees, feeling like I might have melted into the earth, wondering if I had somehow become fused to the dirt itself—if, instead of being condemned to roam the house and grounds, I was now essentially buried alive. Unable to move, but able to look up at the sky . . . to see every raindrop and snowflake that might fall on me. To be gradually overgrown by the tall grasses in the spring.

Then Theo appeared again. I felt a rush of gratitude as he stood looking down at me, his expression significantly softer than it had been before.

"I tried it, too," he said gently. "Just do yourself a favor and don't do it again, all right?"

Theo leaned down and slowly, carefully, helped me ease up into a sitting position. Then he knelt beside me.

His eyes squinted slightly as he stared at the road. "It's early days," he said. "It'll get easier, I promise."

I don't believe you, I thought.

My parents' car seemed to be speeding up a bit. Only about twenty feet of driveway separated it and the gates. In the amount of time I used to spend doing my eye makeup, my family would be out of sight forever. Dad, Mom, Janie, and Uncle James were all looking ahead toward the highway, probably glad to be leaving and shutting the door on this terrible place.

But how could they not know, on some cellular level, that what they were really leaving behind was *me*? How could they not feel it?

I needed something to hold on to. Without thinking, I reached out and grabbed Theo's hand.

He tensed and yanked his fingers out of mine.

"I'm so sorry," I said, feeling embarrassed. I hadn't meant anything romantic by it—that was absolutely the farthest thing from my mind—but things were probably different back when Theo was alive. Maybe the gesture signified more back then. My cheeks burned.

"No, I'm the one who should be sorry," Theo said, staring at our hands, which were inches apart. "It's just that I haven't touched anyone since I died. To be honest, I haven't even talked to anyone." He paused. "Not until you."

I nodded, and then a moment later, I felt his hand reach out and take mine.

He swallowed hard, like there was a lump in his throat, then gave me a self-conscious grin. "You don't know how much you miss something until you get it back," he said.

I was too miserable to smile back. But his touch gave me strength. I thought, *I can do this. I have a friend now.* The unbearable pain of knowing my family was leaving lessened a little.

Until I looked back at the car.

It was halfway through the gate.

Before I could stop myself, I was back on my unsteady feet, staggering toward the gate.

"Come back!" I screamed. "Mom, Dad, Janie—come back!"

Theo grabbed me by the elbow a couple of feet shy of the property line. "They can't hear you," he said. "You're just going to tire yourself out."

All at once, time ramped up to normal speed. And the car

stopped—this time for real. I held my breath as my father's door opened. But then he walked *past* me and grabbed one of the rusted gates, and slowly pulled it through the brush and dirt until it was blocking half the driveway. Uncle James got out of the car and came to help him drag the other side. Then my uncle handed my father a metal chain and a spinning combination lock.

As Uncle James got back in the car, my father stood on the other side of the metal bars, about two feet away from me. And he locked the gate.

"Daddy," I said, my voice crumbling. "Don't do this. Don't leave me."

He kept staring, and I became convinced that he was looking at me, he *had* to be looking at me. I felt myself growing enraged by the thought that he was only pretending not to see me.

"I'm sorry, Delia," Dad said, starting to cry again. "I'm so sorry."

"No!" I roared. "*No!* Apology *not* accepted! *No!*"

"Delia," Theo said, his voice insistent. "Stay away from the gate."

He tried to grab my hand and pull me back, but I shook him off.

"Don't touch me!" I snapped, feeling utterly humiliated.

He stepped away.

I turned to apologize, but his features were set. His jaw clenched and his eyes gazed up into the sky. "You're not the only one, you know," he said, his voice jagged. "We all had people we wanted to see again. We've all been left behind. We're all forgotten. Everyone I ever loved, everyone who ever loved me, is dead. You're . . . you're not the only one."

The car started up again and turned left onto the highway, where the heat from the glaring summer sun turned the air wavy, like a mirage—a vision you could see but never touch.

I watched until the car was gone from sight, and then I stood for a long time staring at the empty stretch of road.

"Come on," Theo said, almost pleading. "Don't keep standing here."

"No," I said. "Leave me alone. Please."

"Okay," he said. His voice sounded hurt, and I knew I'd broken whatever fragile friendship we'd begun. After this, he might never want to speak to me again.

Feeling more regret than I would have expected, I watched him go. As he passed by a patch of trees, a strange light flickered high in the branches, and after a moment, I recognized it as the dancing light I'd seen coming through the window of the day room. It had been Theo I'd seen, back then.

Florence smelled of buttercups. Eliza sounded like bells. Theo looked like light. How many other ghosts had I caught hidden glimpses of? How many of the strange sights and odd little sounds were secret signals that I was surrounded by dead people?

Theo's light moved with him, like a shadow. He passed the house, his reflection glinting off the stone and shimmering off the windows. I watched him until he came to the crest of the low hill and then descended the other side, down into what had to be the graveyard. I knew I should find him and apologize, but I thought I would rest first.

So I lay down in the grass and closed my eyes.

When I opened them a moment later, the world had turned white.

CHAPTER 12

Is this heaven?

No—

It wasn't the pure whiteness of paradise. It was the grayish, interrupted whiteness of winter. Around me, long blades of dead grass lay draped over low piles of snow. A few feet away, a set of delicate animal tracks led toward the trees. Bands of gray clouds rested over the hillside and blended into the snowy landscape, reducing the sun to a weak red ball of light.

I turned back to see the institute. It looked like a picture from an old-fashioned holiday card—the roof draped with white, snowdrifts piled against the front wall. Vignettes of frost clouded the windowpanes. A picturesque winter wonderland beautifully hiding the unrest inside.

I stood and started up the driveway, the frigid air slicing through me like a knife. Knowing I was already dead and couldn't freeze didn't relieve the painfully exposed feeling.

The front steps were iced over, but I ascended toward the front entrance without slipping. Then I stood staring at the door.

How on earth was I going to get inside?

If I called for Eliza and Florence, would they hear me? More than that, did they even care if I was stuck outside? Would they even come?

But as I wondered, the door crept open.

"Hello?" I called out, walking inside and listening for the sound of bells. "Eliza?"

From behind me came a rustling sound.

I sagged with relief. "Thank you," I said, turning around. "I guess I really need to learn how to—"

But what was behind me wasn't Eliza or Florence—it was a ghost.

I mean, it was a *person* dressed like a last-minute Halloween costume ghost, with a sheet draped over its head and covering its whole body—its very short body. Was it a child?

Then I realized—the sheet was solid. The feet peeping out beneath it were not. So . . . it was a *ghost* dressed up as a ghost?

I took a step forward. I was a little nervous, but this—this *thing* looked no bigger than a ten-year-old.

"Hello," I said.

As I reached my hand out to touch the sheet, it swayed slightly, like the little girl inside was nervous. A pang of loneliness went through me as I thought of Janie—poor, sweet, sad little Janie.

"Don't!"

The word was spoken with a distinctly Southern twang. The scent of buttercups crept into my nose.

Florence.

"Back away," Florence said to me. "Very slowly, back away."

The tension in her voice was all I needed to convince me to obey. I stepped backward.

The small ghost moved toward me again.

"*No,* Maria," Florence said, her voice low and threatening. "Leave her alone."

The sheet took one more step toward me.

"What is it?" I whispered.

"It's Maria." Florence frowned. "She's not a nice girl."

The ghost whipped its head toward her and uttered a menacing sound, almost a growl.

"I'm not afraid of you, honey," Florence said, lifting her chin imperiously. "Don't you remember what happened the last time you tried to bother me?"

Another growl.

"Back to the third floor, where you belong. Go! Scram!" Florence stepped forward, stomping her feet and clapping her hands, as if to frighten off a stray dog.

I felt a little guilty watching her. Maria was clearly just a child. How dangerous could she be?

"Delia, stand behind me. Back against the wall, as far as you can," Florence said. "Maria's in a bad mood. Something's got her stirred up. I don't want you getting hurt."

"Ghosts can get hurt?" I asked.

Florence looked at me like I was crazy. "Of course we can," she said. "Now do as I say."

I started to back away, but Maria kept coming for me.

"All right," Florence said, tucking her hair behind her ear. "I guess it's come to this, then."

A noise began to fill the room. It started as a low rumbling but got higher and higher pitched, until my head ached and my ears rang.

Then Florence seemed to explode into light, a violent strobe surrounding her body in a vibrating aura. Her eyes went black and her mouth hung open—the skin seemed to be peeling away from her bones. And slowly, she rose up off the ground, flickering like a phantom from a horror movie.

Without warning, she charged at the little ghost.

It sounded like a velociraptor and a tyrannosaurus coming together in battle. Maria matched the high-pitched sound with her own terrible roar, and for a moment the air around the two of them became blurry and unclear, like a dust storm made of light. I stood helplessly to the side and caught glimpses of arms grappling, heads thrashing.

Then, suddenly, Maria flew back across the room and landed on her back, motionless, with her legs stuck through the wall like the Wicked Witch who'd been crushed by a house in *The Wizard of Oz*. The sheet was in a heap on the floor.

In the next moment, Florence was back to her usual, lovely self—only clearly exhausted. She panted and held up her hand, looking like she was about to fall over. I went to her side and wrapped my arm around her waist just as she began to collapse. She leaned into me.

How can we possibly be dead? I wondered. We had weight. We felt pain.

It took another minute before Florence could speak. "Thank you," she whispered.

"No, thank *you*," I said, trying not to act too freaked out. "You saved me from . . . What is she?"

"She's Maria," she said flatly, as if that were all I needed to know, before pulling away and smoothing her dress. Then she inspected her arms and muttered, "Oh, *perfect*."

I took a step closer and looked at her left wrist, which now had a very clear pattern of tooth marks on it.

But they didn't look like human tooth marks. The points of entry were all just that—points. Not the lines that a human bite would leave.

"Are you going to be okay?" I asked. "Is that going to get infected or something?"

"Oh, I'll be all right," she said, sounding pretty gloomy. "I just try not to get all marked up. You only get one incorporeal body, you know. Might as well take care of it. Do yourself a favor and don't go tumbling down the stairs."

"All right," I said.

Florence continued to inspect the tooth marks, more upset than she wanted to let on. Then she gave me a frustrated, self-conscious smile. "Sorry—Mama always did say I was a touch vain."

"What is she?" I asked. "Maria?"

"Want to see?" Florence walked across the room, grabbed the legs that were sticking through the wall, and tugged them until Maria was back in the room with us.

I almost cried out.

The only thing about the figure before me that resembled a human child was her height—and her feet.

The rest of her was a grotesque mess. The skin of her face was cratered with black sores. Her eyelids were crisscrossed with the scars of old cuts. Her cheeks and lips had begun to rot away, revealing the decaying interior of her mouth—pitted gums and an uneven row of sharp teeth. It gave her the other-worldly perma-grin of a great white shark, even when she was unconscious.

Her arms were just patchy skin over bone, her fingers curled painfully into claws. Her torso, where I could see it through rips in her dress, was twisted and burned-looking.

"Rumor has it she was ten years old when she came here," Florence said. "Killed her father some time in the eighties. She only lasted a few months before she electrocuted herself and a nurse. Nice kid."

Looking at what remained of Maria's old-fashioned clothes, it hit me. "The *eighteen*-eighties?"

"That's right," Florence said. "She was dead long before I came, and I died in aught-two."

This time I didn't have to ask. Nineteen aught-two. "Thanks again for saving me," I said. "And I'm sorry I was rude before."

"Oh, that's all right, I understand. Those first few days are a real head-spinner. Besides, that was a long time ago."

My heart sank. "How long?"

"Six months," she said, glancing out at the snowy landscape.

Six months? I'd been lying outside for six months? I wondered if Theo had passed by, seen me there with my eyes closed . . . and decided I wasn't worth waking.

"Has anyone come looking for me?" I asked.

Florence stared at me blankly, then figured out what I meant. "Your family? No, sugar. Sorry. The police spent some time here in the fall, but not a soul since then. Well—you know what I mean."

"Earlier," I said slowly, "you offered to show me how to go through the wall . . . Is there any way you could help me out with that? I mean, Maria can do it unconscious, and I can't even manage no matter how hard I try."

Florence's face lit up. "Right! That's it. Come over here."

When we were close to the wall, she came up to me. "Now close your eyes. And keep 'em shut."

I did. Then she took me by the shoulders and turned me around and around and around, until I was too dizzy to tell which direction I was facing.

"Sorry in advance if this hurts a little," Florence said.

Then, without warning, she shoved me, hard. I fell backward and landed on the floor with an impact that sent a stunning ache through my backside.

I looked up to complain, but I was alone.

In the hallway.

Florence popped through the wall, beaming. "You did it!"

"Oh yes," I said, getting to my feet and rubbing my rear end. "I totally did it. What talent. I'm clearly a genius."

"You didn't know the wall was there, so you didn't know it could stop you," she said. "Perception rules our kind. That's why—have you ever heard of people putting salt in their windows to repel spirits?"

"I . . . guess so?" I said.

"It works because there's no ignoring salt when you're a

ghost. The smell is so strong that you can never forget it's there long enough to get past it. We can't even touch it."

I sat back. There was so much I didn't know about being dead—about "our kind." It was basically relearning the rules of reality. "So I'm supposed to just . . . forget that the wall is there?"

Florence gazed thoughtfully off to the side. "It's simpler than that. The key is not to try. Just go through, because you can. When you walk down a hallway, you don't think, *Oh, Lord, let me make it down the hall this time.* You just go, right? That's how this works, too. Doors and walls are only barriers because you let them be."

I faced the wall. Then I closed my eyes and walked forward.

I'm just walking, I thought. *Walking walking walking. Nothing to see here.*

When I opened my eyes, I was back in the lobby. Maria was gone, her sheet now discarded on the threadbare sofa.

"Nice work!" Florence said, walking into the room. "You're a quick study."

I tried to suppress my goofy grin, but I couldn't. It was the first time since I died that I felt a modicum of happiness.

"There you go," Florence said. "See, it's not so bad here."

What else didn't I know? I wanted to learn everything there was about being a ghost. Despite my failure at the gate, some part of me was sure that if I tried hard enough, I could find a way off the property. Away from the house. Back to my family.

"Do you want to hang out a little?" I asked Florence, and then I realized that in 1902, people probably didn't *hang out.* "I mean, you know, spend time . . . together?" I felt awkward, like I was asking Florence on a friend date.

"Well, I was just going to—" Seeing my disappointment, Florence's face froze slightly, and then her smile softened. "Tell you what, let's go see what Eliza's getting herself up to."

Eliza, it turned out, was in the nurses' dormitory, getting herself up to lying on one of the beds and gazing at the wall.

When we came in, she sat bolt upright.

"I believe you two have met," Florence said. "Eliza Duncombe, Delia Piven."

"Yes, we've met," Eliza said, staring right at me. "Delia's the new girl with the etiquette problem."

I was about to apologize, but Florence went over and sat next to her. "Now, come on, Eliza. You don't want to be one of those cranky old ghosts. Be gracious. We don't get much company. It'll be nice to have a new face to look at, won't it?"

Eliza looked at me through narrowed eyes. "I'm perfectly content with the faces we're used to."

"Well, she's not going anywhere, sugar, so you might as well get used to hers, too."

I glanced around the dormitory. It was a simple room painted pale yellow, with four bunk beds in a neat line, separated from one another by plain white dressers. Every surface was bare except the farthest dresser, on which was a single figurine. I wandered over to look at it. It turned out to be a little clown with Xs for eyes, someone's old toy. Creepy. Without thinking, I reached over to pick it up. My hand went right through it.

I looked back at Eliza and Florence, who were watching me.

"When do I learn to do that?" I asked them. "Pick things up?"

"It took me a year," Eliza said briskly. "So don't get your hopes too high."

Florence was now curled up on one of the beds, her legs tucked under her. "Well, let's see . . . I died in March, and in December I knocked over the wardress's Christmas tree. So about nine months? 'Course, I didn't spend six of those months lying in the front yard like you."

I sighed at the thought of more helpless months stretching before me. "What's the trick?" I asked.

Florence frowned. "I wouldn't say there's a trick. It's kind of like going through the walls."

Eliza tilted her head to one side. "My first time, I'd been sitting and thinking about something else, and I got distracted and reached for a handkerchief, meaning to wipe my nose. I don't know who was more scared—me, or the living, breathing nurse whose handkerchief it was. She deserved it, though—she was a thoroughly horrid woman."

There had still been living people here in the institute when Eliza and Florence had died. "You were both around when this place was still in business," I said wonderingly. "I forgot that."

"All of us were," Eliza said. Her easy tone tightened a little. "Except for you."

All of us. How many spirits were there? And how many were more like Maria than like Florence, Eliza, and Theo? "Is the whole world just, like, full of ghosts?" I wondered out loud.

"How would we know?" Eliza asked. "We can't leave the house."

"Why not?" I asked, remembering what Theo had said. "Why can I go outside but the rest of you can't?"

They both looked baffled.

"Have you ever even tried to leave?" I asked.

Florence looked shocked by the mere suggestion. "Leave?" she repeated. "Why would we want to do that?"

Dread seemed to pour down my spine like cold water.

"You don't want to leave this place?" I asked. "Not even to see your family?"

"Not particularly," Florence said. "Our families have passed."

"But before they died," I said. "You never thought about getting out of here?"

They were both staring at me as if I'd suggested we all cut our hair into Mohawks and start a mosh pit.

"I tried to go out the front doors *one* time," Eliza admitted. "I failed rather spectacularly. It was . . . unpleasant."

I remembered being knocked to the ground outside, my strength completely drained, wondering if I'd ever be able to move again. "Unpleasant" was one word for it.

"Besides, why should we leave?" Eliza asked. "We don't know what's out there. We don't know what would happen if we were to get off the property. Say we managed to go, and then we couldn't come back. What then?"

"Then . . ." I looked around helplessly. "At least you wouldn't be stuck anymore."

Florence laughed quietly. "Sugar, this is our home. We don't mind being 'stuck' here, as you say."

"But . . ." I fell into silence, trying not to show how disconcerted I was by their quiet acquiescence to captivity. Was it really possible that they were content here? It was almost as if they'd been brainwashed, but I didn't say so. First, because I doubted they even knew what that term meant, and second, because if I started criticizing them, I might find myself friendless for all eternity. "What about Maria? Are there others like her? Bad ghosts?"

Florence shrugged. "Sure, there must be a couple. But don't you worry about that. Mostly everybody keeps to themselves. It feels more natural, you see, to stay in the part of the house where you died."

"But I can go anywhere—and you said Maria is from the third floor. She came downstairs."

Florence arched an eyebrow in disapproval. "Not everybody has the decorum to conduct themselves suitably. All we can do is avoid the unseemly elements and trust things will work out for the best."

I tried not to take her comment personally—as a hint that, if I observed proper decorum, I wouldn't be wandering all over the house and grounds just because I could.

"Oh, I don't mean you," Florence said. "But it's for your own safety, hon. Look at us—we've been here forever and nothing evil has ever gotten to us."

I shuddered. *Evil.* Suddenly, I remembered it—the creeping dark smoke that had overcome me in my room. Right before I fell out the window.

No. I didn't fall. I was pushed.

I was sure of it.

I glanced over at Eliza. I still wondered if she was behind it somehow—after all, she'd been the first ghost I'd seen . . . after. And there was something guarded about her that made me uneasy. She seemed to be hiding something.

"Maybe she's different," Eliza said to Florence, ignoring me. "Because she owns the place. Is that possible?"

Florence didn't seem convinced. "Anything's possible. But in my opinion she'd do well to confine herself to the known parts of the house."

Known by whom? Now I was annoyed. "I don't think I can accept being trapped here," I said. "This is not a good place. I came here, and I saw all this dark smoke, and then—" I paused. "I was murdered."

Florence jolted upright. "Murdered?"

"What could you possibly mean, murdered?" Eliza asked. "You jumped out that window."

"I didn't," I insisted. "I would never have done that. And if I did—for some reason—then it wasn't my doing. It was something in the house. I saw it."

"What do you think you saw, honey?" Florence asked.

I nearly glared at her, but stopped myself. "Like I said, I saw . . . smoke. Coming out of the walls. It came over me and . . . it made me fall."

"You've been through an awful lot," Florence said, a careful slowness to her words, "and nobody can blame you if you went a little batty because of it all."

A familiar old feeling flared up inside me. It took a moment before I recognized it as the feeling I'd had when my parents disregarded what I'd actually said and instead heard things as they expected them to be.

"How do you know I jumped?" I asked Eliza.

She drew back, offended. "Well, I didn't *push* you, in case you plan to start accusing me again. I . . . I was in the room. I heard the commotion and came to see what was happening."

"You saw me fall? And then you saw my ghost?"

She nodded.

I sat up. "Then . . . why was I still inside? If I died from falling? Shouldn't my ghost have been outside?"

She blinked.

"I couldn't breathe," I said. With the memory, my throat tightened. "Right before I fell. I couldn't get air in my lungs."

Florence sighed. "Delia, nobody's trying to tell you this place doesn't operate in mysterious ways. There are plenty of unanswered questions around here. But say there is something in the house that could do that to you—wouldn't it be best left alone?"

"Forget it." I shook my head in frustration. "Anyway, there's nothing stopping me from looking for a way to get back to my family."

They didn't reply.

"Is there?" I asked. I felt increasingly like the two of them were in some clique that I was being shut out of.

"I just think . . ." Florence glanced at Eliza. "I just think you'll be happier—in the long run—if you don't make such a fuss."

"But I . . ." I couldn't even find the words to express the fact that I was completely unable to tolerate the idea of a "long run" spent in this haunted old place. "I guess I'll figure something out."

Then the room was awkwardly silent, and I felt like I should just go find my own spot and leave Eliza and Florence to be BFFs without me. So I stood up and walked self-consciously out of the dormitory, basically reliving all the moments in my life when I'd proved too dorky or smart or unfashionable to hang with the popular girls.

Of all the things I would have guessed about being dead, I definitely didn't expect that it would sometimes feel exactly like high school.

CHAPTER 13

I spent the night sitting alone in the superintendent's apartment. But by the time morning came, I was restless and antsy, and the low, dark ceilings seemed to be closing in on me. I passed into the lobby, headed for the double doors that led outside, and then felt a jolt of shock.

Two wide-eyed teenage girls stood directly in my path, shoulder to shoulder, both with messy hair and in matching long, flannel nightgowns.

More ghosts.

The girls stared in mute fascination until I slipped outside, at which point their shrill giggles echoed behind me.

I rolled my eyes and kept going. A soft snow fell, the kind of big, fluffy snowflakes that land on your clothes as tiny crystals. Except they fell right through me as I passed silently through the quiet morning.

I trudged down the hill to the west of the house, stopping when I came to a row of white marble protrusions sticking up through the snow.

Just as Theo had said—the graveyard.

A few feet away, there was another row of headstones, and another one after that. Those beyond were buried in a deeper bank of snow, which was a relief to me. I didn't especially want to know how many women and girls had met lonely deaths here.

I turned around and nearly ran smack into Theo.

His mouth widened into an almost-smile. "I'd say it's too cold to be outside, but you seem pretty comfortable," he said.

So did he—he stood in a relaxed pose, his hands in his pockets. I realized how glad I was to see him again. After enduring Eliza and Florence's prim politeness, I needed to be around someone who wasn't studying and judging my every word and action.

"It's suffocating inside," I explained.

He nodded. "I can imagine. I like the fresh air, myself."

Only I hadn't just meant the air, or the temperature, or even the smallness and darkness of the rooms. It was the fact that there was no world outside of the Piven Institute—and the fact that that didn't seem to bother the others at all.

"So . . . what have you been up to lately?" I asked Theo.

He laughed. "Well, let's see. Every day I walk the perimeter of the property, and then I sit on a fallen tree over there, in that little patch of woods, and then I wait for it to get dark, and there are a few animals I've been watching since they were small, so . . . that's pretty much the whole story."

We were walking between the rows, basically on top of dead people. I wondered which grave corresponded with which ghost. Did the ghosts feel it when I passed over them? My seventh-grade teacher had told us once that when you shiver for no reason, that means someone's walking over your grave. The class told her she was crazy, because we weren't dead.

Joke's on me, I guess.

"Do you ever think about trying to leave again?" I asked.

Theo shook his head. "Not anymore."

"Why not?" I asked. "What would be the worst that could happen?"

"Oh, I'm not afraid," he said. "I just . . . don't care. It's been a long time since I cared about anything."

"That's it?" I said. "That's what's keeping you here? Not caring?"

His tone was practiced and easy, but I remembered the way he'd choked up when we'd held hands last time. Now he seemed to be trying really hard not to let that happen again—by suppressing any trace of emotion. "I used to care about things. But that's not going to do you any good when you're just a ghost."

I didn't answer. As much as it hurt to miss my family and wish they hadn't abandoned me, I wasn't about to pretend they didn't exist.

"Think about it," he said. "Have you ever known anyone who died?"

"My grandmother," I said. "She died when I was eight."

"Did you love her?"

"Of course."

"But do you think about her every day? Do you remember what she did, her life's work, the things she said to you? We don't do that. We let the memories go. All the moments that you thought were so important . . . it all starts to vanish, the day you die."

There was a touch of bitterness in his voice, and part of me couldn't deny the truth of his words. What was the point of getting all emotional about things and people who were only going to forget I ever existed? But at the same time, he was wrong. I still remembered how my grandmother smelled, and how safe being at her house made me feel. Those things became part of who I was.

Theo made a frustrated sound. "I'm sorry, Delia. That's a terrible way to talk. I don't mean you shouldn't care about people, or that your family—"

"It's okay," I said. "I don't think I agree, but it's okay."

Still, my mood was undeniably gloomier than it had been a few minutes earlier. I kicked at a pile of snow and watched my foot go right through it.

Theo caught his breath. "Now I feel awful. I'll make it up to you, if you like."

"How?"

The smile that followed surprised me with its brightness—and I filed a mental note that his detachment was only a cloak for something that had happened. Something that had hurt him.

"Do you like ice-skating?" he asked.

"Um . . . I'm from Georgia. Not a lot of hard freezes down there. Also, I'm about as graceful as a swan with a broken leg. I'm not really the athletic type."

"Well," he said, taking me by the hand and starting to run, "the good news is, you're not going to die out there."

Keeping up with him was easier than I would have thought. In a couple of minutes we passed into a small stand of trees and reached the edge of a small, round pond. Its surface was a shell of pale-blue ice.

"I've never—" I started to say, but Theo was already pulling me onto the ice. I shrieked and started to slip, but he caught me and set me back upright.

"The other good news is that you don't need skates," he said, gliding past me. "No friction, see? Come on!"

I hesitated, and he circled back, executed a graceful spin, and then looked at me with that infectious smile.

"I thought you wanted more fresh air," he said.

"Fine," I said. "But if I fall through, you have to dive in and save me."

"You won't fall," he said. "But even if you do, you could walk out. This pond has a nice gentle slope, and it's only about twenty feet deep at the center."

I didn't ask him how he knew that. The thought of sinking to the bottom of the frigid, dark water sent a chill up my spine.

"You okay?" Theo asked.

"Yeah," I said. "Somebody must be walking on my grave, that's all."

"They're bound to eventually," he said. "Now see if you can catch me!"

He swooped away, and I pushed off behind him, wobbling a little before managing to find my balance. Then I was sliding, faster than I would have thought possible, across the slick ice. The wind cut through me, but it felt good, bracing, human.

We spent hours racing each other across the pond, and I got to be almost as fast as Theo. By the time the sun began to sink below the trees, I could spin just as well as he could.

"How many times can you go around without stopping?" I asked. "In theory, if there's no friction, you could just spin forever, right?"

With a grin, he pushed off with one foot and began to turn. Then he came almost to a screeching halt.

"Theo?" I asked. A moment later, I realized that time had slowed down again.

How long would I be stuck out here, alone in this slip of time? Without Theo to keep me company, the tall trees and pale sky felt like a terrible wilderness. But after a few minutes, I decided to ride it out. So I stood back and simply waited, watching Theo's slow series of turns take shape in front of me, the delighted flash of his smile sending a trickle of hope into my heart.

If I had to do this—if I had to be stuck here forever—then at least there was someone like Theo . . .

"How many was that?"

Theo stood in front of me. Time had sped up and I didn't even notice.

"You're flushed," he said, a note of concern in his voice.

"It's nothing," I said. "I'm just having fun."

"You are?"

I nodded. "But I lost count of your turns."

"Me, too," he said.

As the sky darkened, we ended up slowly circling the pond. After a while, Theo cleared his throat and stopped. "I guess your feet are pretty cold," he said.

"I can't feel them," I said. "But that doesn't matter, does it?"

He was quiet for a moment, then brushed his hands on his trousers. "Still, you should get back to the house."

"Why?" I asked. "What difference does it make?"

But he was walking in that direction, and with no better options, I went with him.

"Am I really the first person you've talked to since you died?" I asked.

"You really are."

"Well, your social skills are pretty good, considering."

"Thanks," he said. "I think."

We walked in silence toward the main entrance and stopped at the foot of the wide stone stairway.

"This was . . . nice," I admitted. I looked at Theo, wondering if he felt the same.

But the smile he'd been unable to hide all evening had melted away, and in its place he wore an even more serious expression than usual. Behind his eyes was a deep pain, something he didn't want me to see.

So I turned and walked up the steps without saying anything more.

I was shocked to see Florence sitting on the lobby sofa, waiting the way Mom used to wait when I went out with Nic or Landon. When she saw me, her face lit up with concern. "Sugar, you'll freeze out there!"

I brushed my arms off and shrugged. "Still dead. No harm done."

She gave me the kind of look my mom used to give me,

puffed-out lips and a sideways glance—the kind of look that says, *Oh, YOU.*

She frowned. "What have you been doing out there? You weren't talking to that *boy*, were you?"

"Is that a problem?" I asked.

She sighed. "It's just that . . . your place is in here. I'm sure he's lovely, but being out among the trees and the wild animals is no place for a lady."

"Oh, well that's fine," I said. "I'm actually not much of a lady."

She clucked and shook her head. "What I mean is that . . . well . . . I think the house prefers us to be indoors."

I tried to think of a polite way to say that the house could stick its preferences down its stovepipe, but words failed me.

Florence's sweet laugh filled the room. "Sugar, you look sadder than a fat turkey on Christmas Eve. Anyway, I've talked to Eliza, and we have something planned that'll turn that frown right upside down."

I let her shepherd me back to the nurses' dormitory.

Florence's idea, it turned out, was for them to give me lessons on interacting with the physical world—specifically, learning to pick up a brittle old red rubber ball. It was kind of them to offer, but it felt like a consolation prize—one designed to placate me and keep me from asking questions. I pictured Florence cajoling Eliza into helping me: *The new girl is a crazy rebel, bless her heart; let's indulge her a little.*

I didn't want their pity. But I really *did* want to learn. Being able to manipulate objects would help my investigation. I could go back and look over Aunt Cordelia's letters, and when I found her office, I could search for information on the history of the institute.

So I went along with it. I thought it would be like learning to ride a bike. You ride a little, fall off, ride a little longer, fall off, and keep trying until you miraculously don't fall off. But in actual practice it was more like trying to ride a bike that you couldn't even manage to sit on. Repeatedly, I tried to scoop the ball off the table or the floor or from Florence's delicate hand, and every time, I failed completely. After about nine hundred attempts, Eliza and Florence looked like they were sincerely regretting their generous tutelage.

Finally, giving up, all three of us flopped onto the couch.

"I don't think I've been so worn out since I died," Eliza said. "I feel like I could actually sleep."

Florence smiled wistfully. "Oh, that would be wonderful. I want to dream again."

"Dreams," Eliza said. "I had the best dreams. Every night, it was like something out of the cinema—only there was talking, obviously."

Right—living when she did, Eliza would have seen only silent films. I tried to remember what little I knew about the 1920s. Flappers came to mind—women with short, dramatic hairdos and fringed dresses dancing flouncily in jazzy nightclubs. I could easily picture Eliza there, dancing among them.

"Am I allowed to ask what you did—why you were sent here?" I asked, fully expecting to be snubbed.

Eliza made an unhappy sound. "Nothing," she said, a note of protest in her voice.

Florence clucked and laughed. "That old story?"

Eliza reached up and pushed her hair back behind her ear. "I was *thinking* about eloping with an American boy. My father was very British, very old-fashioned, and couldn't stand the thought that I would marry a young man with no family or money. Despite the fact that my father himself had come to America to marry my mother for *her* money, and that was fine."

It confirmed my suspicion about a lot of the patients here; Eliza's misbehavior didn't sound so bad at all. Certainly not worse than sneaking off to Daytona for spring break. I wondered if, had we lived a hundred years ago, my parents would have locked me up here just like Eliza's had. But wondering that opened some dark well of untested emotions inside me, and I suppressed the thought before I could be flooded with feelings I wasn't ready to face.

I focused back on Eliza. "Eloping?" I asked. "You were going to get married? How old were—are you?"

"Seventeen," Eliza said. "Yes, I was eager to be married. The alternative was sitting around and watching my mother do needlepoint and gossip about her friends. It was bound to happen eventually, and I wanted it to be on my terms."

"Oh," I said, trying to imagine a life with such a narrow scope.

"You didn't plan to get married, then?" Eliza asked.

"Well, I don't know." I shook my head. "Maybe someday, down the road. People don't really get married that young anymore. I mean, my parents would have had a conniption if I'd ever talked about marrying my boyfriend."

Eliza and Florence exchanged a glance. "Boyfriend?" Eliza

asked, sounding intrigued. "What was he like? What was he called?"

"*Ex*-boyfriend," I said, correcting myself. "His name was Landon. He was cute and smart. And I thought he loved me, but apparently not."

Florence sighed dramatically. *"Men."*

Eliza leaned forward. "Did you love him?"

I shrugged. "I thought I did."

"Did he make you feel more alive, every time you were near him?" she asked suddenly. "Is that what it felt like?"

"Honestly?" I said. "No. Not really. Mostly I felt sort of nervous, like he was too good for me."

Both Eliza and Florence frowned.

"I don't know," I said, wishing I had an answer that made me sound slightly less pathetic. "I liked being around him, and we always got along. But somehow I did always feel sort of . . . smaller."

Saying it out loud made me realize that it was true.

"What about you?" I asked Florence. "Have you ever been in love?"

Her eyes glazed over. "Oh, yes, I was in love. I *love* being in love."

"Florence is like a fairy-tale princess," Eliza said. "She spends a lot of time sitting in the parlor, reading poetry, and waiting for Prince Charming to show up."

"Old habits die hard," Florence said. "That's how I spent my teenage years . . . sitting around lookin' pretty, trying to catch a man good enough for my mama."

"Prince Charming's not coming here," I said. The only man we had access to was Theo, stuck outside. And something inside me went cold at the thought of Florence turning her considerable wiles on him.

"Don't I know it," Florence said. "I'm so sick of women I could spit. Present company excluded, of course."

We all laughed a little, and I began to feel like they were warming up to me.

"Did it work, when you were alive?" I asked. "Did you catch a man?"

"Well, lots of boys came calling on me, of course. But none of them really got my attention. Then there was one who was different from the others." Florence leaned back and stared at the carved plaster ceiling. "He set my very soul on fire. I would have done anything for him. The problem is . . . he married someone else."

"Oh dear," Eliza said.

"*Oh dear* is right," Florence said. "Talk about a troubled woman."

Then we all laughed, harder this time.

I sat back, contemplating whether what Landon and I had had was even real. It certainly paled in comparison to Eliza's aliveness and Florence's fiery soul.

Maybe that was why he was the one I missed the least.

"Will you tell me more about what it was like to live here?" I asked, still curious. I tried to imagine Eliza arriving and being shown into the wardress's office. My eyes traveled instinctively to her wrist. "Like, why . . ." I trailed off, not sure if the question would offend her.

"My jingle bells?" Eliza's voice darkened. "I kept trying to get away—I was quite good at it, actually; I'd learned how to pick locks from my older brother, Ernest. Eventually they strapped the bells on. Completely mortifying. I'm like a cat. A naughty cat."

"They're not so bad," I lied.

"You know, my family never came back for me," Eliza said, looking at the floor. "Not even to visit."

"That's pretty harsh," I said.

She thought for a moment before speaking again. "Yes, I do think it is. What about you? What was your life like? Aside from the fact that your family doesn't like one another."

I flushed, annoyed. "We do like each other; it's just . . . complicated. Different from when you guys were alive. Families don't always get along."

"That's not different," Florence said with a small laugh. "That's the way it's been since Cain and Abel."

"What's different, I think, is that everyone seemed so *rude*," Eliza said. "The way you treated each other."

"We weren't always like that," I protested. "I was having a really bad day." Which was a bit of an understatement.

No one spoke for a long time, and when I glanced back over at Florence, she was gone. Eliza was beginning to fade, too.

"How do you do that?" I asked. "Fade in and out."

"It's not just us," she said. "You do it as well. It's like . . . when you're alive, you can walk into a room and not attract any notice. And then you say hello or spill your drink, and people notice you. For ghosts, it's a bit like that, only you fade in and out."

"So you can't always see me, even when we're in the same room?"

"Not always," Eliza said. "But I should warn you, I *hate* surprises. So don't creep up behind me."

"Fair enough," I said. I was starting to think she found me just tolerable, which was a big step up from before. Her next words floored me.

"What color was the smoke?"

I looked up at her, startled.

"The smoke you saw before you jumped—I mean, fell," she said. "What did it look like?"

"It was dark, practically black," I said.

"And it was almost . . . shiny?" she asked. "Like a piece of oiled metal?"

I nodded and saw a gleam of recognition in her eye. I waited for her to say more, to tell me why she'd asked. But instead, she nodded curtly and disappeared.

I was worn out, too, but I felt stubbornly determined to accomplish *something*. So I went through the hall door and down the dark corridor, illuminating it with the pale blue glow that emanated from my body. I'd been through every door except the one at the far end—the visiting parlor—so that was where I headed.

The room was large and gracious-looking, with wood floors and a fancy sofa against one wall. Apart from the superintendent's apartment and the lobby, it was the nicest room I'd seen in the house, which made sense, considering it was for visitors.

There was a large bookcase against one wall, and I let my eyes drift across the authors' names embossed in gold on the spines—Byron, Tennyson, Dickinson, and a whole row of dark green texts with gleaming silver spines—*The Selected Works of Lord Lindley*. I tried to remember the last book I'd read as a living person, and cringed as I realized it had been the Cliffs-Notes of something my teacher had assigned at the very end of the school year. Maybe someday I'd be able to pick up and read these books. Maybe even today.

I bet for something as noble as poetry, I'll be able to touch the books, I thought. Eyes closed, I slowly reached my hand toward the shelves.

Nope. My fingers went right through the spines of the first three volumes of Lindley. I slumped in disappointment.

Then a distant sound caught in my ear, a faraway rumble . . .

I perked up. I knew that sound.

It was a car.

I ran back to the lobby, where Florence had reappeared on the sofa. She gazed dreamily out at the grounds.

"Someone's here!" I said, racing to the window.

"That happens from time to time," she said, waving her hand languidly.

Off in the distance, kicking up snow as it came up the driveway, was a silver SUV.

Despite her blasé pretense, Florence came and stood next to me. "Who is it?"

"I don't know," I said breathlessly. But an impossible hope grew in my heart—

It's my family.

I ran through the front door and down the snowy steps just as the car reached the circular drive in front of the house. The glare of the sun on the windshield obscured the faces of the people in the front seat, so I ran around to get a better look at my dad.

But when I saw the person behind the wheel, I stopped short.

The driver of the car wasn't my father.

It was Landon.

CHAPTER 14

I stood staring at Landon's face so intently that it took me a moment to notice who was sitting in the front passenger seat.

Nic.

"Oh!" I cried, and the word ended in a choked sob.

"Who is it?" Theo had materialized next to me. He stared into the car, shading his eyes with one hand.

"My best friend," I said, trying and failing to keep my composure. Tears streamed down my cheeks, though I couldn't pinpoint which emotion had motivated them. "She came. She didn't forget me."

Theo frowned in Landon's direction. "And who's he?"

"That's . . . nobody," I said. "He's not important."

I ran up to Nic as she got out of the car and threw my arms around her in a bear hug, even though she couldn't know I was doing it.

"Nic, I'm so happy you're here!" I spoke loudly, as if she were hard of hearing. On the off chance that she could understand me, I was going to make sure I said everything I'd ever wished I could go back and say. "I've missed you! I love you! Thank you for not forgetting about me!"

But she didn't seem to hear my words, and she definitely didn't take comfort from them.

She stared up at the house like it was something horrible, a cavern filled with angry dragons, and shrank into her thick winter jacket. Seeing her so miserable took the happy wind right out of my sails.

Landon came around the car, looking more than a little uncomfortable. When he touched Nic's arm to get her attention, she practically jumped out of her skin.

"Are you sure you want to do this?" he asked. "You don't have to."

She swallowed back her tears and wiped her nose with a tissue. For a girl who usually went around looking like a Hollywood starlet, with dark Renaissance-princess hair and perfect white teeth, Nic was the world's ugliest cryer. Her nose went tomato red, her skin got all splotchy, her eyes squinched up, and her lips pulled back. It was a sight to behold, the perfect representation of who she was—over-the-top, emotional, big, blustery, and completely the most loving and lovable human being on the planet.

"I do have to," she snuffled, a steel rod of resoluteness in her voice. "I *do*. I owe it to her."

Landon sighed and stuck his hands in the pockets of his preppy navy-blue corduroy peacoat. "All right. But remember, we can leave anytime."

She nodded and went up the stairs toward the entrance.

The doors were locked, of course. Nic stood back and paused, then went back down the stairs.

For a second, my heart seized—I thought they were going to get back in the car and leave. But then she started around the side of the building. I followed her.

"Good-bye, then," Theo called to me.

"Oh, sorry—I'll see you later!" I replied, forgetting all about him as I jogged after Nic.

"Where are you going?" Landon shouted, and for a second I had this brain hiccup where I thought he was talking to me.

"There's supposed to be another door over here," Nic said over her shoulder, not slowing down. I stayed close behind her, listening to the crunch of her shoes in the snow. "There should be a key under a flowerpot."

"A key?" Landon jogged a little to catch up to us, his breath a faint mist in the cold air.

"Yeah," she said. She stepped onto a slab of concrete and knelt to lift one of the flowerpots, revealing a tarnished key. "Janie said they left a key, in case any lawyers or realtors came by."

Landon was quiet for a second. "Isn't Janie a little . . . ?"

A little what? I waited to hear what he would say about my sister. I wanted news of my family. I wanted to hear every little detail of their lives.

"She gave me the combination to the gate lock," Nic said. "I think she knows what she's talking about."

Landon shrugged and looked up toward the roof. "So are their parents going to sell this place?"

"Not yet," she said. "But maybe someday. I mean, what else would they do with it? Janie said her dad moved out the day after Thanksgiving. They're probably going to get divorced."

What? My parents were getting a divorce? I reeled at the thought. How could that be? They bickered sometimes, but in general they'd been an infuriatingly unstoppable team for my entire childhood.

"They say there are some things that break marriages apart," Landon said quietly. "I guess losing a kid is probably one of those things."

"It broke me apart," Nic said softly, and I realized how self-ish I'd been when I'd imagined her reaction to my death and fretted over being replaced by someone new. Losing your best friend would be something you'd never recover from. Even if you moved on, found a new college roommate, chose a new maid of honor . . . some tiny piece of you would always be missing. I thought of what my life would have been like if Nic died, and the bleak misery of it made my stomach ache.

Nic unlocked the door, Landon pulled it open, and they entered in silence. Then Nic went to the little table by the door and pulled a large key ring from the drawer.

"Right where Janie said it would be." She turned to Landon and tried to hide a shiver. "Shall we?"

He nodded, unenthused.

"I think she said it was this one . . ." She opened the door to the main hall, and I slipped through behind them. They'd come prepared—Landon held a huge torch-style flashlight, and Nic carried a little electric camping lantern. Nic moved as if she knew exactly where she was going. I got closer and realized she was looking down at a photo of a hand-drawn map on her phone.

The labels on the map made my stomach clench. They were in Janie's handwriting, but it seemed, to my eye, less loopy—

less like the perky preteen scrawl I knew and more like the writing of a young woman. Like she'd grown up in a hurry.

The map led us to the back stairwell and up to the second-floor day room. I hadn't been back up there since the day I died. But being with my best friend and boyfriend (all right, my *ex*) felt almost . . . normal.

Nic stood in the center of the day room and took in all the details, then strode ahead. Landon watched her, not quite knowing what to do or say. Her single-mindedness seemed to alarm him slightly.

"Through there," she said, gesturing toward the ward door.

But before she could go forward, Landon blocked her path. "Are you *sure* you want to do this?"

She was silent for a long time, and then she nodded, her eyes fixed on the door.

"Delia."

The sound of my name startled me. Eliza stood a few feet away, looking at me anxiously. "Are you okay?" she asked.

"Of course I am," I said, noticing that Nic and Landon had ventured into the ward hall. "But I have to follow them, sorry."

"No, wait—"

But I left her behind. When I caught up to Nic and Landon, they were standing and staring at the door to Room 1.

It was crisscrossed with police tape: CRIME SCENE DO NOT CROSS.

"We don't have to go in there," Landon said.

"Yes, I do," Nic said. "I really, really do. Don't you understand? She was my best friend. And her being here was my fault. That *stupid* trip . . . I knew she didn't want to go."

"Nic, come on," I said. "It's nobody's fault. I mean, if we're going to start pointing fingers, it's way more Landon's fault than yours."

She tore down the crime scene tape and went inside. Landon tried to tidy the dangling strips of yellow plastic before following her.

Though the prospect of being in that room filled me with dread, I was curious enough to go in after them.

"Delia!" Eliza's unhappy voice echoed from the hall.

The room was mostly dark, with stripes of dusty sunlight streaming between the boards that covered the window.

Nic shivered. "It's freezing."

Landon shrugged off his coat and draped it over her shoulders. They looked around for a minute, and then Nic walked the perimeter of the room, trailing her fingers along the wallpaper.

"Do you think she wished we were here with her?" she asked.

"I don't know," Landon said. "*I* wish we'd been here."

Nic nodded, staring at the boarded-up window. "I can't even remember the last thing I said to her. I think I called her a loser or something."

"That's just what you guys did," Landon said. "You can't feel bad about that. What was it she always called you?"

"A weenie," I said.

"*Weenie,*" Nic said, half laughing and half crying. "She always loved Halloween because for a whole day she got to call me *Halloweenie.*"

Landon snorted, and then they dissolved into low laughter.

"I could never think of anything for *loser*," she said. "So I just said March seventeenth was St. Loser's Day. But it wasn't the same."

"Yeah, not as good," Landon said.

Nic let out a long sigh, and the audible expression of her pain made me want to curl up and die. Again.

"Let's go outside," she said suddenly.

"Come on," Landon said, scratching his chin unhappily. "Why torture yourself?"

"Because I want to. I need to see . . . the place where she fell."

"But why?"

"Because if I don't see it," Nic said desperately, "I'll never believe it actually happened. I'll never believe that she's not just hiding someplace. You know how desperate she was to get away from her parents." Her whole face lit up. "What if she was here now? Like, hiding in the closet or something? Wouldn't that be hilarious?"

Landon looked doubtful. "Not sure that's the word I'd choose."

"You know what I mean. It would just be so . . . so Delia. If there were a cupboard under some stairs, I'd just about put money on her being in there."

He didn't look convinced, but she wasn't paying attention to him anymore.

"Come on," she said. "There's an exit through the kitchen."

Apparently, Janie had learned more about the house than I knew, because her map clearly showed a door leading out through the industrial kitchen. I trailed behind them, past the shelves piled high with stacks of giant pots and pans, past the hulking ancient stoves, and out a door with a thin coating of rust covering its entire surface. From the dark kitchen, we emerged into the crisp winter air.

Nic marched to the space under the boarded-up window. The ground was covered with snow, but she nudged her boot through it, kicking the white powder out of the way, until a patch of muddy, dead earth became visible.

Then she knelt, touched her hand to her mouth in a gentle kiss, and set her fingers in the mud.

"I miss you so much, you stupid loser," she whispered.

"You too, Weenie," I said.

Then her pain came pouring out, flooding the air with sobs. Her sorrow seemed to cut me in two, leaving me feeling pinned and helpless, weakened by my own reflection of her feelings.

Landon leaned over to touch her shoulder, but she pushed his hand away. Her sobs were gasping, choking sounds, echoing in the cold, empty air. Gradually they subsided, and she tried to speak.

"What?" Landon asked.

"I—I said . . . How could she?" Nic sat herself up. She looked terrible (and I can say that because I'm her best friend). "How *could* she?" She jumped to her feet. "How could you?!" she shouted up at the window. *"How could you do this to me, Delia?!"*

It took a second for the words to sink in. And then our shared sorrow melted away, leaving me feeling . . . angry.

"Do this to you?" I yelled back. "To *you?* Are you kidding? I didn't do anything! I'm the victim here!"

"It's okay," Landon said, trying to grab her arm. "Nic, it's okay. Come on, let's go inside. You're gonna freeze to death out here."

Grudgingly, she let him guide her back into the kitchen and through the maze of rooms to the superintendent's apartment, where she sat on the couch, sniffling and wiping her nose with a well-used tissue.

Landon flicked on the lights, then walked over and sat on the same couch, leaving a good-sized space between them. I hovered nearby, still hurt by her words but hungry for more conversation. I wanted to hear about my parents, my sister, the school year. I yearned for delicious, inconsequential little details—who won Homecoming Queen, what were the new trends, what books people were reading, which teachers were being extra strict this year, where our friends were applying to college. They were halfway through senior year. I wondered if Nic had to lie to her parents to be allowed to come here.

Landon fidgeted, his fingers tapping out an irregular rhythm on the arm of the couch, his eyes darting around the room. He'd always fidgeted. I wondered how many times I'd leaned against his warm chest, my eyes closed, thinking he was enjoying our time together—when really he was just looking around, wanting to be somewhere else.

"So . . ." he said finally. "Should we get going?"

"No," Nic said. "Not yet."

"Listen, you can't do this to yourself," he said. "You know that whatever she was going through wasn't your fault. Any more than it was mine."

"But what if she—"

"Delia, *come here right now*." Eliza's voice rang out from the opposite side of the room, urgent enough that I actually went to see what she wanted. But when I reached her, she simply shook her head. "You don't need to see this."

"See what?" I repeated. Was she jealous because my friends actually came to look for me? "See my best friend, who came to look for me and get closure? Don't *I* get a little closure?"

She stared at me incredulously. "You honestly think that's what you're going to get by watching those two—closure?"

"Those two"? What did *that* mean . . . ?

Then I turned to look at them.

Landon had edged closer to Nic.

My heart stopped.

No way.

I couldn't keep myself from walking back toward the couch.

"Nicola," Landon whispered.

My whole body went stiff. "Since when do you call her that?" I asked. "Nobody calls her that except her grandma. She hates it."

But instead of correcting him, Nic angled her head . . . and rested it on his shoulder.

Then he reached for her hand, wrapping her fingers in his own.

Come on.

She pulled her hand away. "It doesn't feel right."

"Oh," I said, "you *think*?"

I stared at them, a hundred horrible thoughts invading my brain at once.

Had Landon and Nic . . . had they liked each other all this time? Had my *best friend* been part of the reason he broke up with me? Did he bail on Daytona because he was afraid to be around us both at once? Was the camp girl just an invention to hide their secret?

"Listen," Landon said. "Neither of us knew what was going to happen. And we were both devastated. You lost a best friend, I lost a girlfriend—"

"Oh, please!" I snapped. "You lost a girl you dumped. Over text. Like a slimy coward!"

"We both loved her. And she loved us. And the thing is . . ." He reached up and gently touched her cheek. "She would want us to be happy."

"But not this way," Nic said. The pitiful note in her voice wasn't enough to buy my sympathy. She should have gotten up off the couch, slapped his hand away from her face. Instead, she just sat there like a traitorous lump.

"You're right, I don't," I said. "I don't want you to be happy this way. Have some respect for the dead!"

"Can't you feel it, though?" His fingers trailed down to her neck. "She's at peace. Wherever she is, she's peaceful and happy."

Nic's eyelashes fluttered. "Do you really think so?"

"No," I said.

"I know so," he said, starting to lean toward her.

No, no, no, no, NO.

NO.

"No!" I cried out. *"NO!"*

But then, in front of my eyes, they were kissing—a sweet, soft, slow kiss. The kind Landon and I used to have. The kind I used to describe to Nic, who listened with starry eyes because she hadn't had a boyfriend of her own yet. The kind that made me believe that Landon and I might be one of those couples who lasted forever.

When the kiss was over, he started to pull away.

But Nic—*my best friend*—pulled him back.

As I stood there, drinking in the sight of two people who should have, at the very least, had the grace not to kiss in the very place where I had *died*—something began to vibrate inside of me.

Only when the vibrations became so strong that I had already lost control of them did I understand what the feeling was:

Rage.

MY FAVORITE MEMORY OF NIC

Gym class, first day of sixth grade. As if being eleven years old in a pair of baggy blue gym shorts wasn't hideously humiliating enough on its own, Coach was calling us up, one by one, to assess our physical fitness level.

I sat a few rows back on the bleachers, listening to the clump of mean girls in front of me verbally eviscerate everyone who wasn't one of their own.

"Thunder thighs," they would whisper, or, "Jelly belly. Ugh, that hair. You can tell just by looking at her that she *smells*."

I was petrified, waiting for my turn to make the walk of shame and be judged for my shortcomings.

"Pisani, Nicola?" the coach called.

A tall brown-haired girl with thick glasses and rainbow-hued braces stood up next to me. The mean girls' heads swung around to get an early look at her.

"Excuse me, Coach," Nic said. "I don't actually care to walk up there and be mocked and ridiculed by this pack of cackling witches. I already know what's wrong with me. I have bad teeth, ugly glasses, and a big butt. So . . . can you just write that down?"

Everyone was speechless.

But one of the mean girls couldn't resist. "Don't forget hairy arms," she said.

And the mean girls spent the rest of the class running laps around the gym.

When Nic came back from talking to the coach, she sat down. "Your butt's not big," I said.

"Sure," she said with a shrug. "Not compared to yours."

From that moment on, we were best friends.

CHAPTER 15

I saw Nic and Landon as if I were watching them through a telescope—singled out, in perfect focus, while everything around them melted into darkness.

"STOP!" I roared, plunging forward past a little table with a heavy, old-fashioned phone on it. Without thinking, I swung my arm in its direction. The shock of contact reverberated through me, and the phone went flying and landed heavily on the floor with a discordant crash of its bell.

At the sound, the lovebirds on the sofa jumped apart.

"What was that?" Nic searched the room. When she saw the phone on the floor, her eyes widened with fear.

"Oh, are you scared?" I cried. *"Good!"*

Nic's gaze traveled back and forth, as if she was waiting for something else to happen.

I grabbed the little table by one leg and tossed it onto its side. It landed on the floor with a tremendous clatter. Then I stormed over to the dining table, grabbed the closest chair, and hurled it across the floor.

"What's going on?" Nic wailed. She retreated until her back was pressed against the narrow strip of wall between two large

windows, while Landon stood a few feet away, looking around helplessly.

Pathetic.

I swept a decorative bowl off the dinner table and hurled two more chairs in their direction.

Nic's thin scream of terror echoed through the room. Her fear filled my head . . . and fed my fury. My anger and the power it gave me were like a drug.

I stalked over to where she stood, made a fist, and propelled it through the panes of the window to her right—

One, two, three, they shattered. Glass showered the floor around her.

"Oh my God!" she cried. "Landon, what's happening?"

"What's *happening,*" I said, "is that you stole my boyfriend!"

Landon was rather un-heroically frozen in place. "Nic, get away from the window!"

She ducked her head and started to run forward, her hands covering her face, but I pushed her back. She hit the wall with a frightened yelp and then tried to escape a second time. Again, I simply reached out and pressed on her shoulders. She couldn't see me, so she couldn't dodge or duck away from my touch.

She slammed back into the wall, then gave up and helplessly sank to the floor.

Finally, Landon leapt into action. He raced toward her—but all I had to do was shove his chest to send him flying backward, tripping over the scattered chairs and landing in a heap.

I turned my attention to the second window, the one on the other side of Nic, and *one, two, three!* punched through the glass. Then, because releasing the energy felt so incredibly satisfying,

I kept going—*four, five, six, seven!*—until I'd rammed my fist through every single pane.

I was beyond hearing Nic's terrified weeping, or Landon's dismayed moans. All I could hear was the voice in my head—a monstrous voice fanning the flames of my wrath.

Traitors, it said. *Filthy, disgusting, bottom-feeding traitors. They deserve this. They deserve the pain, the fear . . .*

They deserve to die.

Then they'll know how it feels.

Finally, I caught myself and staggered back, surveying the scene.

Landon sat on the floor, cradling his left arm close to his chest. Nic was bent into a quivering little ball on the ground.

Eliza hurried by, elbowing me out of her way. Her voice was icy and filled with righteous judgment. "What have you *done?*"

I didn't answer. I stared at my best friend, who hadn't even raised her head to look up.

"Nic," Landon grunted. "I think my wrist is broken."

There was no answer.

"Nicola?"

Still, she didn't answer. Eliza knelt by her side.

"Nic?" I asked, stepping toward her.

"Delia," Eliza whispered, her voice chilled. "Get the boy's attention."

I stared. "Why?"

"*Get the boy's attention!*" she snapped. "Now!"

"How?" I asked. I reached for a stack of magazines on the little table behind the couch, but my hand whooshed right through them.

"It hurts," Landon muttered to himself.

"Oh, for the love of—" Eliza said. "I'll do it."

She stood up, reached through the broken window, and sent a small shower of glass tinkling to the floor.

"Nicola?" Landon asked, looking up and then hesitantly coming closer. "What's—"

Suddenly, Nic raised her head and looked at him. Her skin was dull gray but her eyes were bright and surprised looking. Her left hand held tightly to her right wrist.

Only then did I see the puddle of red spreading on the floor by her—blood. Blood that came pulsing out of a gaping wound on her forearm.

Landon gasped.

"You think it's an artery?" Nic asked faintly. "It's . . . kind of a lot of blood, isn't it?"

"Nicola, oh my God. Oh my God. Here—" Landon ripped off his shirt and ran to her side. "Raise it above your heart. Can you raise it? Let me . . ."

He tore the sleeve off the shirt and wrapped it around the wound. Immediately, it was soaked through with dark, brilliant red.

"Hold that," he said. "Hold it tightly. I'm going to call an ambulance—"

"No cell service," she whispered.

"Okay, okay." He was panting, on the verge of panic, trying to make a plan. "Then we'll have to drive, but the car's parked out front. Can you walk that far?"

"I'll wait for you," she said.

"I can carry you—"

"No, I'll wait here," she said softly. "Go get the car."

He looked at her helplessly, then ran out the door, shouting over his shoulder: "Keep the pressure on it!"

She nodded and took a few weak breaths, straining the air through her teeth. But after he'd gone, the grip she held on her wrist slackened, and her head fell limply to one side.

"She's passed out," Eliza said. "She's lost too much blood."

I dropped to the ground and reached for Nic's wound, trying to press my own hand on it.

But I couldn't even do that much. My hand wouldn't make contact with the soaked shirt.

Oh God, she's going to die. I killed her.

I killed my best friend.

"Please, Eliza, help me," I said. "Please!"

"Get out of the way," Eliza said, and she crouched at Nic's side. As if it were the most natural thing in the world, she pressed her fingers on the dressing and held firmly. "If he can get her to the hospital soon enough, she'll probably be okay."

"But it's snowing," I said. "The roads are iced over."

"Well, you should have thought about that before you tried to murder her!" Eliza barked. "Honestly, Delia. She could die here, and it would be *your* doing. I thought you said she was your best friend."

"I know," I said, and then I started to shake. My whole body quaked so violently that my vision blurred. "It was an accident— I never meant to—"

Eliza looked away, as if it embarrassed her just to witness my feeble uselessness. "Hold yourself together," she said quietly.

145

"The very least you can do at this point is not make things worse."

I nodded and shut my mouth, but I couldn't stop the tremors that coursed through me. I stared at my best friend's pale, unconscious face, wondering if some part of her knew it had been me who did those terrible things.

What kind of best friend was I? Nic wasn't stealing my boyfriend. He wasn't even my boyfriend anymore. And more significantly, I was *dead*. You can't steal anything from a dead person.

What had I done?

I was desperate for Landon to return, to put her in his car so they could race to safety. I ran to the front window and watched the SUV come around the corner of the house. Leaving the engine running, Landon jumped out and came inside.

His face paled when he saw Nic slumped over, but after finding her pulse, he relaxed minutely. Groaning with effort, he pulled her away from the window in an attempt to lift her. But his left arm was limp and useless, and as he tried to pull her up, he let out a primal yell of pain.

"You need to wake up," he said. "Nicola, come on, wake up."

She stirred, but her eyelids didn't even flutter.

Again, Landon tried to hoist her off the floor, and again he cried out in pain.

"Please, Nicola, come on," he begged. There was a tone in his voice I'd never heard before . . . a tenderness he'd never used with me. And it was mixed with crushing fear. When I looked at his face, I was shocked to see terrified tears streaming from his eyes.

He genuinely cared about her. More than he'd ever cared about me.

"He can't pick her up with that arm. She needs to wake up." Eliza stared at the ground for a second, came to some decision, then shot a sharp glare at me. "You stand well back."

"Why?" I asked. "What are you going to do? Are you going to carry her for him?"

She looked at me like I was crazy. "Carry her? And how would that look? You don't understand anything about how the world works, do you? Do you want spiritual mediums and two-bit psychics crawling all over this place? Now, *stand back.*"

I stood back.

"Farther," she said. "On the other side of the table. I don't want her to see you."

To *see* me? I obeyed wordlessly.

Eliza closed her own eyes and inhaled—but instead of taking in air, her body seemed to breathe in light. She glowed slightly, kind of like Florence had in the lobby with Maria. But that light had been fierce and vivid—this had golden warmth to it.

She leaned forward and placed her hands on Nic's cheeks.

"Wake up, then," she whispered. "Come, Nicola, wake up."

Nothing happened.

Eliza leaned forward so her forehead touched Nic's, and a bit of her glow ignited a flush of warmth under my best friend's graying pallor.

"Wake up, sweetie," Eliza said, a bit more tersely. "Enough of this foolishness. Wake up."

But nothing happened.

Eliza shot me a despairing look, then turned back to Nic. Her voice rose and became firmer. "Nicola—*wake up!* Wake up, you idiot! Trust me, you do *not* want to die here! Wake up!"

Nic's eyes suddenly popped open.

She stared right at Eliza.

"There's a good girl," Eliza said, stroking her cheek gently.

Nic was transfixed, staring at Eliza with wonder in her eyes. Then Landon grabbed her face and, pulling it toward his own, smothered her forehead with kisses.

"Oh, God," he said, his voice thick with tears. "I thought I was losing you."

Nic looked surprised to see him, and then she turned her gaze back to where Eliza had been sitting—where she still sat, though she was invisible to Nic now.

"Let's stand up. Wrap your arm around my neck," Landon said. He shuffled her into position, and she got to her feet, swaying slightly.

"Where'd she go?" Nic asked, looking around the room. "The girl with the dark hair . . . did you see her?"

"No, I didn't see anybody," Landon said. "I'm sorry. I don't know what you're talking about."

They reached the door, and Landon pushed it open with his foot.

Just before they stepped outside, Nic made one last visual sweep of the room.

And she called out, "Delia? Are you here, too?"

Then the door closed.

I stayed in the corner, where I'd been since Eliza ordered me there. Through the frosty windows, I watched Landon load

Nic into the passenger seat and then run around to the driver's side. The car bumped away from the house and disappeared around the corner.

Eliza sighed and sat back. She looked drained.

"Thank you," I said. "Thank you for saving her life."

"Well, it wouldn't have been necessary if—" Her harsh words cut off suddenly. I saw deep sadness in her eyes, and I saw them grow even sadder as she stared into mine. Slowly, she got to her feet. "Delia, you need to be more careful. You can't go on this way."

"I know," I whispered. "I'm sorry."

She nodded, and I could tell her thoughts had strayed to something heavy and painful, from some distant time.

"Why did you ask me about the smoke?" I asked. "Did something happen to you when you were here?"

"It doesn't matter anymore," she said. "The past is in the past. And if you're wise, you'll learn to accept your place and stop trying to change the way the world works."

"But why?" I asked.

"Because," she said. "You're still just a child, aren't you? And there's no limit to the destruction that a child can cause."

Her words went through me like a knife. For once I saw my actions from someone else's point of view. Saw the stupidity of my recklessness.

"If the past is kind enough to disappear into oblivion, we should be grateful," Eliza said, staring at the floor. "We should take it for the gift that it is. Trust me . . . I know."

Then she walked away and disappeared through the wall, leaving me alone in the wrecked and bloodied room.

CHAPTER 16

I stood in that spot until the shadows grew blue and long. Until the sky began to turn purple and orange and the night mist crept up from the horizon and enveloped the world in an eerie glow.

I don't know how long I would have stayed there if I hadn't heard the voice:

"Delia . . ."

It seemed to come from nowhere and everywhere all at once. I may have been in a daze, but I was aware enough to be frightened. The problem is, when you don't know where something is, it's impossible to run away from it.

"Delia . . ."

"Hello?" I said.

I dashed through the wall, into the dark hallway, and continued through to the kitchen. There, I found myself looking at a ghostly woman dressed in a crisp white-aproned nurse's uniform. Her name tag read NURSE CARLSON and she carried a metal tray—judging by the distinctive rust spot on one side, it was the exact same metal tray that I'd seen in the superintendent's apartment and in the nurses' office.

This lady really got around.

Her eyes were encircled with bluish-black bruises. Had *she* been the one saying my name?

She scowled at me. "You'd better get back to the ward before Dr. Normington sees you—whoever you are!" she snapped.

I stared at her without answering. She definitely hadn't spoken my name before. She didn't even *know* my name.

"Go!" Her voice rose to a shrill howl. She dropped the tray to the floor with a deafening clank. "Go! You're bad, just like the rest of them! You're all bad! You deserve what you get here! Bad, crazy girls! Look what you *did* to me! Just *look* at me!"

I didn't want to look at her. I didn't want to do anything but turn and run the other way. So that's what I did—out of the kitchen, down the hall, and up the stairs to the second floor.

"Delia . . ."

The voice was like the breath of a stranger on the back of my neck. It made me feel like I was being smothered by something I couldn't even see.

There was nowhere left to run.

Except up. To the third floor.

On the third-floor landing, I paused outside a door painted in layers of peeling paint. The metal sign, which had nearly crusted over with damp-looking blue corrosion, proclaimed LONG-TERM CARE.

I pushed it open and found myself in a large room. With the exception of a few wood benches bolted into place under the windows, which were covered in a thick mesh of chicken wire, the space was bare—there was nothing here except the stained tile floor and sickly green walls. There wasn't a single picture, no chairs. No fireplace, rug, piano, tables, or lamps. Nothing to suggest comfort or a sense of home. This was the day room for the lifers.

The dust was so thick in the air that it looked like a school of plankton swirling and dipping in the late-afternoon sunshine.

There was a door marked NO UNAUTHORIZED ADMITTANCE in a little alcove to my left, and another door across the room, with a dirty-looking stamped metal sign that read WARD.

I went through the ward door. Like the day room, the hallway was laid out similarly to its second-floor counterpart—same length and width, same number of doors—but with a few striking differences. The nurse's station was guarded by sturdy metal mesh, bolted into the walls. The closest door was open to reveal a filthy-looking bathroom with a row of exposed toilets, three grimy sinks, and a pair of bathtubs. There wasn't even a curtain for privacy.

No dignity for the troubled women on the third floor.

In each bedroom was a metal bed frame holding a limp, discolored mattress, most with rotting foam spilling out from their torn seams. A network of cracked and crumbling leather straps was clearly visible: two for the wrists, two for the ankles, one to go across the chest, and one to go across the upper thighs. Just looking at them gave me phantom sensations of pressure on my wrists and a tight feeling in my chest.

Things were much less luxurious up here, which made sense: for a woman to be confined to the third floor, she probably showed some signs of actual mental instability. Unlike the second floor, where the residents were just troublemakers, the families of the third-floor women didn't have to do any soul-searching about leaving them at the Piven Institute. There was no need for cozy bedding or snug-looking rooms to entice guilt-ridden parents or husbands with the promise of comfort.

The third floor wasn't just for show.

With a shudder, I walked toward the window at the end of the hall, where I stood staring outside at the moonlight luminescing off the snowbanks that covered the grounds.

I stepped back from the window.

But when I turned to head downstairs, something was wrong . . .

The hallway had shrunk.

Before, it had been wide enough that I could have lain down across it and still had a couple of feet between my head and the wall.

Now, stretching my arms out to the sides, I could reach both walls with my fingertips.

Just ignore it, I told myself. *Ignore it. It wants you to react. It's trying to scare you.*

My first instinct was to scrunch my eyes shut as hard as I could and run for it, but I knew that would be a mistake. What I had to do was act like I hadn't even noticed and sail right through the hall. Keep my head high all the way back to the first floor.

But when I took a step, I was immediately engulfed by a sick, dizzy feeling. My vision seemed to ripple. I rubbed my eyes to clear them, and when I looked up, the walls were even closer. With my arms extended, I could have rested a flat palm on either side.

Another step. Another wave of nausea rang through me like a gong.

If I stood still, the awful feeling subsided. If I moved, it pressed in on my face and my cheekbones and turned my stomach.

Two more paces forward. I leaned over and retched.

When I stood up, the hallway was less than three feet wide.

Finally, I closed my eyes, stretched my arms out in front of me, and ran.

I made it about ten steps before my shoulder slammed into something, and I recoiled, only to slam into something else on the other side. Now the space was only as wide as my body. And there were still six feet to the door.

I paused and then turned just my head to look back over my shoulder. Surely I'd see that this was all just an illusion. There would be a spacious, bright hall behind me.

But there wasn't. What I saw was like a view through a fun-house mirror. The narrow walls twisted off out of view, squeezed together and distorted.

What's more, they were still getting closer—as if a zipper was dragging them together.

As if *I* was the zipper.

I was paralyzed by fear, afraid to go forward and afraid to stay where I was. What would it do to me? Smash me flat? Leave me horribly maimed and disfigured, the kind of ghost that other ghosts chase back to the third floor?

I felt like a mouse being tormented by a cat. Like the house itself was batting me into a corner, playing with me—just because it could.

As if it was showing me who was boss.

Just go, I thought. They were just walls. I could get through walls. What was the problem? But they were solid against my body.

Suddenly, there was a blast of cold air, so cold it made my whole body ache.

And something slammed into me from behind, pushing me into action.

I plunged ahead, pivoting sideways when the walls were too tight to walk straight. I made it to the door, closed my eyes, and pushed through, throwing myself into the dreary day room in the last possible moment.

With no sign of what had caused it, the cold air dissipated.

"Hello?" I called. "Hello—who's here? Who are you?"

There was no answer.

But there was something on the floor that hadn't been there before—a tiny image, carefully cut out of a magazine: a little box of cat food.

Weird.

I slumped back against the wall, my energy almost totally gone. Being tired as a ghost was different from being tired as a person—it almost felt like I was beginning to fade away, to lose parts of myself. My body seemed somehow more translucent, and my thoughts jumped around. I couldn't focus.

I need to rest.

I walked through the day room, noticing as I did that a woman about my mom's age now occupied one of the benches. She was wearing a flimsy cotton nightgown, carefully counting her own fingers. I tried to get past without attracting her notice, but she looked up as I passed by. Her eyes were empty and hopeless, her expression blank. She didn't seem angry, or sad, or even confused. She was just . . . there.

I averted my eyes, like you're supposed to do around an aggressive dog. But it probably wasn't necessary. The next time I dared peek at her, she'd gone back to counting.

Then something caught my attention . . .

Music. A simple melody so sweet and soothing that it might as well have been the smell of freshly baked cookies.

It was coming from behind the other door—NO UNAUTHORIZED ADMITTANCE.

I went through it and slipped down a long hallway. As I passed each doorway, I only paused to peer inside—I didn't want to stop. I had to find the source of the music.

This was the part of the building where the patients had been treated—doors labeled EXAM, HOLDING, and THERAPY. The exam rooms each held a hospital-style bed with straps just like the ones in the bedrooms. But there were also counters and cabinets still stocked with antiquated medical supplies.

The holding room was a full-on padded room, where you stash people who are so crazy you're afraid they'll bash their own brains out against a regular wall. Every visible surface was covered in rough-woven fabric—canvas, maybe—tattered and rotten with age.

The therapy room was closed, as were a few unlabeled doors on either side of the hall past it. Which was fine with me. I wasn't exploring—I was chasing that song.

The music grew louder as I followed it down to the last door on the left: PROCESSING. As soon as I went through the wall, the song cut out discordantly, leaving me standing in a room that was quiet and cold and filled me with prickly revulsion.

Shelves lined one wall, holding a Tetris-like arrangement of antique suitcases. On the other side of the room was a cabinet whose worn doors gaped open, revealing stacks of folded cotton garments. A few had fallen to the floor, and despite their shapelessness I could tell that they were the same as the nightgowns some of the ghosts were wearing.

In the far corner was a curtain on a metal frame that reached about neck-high. A new patient would be sent behind it to take off her old clothes and put on one of the cotton nightgowns, at which point her old things would be packed away and set on the shelf until the day she claimed her suitcase and left . . .

Or the day she didn't.

Staring at the squared-off leather and canvas bags, I wondered which ones might have belonged to Eliza and Florence and Maria. Or the other ghosts I'd caught glimpses of in my time there.

A sick feeling rose in my stomach again, and I wandered over to the small window in the corner in hopes of quelling the trapped, boxed-in sensation that had come over me. Squares of pale winter light formed a grid on the walls. I rested my forehead against the glass and looked out over the snowy landscape.

Off in the distance, a figure moved across the snow, casting no trace of shadow on the white ground.

Theo.

I thought for a second about going down to talk to him, but what if he didn't want anything to do with me? He must have seen what I did to Nic. What would he think of me? The same thing Eliza did, probably—that I was immature, out of control. I was afraid he would look up and see me watching him, so I started to back away from the window. But as I did, I tripped over something.

I was so captivated by the cascade of delicate musical notes that spilled into the air that I forgot my inability to interact with the physical world. I'd done it when I was angry, but that was different. That came from some dark force inside me—a force I couldn't control and didn't intend to release again.

This had been accidental. I told myself it was a fluke. But when I bent down, I was able to pick up the object I'd tripped over: a tiny silver music box, with a cylindrical barrel and a miniscule handle. When I turned the handle, little nubs on the barrel pinged against a row of thin metal strips and softly played a few musical notes.

It was such a novelty to hold something in my hands that I turned it over and over, enjoying its weight and texture, the cold hardness of the metal.

Then I started slowly turning the handle.

The song began as one note . . . then another . . . slowly, slowly, they rang through the quiet room, and only once I started turning the handle more quickly did I start to comprehend what I was hearing.

I could still imagine my sister's voice.

Beautiful dreamer, wake unto me.

Starlight and dewdrops are waiting for thee.

The notes were so simple and lovely. And it was so comforting to have something, at last, to *do*—to actually do with my hands, with my fingers, with my time.

I sat on a little wooden chair by the window, leaning forward to look over the grounds again, my fingers still turning the tiny crank.

Theo was gone. Off to wherever he went, to do whatever he spent his days and months and years doing.

Beautiful dreamer, wake unto me.

Beautiful dreamer, wake unto me.

The gray sky began to glow with moonlight reflected off the snowy earth.

And I went on turning the handle of the little music box.

The snowdrifts melted away, revealing dead, brown grass and puddles of mud. Rainstorms rolled through and coaxed new, green life out of the hillside. A bird searched for twigs for her nest and then worms for her babies, and a raindrop fell, millimeter by millimeter, from the eaves.

And still I played the song.

CHAPTER 17

Wow," said a voice. A man's voice.

I didn't turn from the window. But I let the music box rest silently on the windowsill.

"Carlos, come check out these suitcases," the voice said. "Wild."

"Hang on," said a second voice. "I'm just checking the readings . . ."

I looked over at the entrance to the room, where two men in their late twenties stood studying a complicated-looking hand-held meter, the kind with the needle that swings from red to yellow to green.

"Clear," the scruffier one—Carlos—said. "Dude, I'm telling you, this place is clean."

They were both wearing khaki cargo pants and long-sleeved T-shirts. Carlos's was from some event called Phoenix Conspiracyfest 2013. The other guy's shirt read I WANT TO BELIEVE. He was clean-shaven with a buzz cut and carried a camera. Over his shoulder was slung a backpack labeled JASON.

"Is this the last room?" Carlos asked. "There ought to be stairs out that door."

Jason nodded, then raised the camera to his face and began taking a video of the room. He panned across the suitcases, toward me.

I froze, wondering if he would somehow sense my presence. But he didn't seem to.

He finished the pan, holstered the camera, and shrugged. "I agree. Clean."

Carlos looked troubled. "How do we explain the Christmas incident?"

"I don't know," Jason said. "Those were just dumb high school kids. They probably trashed the place and then made up a story to keep from getting in trouble."

High school kids? Were they talking about Nic and Landon?

Did that mean she was alive? Surely they would have said something if she wasn't.

"It's been two years since then, with no other reports of sightings. The repair guys were here, the insurance guys, the cops . . . nobody's seen a thing." Jason sniffed. "Not to mention our readings show zero paranormal activity."

Wait a second. They were measuring paranormal activity? These guys were ghost hunters.

"Let's send the report to the investors tonight," Carlos said. "And tell them to put the check in the mail. There are no ghosts here."

. . . Really, really incompetent ghost hunters.

Jason wandered over to the shelf of suitcases and cracked one open. "Why'd they shut this place down, anyway?"

"If you read the articles I sent you—"

"I didn't," Jason said.

"It was a private sanitarium," Carlos said. "The old-fashioned version of what the developer's looking to do with it now. Designed mostly for short-term rehabilitation. But at some point the state noticed that people weren't being rehabilitated. They just got worse with time. That was back when they'd lock you up for being a party girl, you know, just to scare you back to good behavior. But the party girls went crazy. They all went crazy. And more than a few of them died under mysterious circumstances."

Jason was holding an old shoe he'd pulled from one of the bags. It was coffee-colored leather, with a sturdy two-inch heel, and it looked stiff and shrunken with age. Suddenly, it seemed to occur to him that an actual person had once worn that shoe—a person who may have met a terrible end in this very building. He shuddered and gently put the shoe back.

"This place *should* be haunted, then," he said, looking around. His demeanor had changed. He looked uneasy. "Shouldn't it?"

Carlos was making a notation on his phone. "It's not."

"But maybe we should do one more walkthrough," Jason said. "Since we're talking about bringing *more* troubled kids here. If we missed something—if there were some kind of super-natural presence—it could easily feed off—"

"No way," Carlos said. "Look, dude, we've been here for five hours. It smells and it's giving me a headache, so I'm going back to the hotel. You're welcome to stay and host a séance. But I'm leaving. This place is clear. There are no ghosts here."

Were Carlos's words true? Were my parents going to sell

this property to a developer who wanted to put *another* mental hospital here?

I thought about getting up out of my chair, creating a disturbance, getting their attention somehow. I tried to will Jason to stand his ground.

And then, behind me, I heard one clear note from the music box.

Jason tensed. "What was that?"

But Carlos laughed and ran a hand through his scraggly hair. "Buddy, you're getting paranoid. Let's go."

No.

Wait.

Stay.

But no part of me took action to keep them there. To draw their notice.

The door closed behind them, and I remained in my seat. The music box played a couple of enticingly clear and lovely notes, and in spite of my intentions to do otherwise, I reached over and gently picked it up, holding it in my lap.

I'd been holed up in that room for two years. Was that even possible?

Briefly, I considered going downstairs and finding Eliza or Florence. Telling them about what the ghost hunters had mentioned—that the house would soon have more troubled young adults in its grasp. And while I wasn't sure exactly what would happen, I knew to my core that it would be bad.

The house holds on to troubled girls, I thought. *It doesn't want to let them go.*

The thought hit me with such clarity that I recognized it immediately as a solid truth.

That was why the house—the presence—the dark smoke, whatever it was—had come after me. Killed me. Because I was trying to leave . . . when I "belonged" here. So what would happen when more troubled teens came?

Disaster, that's what.

But what was *I* going to do? I couldn't stop it. I couldn't save anybody else. I couldn't even save myself.

Without thinking, I'd begun to turn the crank on the music box again.

Out front, Jason and Carlos were packing up their car to go. Theo stood a few yards away and watched them. Then they started the car and drove straight through him.

Worst ghost hunters ever.

I didn't move from my chair. The grass in the fields grew strong and tall and green, and the days got longer. The sun's path widened in the sky, and the stars made arcs over the horizon. I half believed that I wasn't stuck in a house at all, but on a journey across the ocean, on a huge, creaking ship. And the rippling grass below me was the moon frosting the tips of the indigo waves.

My body, buried somewhere hundreds of miles away, gave itself back to the earth.

My soul began to peel away from my consciousness, until I began to feel that there was nothing left of me.

The music was everything I needed or wanted. It was all.

In this way, lost in my daydreams, bearing witness to the seasons on the hillside, and always, always carrying in my mind the lilting song from the music box, I passed another year and a half as if it were a single mildly interesting day.

A car door slammed.

I sat stunned and motionless, looking down at the music box in my hand.

A choice lay in front of me. If I kept turning the crank, I would never need to go and see who had come here. I would never face the uncertainty or heartbreak of being reminded at every turn that I was gone, forgotten. So what if the house wanted more victims? Why was that my business?

The temptation to ignore the living altogether, to let the fog of death rise around me and contain my existence, was real and nearly irresistible. I didn't have to resist—I could be one of the ghosts who sat in the background, counting her fingers.

I'd be the one on the third floor with the music box.

It would be so simple, just to surrender myself and my thoughts. Let the house have me, let time carry me forward like a river. What difference did it make? Besides, what was the alternative?

Pain and rejection. Sorrow and heartbreak.

How could you know that? You haven't even tried.

All I'd ever done was mess things up. Massively.

Maybe you were a dumb kid. Maybe you did make stupid, irresponsible choices. But you don't have to be that person forever.

But the person I decided to be right here, right now—that would be the person I was forever.

I looked out the window. All I could see was a red car, an unfamiliar model that hadn't existed when I'd died. With a flutter of anxiety, I wondered if it was some hapless troubled kid forced here by her parents. But the grounds were still decrepit, the grass still dead.

A few feet from the car, watching it carefully, was Theo. He glanced up at the house, and he noticed me and waved.

Slowly, I waved back.

And then I stood up and left the music box behind.

CHAPTER 18

I skipped down the stairs two at a time, and the air moving through my body felt warm and inviting. Some distant part of me recalled how it felt to step outside on a summer day and feel the sun kiss my skin.

I made my way to the lobby, where Florence and Eliza stood at the window, looking outside.

"Hello," I said. "Long time no see."

"Three and a half years, give or take," Florence said. "What have you been doing with yourself?"

I shook my head. It suddenly occurred to me to be ashamed of how I'd spent my time.

"It's all right, sugar. It did you good. You look refreshed." She gave me a smile.

"I came to see about the car," I said.

"More visitors. Oh dear—it's a girl." Eliza still hadn't deigned to look over at me. She sighed disapprovingly. "Girls shouldn't come here. This place is inhospitable."

The "girl" could more accurately be described as a teen-ager. Her hair was black with a magenta streak, shaved close on one side and long on the other. I couldn't see her face, but I could tell by the way she moved and walked that she was unhappy.

"What do you think happened to her?" Eliza asked. "Why is her head shaved? Some kind of head injury?"

"No, that's not an injury," I said. "It's just the style. She's Goth."

"*Goth?* Short for *Gothic?*" Eliza studied the girl. "I take it that's a mode of fashion?"

"Basically," I said, looking at her long-sleeved black shirt and roughed-up black jeans. On her feet were black rubber flip-flops, and even from this distance I could tell her toenails were painted black. "For some people it goes a little deeper than that."

"She looks like a vampiress," Florence said.

Then the driver got out of the car.

I gasped.

"I suppose being Gothic doesn't run in families, then," Eliza mused. "That woman looks quite normal."

I leaned closer to the window, hardly able to believe what I was seeing. "*'That woman'* is my mother!"

"Oh?" Eliza said, looking more carefully. "Oh . . . yes."

"She looks like you," Florence said. "Very pretty."

And if the woman was Mom, then that meant the girl was . . .

"That's my *sister?*" I said. "Oh my God—that's Janie!"

"Are you quite sure?" Eliza said. "It doesn't look like her at all. I remember her being a sweet little thing. Blond, wasn't she?"

I ran outside and down the steps, desperate to get a closer

look at my little sister. When I reached her, I practically skidded to a stop.

This . . . this couldn't be Janie.

When I was alive, my sister's favorite colors were pink and hot pink. Her blond hair had always been her favorite feature.

No way had that sugary-sweet aspiring pop princess turned into this creature of the night.

But when she lifted her face, there wasn't a speck of doubt left. Despite the dark, asymmetrical hair and the eggplant-purple lips and the eyes ringed with smoky circles of gray makeup, this was definitely Janie. *My* Janie. I was so enthralled by the sight of her that I stood about a foot away and stared at the curves of her cheeks, the slight upturn of her nose.

"She's not a little girl anymore," I said out loud. "Look at her. She's so . . ."

"Scary," Theo said. He had come up behind me.

"Beautiful." I shot him a cool look. "She looks like a model."

"Well . . . not like any fashion model I ever saw in my time. But if you say so."

I went back to studying my sister. How old was she now . . . fifteen? Nearly the age I had been when I'd died here. If I'd lived, I would have been twenty. An unexpected zap of jealousy went through me. Janie was growing up. Soon she'd be older than I ever got to be. Then she'd go to college, have a career, start a family.

Stop it, I scolded myself.

"Don't forget your mother," Theo said. "She's here, too."

After another few seconds spent staring at my sister, I

turned to look for Mom. At first glance, she looked as she always had. Her hair was the same, she wore the same pale rose shade of lipstick, and I even recognized the gray T-shirt she was wearing as one she'd owned back when I was alive. But when I got closer, I realized that my initial impression was wrong. She'd changed. Something was different.

Something was . . . gone. It was like a piece had been removed from her soul. When she looked warily up at the house, I could see that some part of her was far away, searching. Sad.

Because of me.

Instinctively, I looked around for my father. Then it hit me—if Mom and Dad had separated three years ago, he was probably completely out of the picture by now.

"Why do you think they came back?" Theo asked me.

I didn't really care, honestly. They could have been there to start a bunny-worshipping cult, and I would have been thrilled to see them. I felt buoyantly happy, and was suddenly struck by a strange and wonderful idea.

"What if they're going to *live* here?" I said.

The scenario unfolded in my mind: Mom needed a change of scenery. Maybe she'd decided to finally work on the novel she'd always wanted to write. And this place was sitting empty, so they figured *why not?* Stranger things had happened, right?

"That would be terrible," Theo said. "Don't even wish for it."

My mother put her hands in her pockets. "I guess we should get everything inside."

Janie shrugged and trudged through the knee-high weeds toward the front steps, but Mom called out to her. "Jane? Could you help me with the bags?"

Jane? She went by Jane now?

It's fine, I thought, even though it felt like the floor had just dropped out from underneath me. *Kids grow up. She's not a baby anymore. She's a teenager.*

But Janie—sorry, she'd never be *Jane* to me—didn't hurry back to help our mother. Instead, she froze, her shoulders rigid, and stared at the door for a second before she spun around, stalked back to the car, and wordlessly waited for Mom to pop the trunk.

"I know this isn't your first choice—" Mom started to say. But Janie cut her off.

"I just don't see why I have to be the pack mule when you're the one who decided to bring almost everything we own." She hoisted a bag over her shoulder and frowned. "Where are the keys?"

Mom's lips pressed into an unhappy line, but she handed over the key chain. Then Janie reached back into the trunk and pulled out a scraped-up red suitcase.

I gasped. That had been *my* suitcase.

Trying desperately not to show that the stuff she was carrying was almost too heavy for her, my sister tottered up the steps and unlocked the front entrance. Then she went inside. The doors gaped open behind her, and I quickly moved to follow her into the house.

"Delia, hold on," Theo said softly. "I think we should talk."

I glanced back at him. There was something like worry in his expression. The prospect of spending time with Theo was tempting. But I didn't have time to chat. I had my family back.

By the time I got inside, Janie had opened the door to the

superintendent's apartment and set down her bags. Mom came in carrying everything else—cleaning supplies, groceries, her laptop, pillows, sheets, blankets, a tote full of books (my mother never went anywhere without books). Then she ducked into the kitchen to put the food away.

When she came out, she looked around.

"Jane?" she called.

No answer.

"Jane!" I detected thinly-veiled panic in her voice. Could you blame her? Alarm rose inside me, too, like a tiny, quaking creature.

Mom dashed out to the lobby and threw open the front doors to look outside—was she making sure the car was still there? Then she went back inside and down the main hall, pausing to listen for any sign of my sister. Finally, she climbed the stairs and walked across the day room to the ward door. I trailed close behind her.

In the ward, she made it almost all the way to the end of the hall before stopping outside Room 4 and letting out a massive sigh. Over her shoulder, I saw Janie sprawled on the bed, her eyes closed and earbuds in, with tinny music spilling out of them.

"*Jane,*" Mom said loudly. My sister lazily opened her eyes, and plucked out one of her headphones. "Honey, why didn't you tell me you were coming up here? You can't just run off by yourself. You could get lost in this place."

Not likely. I remembered the hand-drawn map on Nic's phone. At some point, my sister had done some unauthorized exploring.

"Please," Janie said. "I'm not a little kid."

"Why don't you come downstairs?" Mom asked.

But Janie just stuck the earbud back in her ear.

"Why on earth have they returned?" Eliza asked, popping in by my side.

I looked at my mom, who was clenching her fists in an effort not to lose her cool.

"To get the place ready to sell, I guess," I replied.

"How would you know? Have they said?" Eliza turned her reproachful gaze toward my mother. "Surely someone else could have handled the details for them."

"Who knows?" I said. "Maybe they don't have enough money to hire people."

After all, with Dad out of the picture, Mom was having to make ends meet with one salary instead of two.

But a plaintive, embarrassed voice deep inside me said, *To see me. To be near me.* I mean, sure, I was dead, but wouldn't they naturally want to spend time at the place I'd died? To sort of . . . cherish my memory or something?

"Well," Eliza said, bells jingling as she placed her hands on her hips, "I hope for their own sakes that they don't stay long."

I bristled with indignation.

"Oh, don't get grumpy," Eliza said. "You know what I mean. This place isn't safe."

I turned on her. "And yet you keep saying it's fine."

"I don't—" She colored slightly. "It *is* fine, in some ways."

"Like if you're dead?"

"I suppose."

"Yeah, well, news flash," I said. "I wasn't dead until I came here."

She narrowed her eyes. "What's a 'news flash'?"

"Forget it," I said.

"Anyway, whose side are you on?" she asked. "Do you want them to stay or leave?"

I stared at Mom for a beat. She and Janie had just finished a mini-argument that left them both hurt and angry.

The answer was blindingly obvious.

My mood sank instantly. "To leave," I said. "They need to leave and never come back."

"All right, then," Eliza said. "What are we going to do to make that happen?"

I looked at her, feeling equal parts gratitude and confusion. "We?"

The pink in her cheeks intensified. "I couldn't help *you*," she said. "I might as well do what I can for your family."

Mom cooked dinner in the superintendent's kitchen and served it on paper plates. Janie took her food and went to eat by herself on the couch while Mom sat at the table with a paperback. After they'd finished eating, my sister got the red suitcase and started for the door to the hallway.

Mom jumped to attention. "Are you going upstairs now? I'll come."

"Mother, could you just . . . not?" Janie said. "I'm fine. I can be alone for five minutes without you fawning all over me."

Mom tried to look light and carefree, but the effect was miserable. Her face contorted like a sad mask. "Sorry. Are you sure you're okay up there alone?"

"Relax," Janie snapped. "You're making me so nervous."

Mom was silent, and my sister relented.

"I'll be fine," Janie said, flipping her hair the way she used to—only now it was habit, not affectation. "It's fine."

Her niceness seemed to soothe some wild fear in our mother. "Okay," Mom said, her face still plasticky bright. "See you in a bit, sweetie. I guess you can text me if you need anything. Thankfully they put in that cell tower up the highway. It's like we're living in the twenty-first century again!"

"Sure," Janie said. Then she walked out.

My mother gave a little sigh and went back to her book.

MY FAVORITE MEMORY OF JANIE

It was almost Halloween, which is one of those holidays that's extremely important to kids and extremely useless to parents. Mom and Dad had a history of forgetting to get our costumes until the last possible minute. When I was thirteen and Janie was eight, we decided to take matters into our own hands. So one day after school, we raided their closet.

I grabbed an old flannel shirt Mom had never thrown away and put together a nineties grunge look, but we were having a harder time finding something for Janie . . . until we dug through an overflowing shelf and found a ruffly apron. I remembered seeing it on pictures of my great-grandma. We hauled it out and then unearthed a full skirt and a simple white blouse.

"Voilà," I said, tying the apron strings into a bow behind her back. "You're a housewife."

She wrinkled her nose at herself in the mirror. "It's not enough."

"Come on, then," I said, leading her out to the kitchen and opening the pantry door. "We'll get you some props."

I handed her a broom, which she rejected with a sneer, so then I gave her a mop, which, for some reason obvious only in eight-year-old logic, was acceptable.

"What else?" she asked.

"You need a hand free for your candy," I said.

"I can wear a purse on my arm and put the candy in that," she said. "But I need more. I still don't look like anything."

"I know!" I said. "Wait here."

I ran back to my room and dug through my jewelry box for a strand of fake pearls. When I got back to the kitchen, Janie was holding the mop in one hand and a teapot in the other.

"Better now," she said.

I didn't want to laugh at her, but I couldn't really stop myself. "You look like you're hosting the weirdest tea party ever."

She set down the teapot, then opened a cabinet and pulled out a frying pan, struggling to manage everything with the mop wedged into her armpit.

"Better?" she asked. "Like, for making cookies?"

"What—? *Janie.* You honestly think cookies are made in frying pans?"

She blinked at me, clueless.

"Here," I said, picking the teapot up and tucking it in the crook of her elbow. "Now. You're the perfect housewife."

For a second, she believed me, and then I busted out laughing so hard that tears exploded down my face. Janie took a few seconds to decide whether to be angry, and then she started laughing, too.

Mom came home a couple of minutes later and stared at us, confused, as we gasped and wheezed for air. "What are you girls doing?"

"What?" I asked. "Don't you want some of Janie's fried cookies?"

Janie waved the mop at Mom. "Come to my tea party!" she said, in a demonic, gravelly voice. *"Come to my tea party and mop my floors!"*

And then we basically lost our minds laughing while our mother, who had never taught us anything about housewifery and therefore only had herself to blame, stared at us as if we'd turned into aliens.

CHAPTER 19

I caught up with my sister on the stairs and stayed a few paces behind as she pushed open the door to the day room. She stood in the doorway for a little while, looking around. Then she circled the room, examining the chairs, running her finger along the dusty window ledge, and staring up at the ceiling. Her thoughtful curiosity read, to me, as confidence. Misplaced confidence. She ought to be just a *little* careful.

She paused by the piano and made a soft *Hm* sound.

She'd found the stack of Aunt Cordelia's letters that I'd left there four years ago.

"No," I said, hurrying over to her and trying, uselessly, to wrench them from her hands. "Those aren't for you. Put them down."

But of course Janie, lips slightly parted in surprise, carried them to the small, still-dustless table and sat down to read them.

Since I couldn't stop her, I positioned myself to read over her shoulder.

Dear Little Namesake,
I hope you had a nice Christmas. It was very cold here and

I did not have a tree. By the time I thought to get one, I had run out of time. Anyway, it doesn't signify much because there would be no one to enjoy it but myself. There is a lovely fir on the lawn that I can see from my desk as I write this, so I pretended that was my tree. Although if Santa Claus left any gifts beneath it, I'm afraid the squirrels must have taken them!

I remembered this one. I'd felt bad for her, for not having a tree or anyone who cared enough to help her get one. In my next letter I drew her the fanciest Christmas tree I could fit on the page, complete with a generous sprinkling of glitter that, in retrospect, probably got all over everything she owned.

But what got my attention reading the letter now wasn't her loneliness—it was the clue. Of course. I needed to find the tree, and that would be one more hint as to where her private office had been. I went back to reading:

Did you ever decide which jacket you wanted? Red and purple are both lovely colors. I don't blame you for having a difficult time with the choice. It's all right if you decided based on what your friend Nicola wanted. Friends are an important part of life. It's perfectly fine to depend on others, once they have earned your trust.

—said the woman who spent her whole life living alone.

The problem sometimes is learning who you can trust, and who you can't. Always remember that those around you aren't always what—or who—they seem to be.

The rest of the letter was basic stuff: weather, mostly, mixed with her usual well-wishes for my family and me. Janie folded it and slipped it carefully back into the envelope. She opened the next one in the stack, which also happened to be the very last letter I'd received from Aunt Cordelia.

Dear Little Namesake,

It's wonderful that you are so excited for summer, and that you are hopeful for good marks from your teachers. I was never a very good student. I always wanted to be doing something else besides reciting and memorizing. I do believe things are different now, that they are more aware of what children like and how they prefer to learn.

I have been pondering whether to tell you something very important, and I think I have decided that I will, in part because your excellent grade card demonstrates a good deal of maturity. So I will include it either here or in my next letter. I haven't made up my mind yet.

But at the end of the letter, where the important announcement should have been was a little bit of backtracking and a promise that she would tell me "everything" the next time she wrote.

Only there never was a next time. I guess I got too busy to write back to her. I was busy with summer camp, and hanging out with my friends . . . without the bonus of getting extra credit, writing letters just didn't seem like a priority. Cordelia must have assumed I wasn't interested, because she never did tell me her important message.

Janie scanned the rest of the letters, pausing when she came to the one with the description of Aunt Cordelia's little "sanctuary." She studied the page carefully, then set it on the table and pulled out her phone, examining the familiar hand-drawn map.

As she stared at the lit-up screen, there was a rustling sound.

All of the letters had fallen off the table.

Janie cocked her head, like a curious puppy, and leaned down to pick them up. She set them in a neat pile and went back to the map.

Flutter flutter.

She jerked her head up to see the empty surface gleaming in front of her.

Again, the letters lay in a pile on the ground. Some invisible ghost was messing with my sister. The same ghost that had messed with me years earlier, pushing my sweater to the floor.

"Who's there?" I demanded. "Who's doing this?"

"*Sh!*"

The sound seemed to have no source, but suddenly the light on the other side of the table began to waver.

Then there appeared a woman who looked to be in her early forties. Her gray-streaked black hair rested in a large topknot at the crown of her head. Her dress was dull blue, floor length, and partly covered by a dingy white apron with threadbare edges. A pair of wire-frame reading glasses rested on her nose. She was one of those people who could have been pretty, if there had been any spark of light or joy in her eyes. But instead, there was an aggressive kind of bitterness, and it made her look plain and tired.

She glared at me, then went back to her work, moving her hands in intricate motions, making delicate adjustments and small, pulling gestures. It was some kind of knitting . . . only without any actual needles or yarn. Her movements were hypnotic, and I lost myself in watching her fingers deftly maneuver their invisible tasks.

She studiously ignored me.

My sister carefully placed one letter back on the table.

The woman glanced at the offending envelope, then swiped at it with a swiftness approaching violence. It tumbled off the side.

Janie let out a nervous, disbelieving laugh, then seemed to remember how utterly freaky this was and took a few steps back.

After a minute, she leaned forward and delicately set one of her (many) skull rings about an inch away from the edge of the table.

For nearly a minute, nothing happened. Janie visibly relaxed. But then the woman reached out and knocked the ring to the floor, where it bounced and skittered before coming to a stop just past my sister.

Janie gasped.

"What are you *doing*?" I said to her. "Why are you just standing there? Go! Go down and see Mom! Tell her about this! Tell her you want to leave!"

Except . . . my sister didn't want to leave. She scooped her ring off the floor and came right back. This time she set the ring dead center on the tabletop. The old woman shoved it off with so much force that it shot up and hit Janie squarely in the side of the jaw.

Enough.

"Hey, lady!" I snapped, anger rising inside me. "That's my little sister!"

The woman finally looked up. "Go away! Leave me alone!"

"Don't you *ever* try to hurt her again," I said, standing right above her. "Do you understand?"

She scowled.

"That scarf you're knitting?" I said, feeling the power of my anger growing like a flame inside me. "I'll—I'll tear it to shreds. I'll set it on fire."

The woman's snarl turned to a confused, frightened expression, and she cradled her imaginary knitting close to her body. "It's not a scarf. It's a blanket. For my little girl." She bundled it up and clutched it to her cheek. "She needs it. She's so cold without it."

Her tone was so woeful that the heat of my anger cooled. "I won't touch it," I said. "But you need to be nice. Don't try to hurt my sister."

The woman looked down at the blanket.

"Okay?" I said. "Say okay."

"Okay," she said, pursing her lips. "But I don't see why you have to threaten me."

"Sorry," I said. "You were acting pretty crazy."

She cracked a small smile and looked at me through eyes that looked less insane than just plain exhausted. "We're all crazy here," she said.

"Yeah, well," I said. "Maybe not all of us."

She inclined her head toward Janie. "You'd better keep an eye on her," she said.

"Trust me, I know," I said. "So what's your name?"

"It certainly isn't *Hey, lady*." She gave me a rueful smile. "I'm Penitence."

"Delia," I said. "Nice to meet you."

Penitence nodded and turned her attention back to the invisible blanket, an impossible hint of a smile on her thin gray lips.

Janie, done playing with the forces at work near the table, stepped toward the wall and rested her palm on it. All the stubborn resoluteness went out of her. She looked like a rag doll, her eyes overflowing with tears. Her head dropped forward, and her fingers curled into a trembling fist.

"I'm sorry, Delia," she whispered. "I'm sorry for everything. It's my fault."

"No, Janie," I pleaded. "Don't say that. It had nothing to do with you."

She rushed into the ward hall. I had to run to keep up with her. She went straight into the bathroom, splashed water on her face, and gulped in deep gasps of air.

Then, as she stared at herself in the mirror, something in her face changed. Her jaw clenched. Her eyebrows pressed into straight lines. Like she was loading up on strength.

What struck me the most was how practiced the gesture was. As if she'd been breaking down and then shoring herself up this way for years.

For four years.

From the bathroom, she went back to the day room and stood at the piano, turning the letters over in her hands. Finally, she grabbed her phone and loaded the hand-drawn map again.

Then I got it.

She was trying to figure out which room had been Aunt Cordelia's.

I watched as my sister went out into the stairwell . . . and started to climb to the third floor.

Perhaps disturbed by the presence of the living among us, the third-floor spirits crowded the hallway. Even the shiest ghosts, sad-looking girls and women wearing limp asylum nightgowns, had come to investigate. A few reached out to Janie, whispering or moaning—I watched tensely but didn't interfere. Most seemed ultimately harmless. A couple, though, looked more dangerous—more focused.

At one point, Maria scuttled by on all fours.

I moved to walk in front of Janie, turning sideways so I could watch her.

Studying her map, my sister walked to the door marked THERAPY . . . and started searching the key ring for the key to unlock it.

I'd never been in that room before, so I went through the wall to check things out before my sister could get herself into trouble. But just as I stepped in, Janie got the door open.

"Holy . . ." she whispered, awed into speechlessness.

It looked like a medieval torture chamber. A wooden chair in a permanent reclining position dominated the center of the room, and next to it was a complex board covered in dials and buttons. Connected to that by wires was an elaborate frame, and dozens of wires with small electrodes at their ends dangled from the frame.

In a dubious effort to make the room more cheerful, the walls had been painted a pale blue. But they were barely visible between the hundreds of taped-up newspaper and encyclopedia articles. Stacks of books overflowed on the counters and filled the scratched white sink basin.

Pushed up under the window was a small writing desk, its contents neatly organized in marked contrast to the chaos of the rest of the room: a little pen jar, a box of stationery, and a leather desk blotter. A small swivel chair was neatly parked under the desk.

Janie had found Cordelia's office.

I started to cross toward the desk, but halfway there, *Bang!* I smashed right into an invisible wall.

An acrid scent seeped into my nose. I looked down and saw a thick line of white granules on the floor.

I recalled Florence telling me about salt—about its power over us ghosts. Just being near it turned my stomach, so I retreated, watching helplessly as my sister pressed on toward the desk.

Janie paused, her fingers spread wide like a spider's legs, gently resting on the blotter. She inspected everything with a care I myself would not have used. In fact, I was beginning to grow impatient with her minute examination of the pens, the stationery, the blotter itself . . .

Until her attentiveness paid off. Something I would never have noticed caught her eye. She lifted the corner of the blotter to reveal a piece of paper covered in writing that I recognized as Aunt Cordelia's old-fashioned scrawl. Another letter.

The first line, unmistakable even from halfway across the room, read:

Dear Little Namesake,

"That's mine—bring it here!" I demanded. Without thinking, I lunged forward but slammed into the invisible barrier again. This time, the impact sent a shock of pain through me, and I stumbled backward, knocking into the counter.

A stack of books tumbled to the ground.

Janie whipped around to look in my direction. Wariness clouded her face when she caught sight of the mess.

She glanced back at the letter for a moment, then tucked it into the front pocket of her jacket and started for the door.

As she tread on the salt, there was a slight crunching sound. She knelt to look at the white line, which she'd tracked across the floor in the sole of her shoe. I hoped she would brush it out of the way so I could get closer to the desk, but instead, she very carefully repaired the line and stood up.

She took one step forward, then stopped short and swung back. She crouched down and, using her pointer finger, separated a thin line of salt from the thicker line. Then she leaned down and brushed it into her palm, until she held a decent handful of salt.

I tested the barrier that remained and found it just as strong as before.

I followed Janie out of the room and down the hall. The ghosts that had come out earlier to watch her were all gone . . . but the hallway still had an air of occupancy.

Something was there with us. I just wasn't sure what it was.

Back on the second floor, Janie disappeared into the ward

just as our mother came into the day room, loaded down with her wheeled suitcase, her laptop bag, and the tote full of books.

After setting everything down just inside the door, Mom took a minute to look over the room. A shudder set her body trembling, but she took a few slow, deep breaths and seemed to calm herself down.

"You can do this," she said softly. "It's only a week."

"Do what?" I asked. "What are you trying to do?"

There was a soft, cackling laugh, and I looked over at Penitence, who bent over her work.

"She can't hear you," she said.

"I know," I said. "I just kind of hoped that if I keep talking to them, they'll . . . understand me, somehow."

I expected her to laugh again, but she was quiet for a long time and then said, "There are ways. But you can't simply speak. You must be subtle."

"Subtle how?" I asked.

"Subtle," she said, "in a way that can only come from watching and waiting. Subtle in a way that can't be explained."

She turned and looked at my mother, puffed up her cheeks, and exhaled a thin whistle of air. Mom shivered and pulled the sleeves of her sweater down over her wrists. Then she hastily gathered her things and went on into the ward.

CHAPTER 20

In her room, Room 4, Janie sat down on the bed, turned on her music, and closed her eyes. Within a minute or two, the tension went out of her arms and her breathing turned slow and even.

Dancing light came through the window and shone on the opposite wall. I looked down to see Theo outside. He waved up to me and then beckoned me to come out. I glanced over at my sleeping sister, then nodded to Theo.

The two nightgowned girls were back in the lobby. At the sight of me, they nudged each other until one of them said, in a halting voice, "Who are they? The new ones?"

"My family," I said. "Please leave them alone."

"We leave everyone alone!" the second girl said, and then she giggled shrilly.

"What are your names?" I asked. "I'm—"

But they'd already vanished.

Theo waited for me by the fountain with his hands on his hips and a deep frown etched across his face.

"They can't stay," he said.

"I know."

"No, I'm being very serious, Delia," he said. "You can't let them—"

"I get it," I said. "It's dangerous. Well, I don't know what to do about that. I didn't ask them to come."

He gazed at the ground, clearly playing out some internal debate. Finally, he looked up at me with his amber-flecked eyes. "The first time we met, you asked if I ever saw my family after . . . after. And I said I'd seen my brother. But I didn't tell you what happened."

I nodded, casting a quick glance up at Janie's window.

"We were twins," Theo went on. "Theodore and Edward. Theo and Ted. We were best friends; we did everything together. We were working together on the land survey and planning to start our own business, doing that kind of work for private clients—department stores, hotels. About a year after I passed, Ted came back here. I thought he was here to visit the place I had died. Just to say hello. I missed him so much. It felt like part of me was lost."

Theo's eyes sparkled as he spoke. Then, all at once, the light went out of them, and his expression turned dull and distant.

"He came only for himself," he said softly. "He didn't really think I was here. But he talked, you know, the way people talk to make themselves feel better. He filled me in: Mom's roses won at the garden show; Dad was a deacon now . . . But the real reason he came was . . . he wanted my permission to marry the girl I'd been engaged to before I died. He told me their plans— his and Barbara's. He gave me a story about how they hadn't even seen each other after the funeral, only he ran into her about six months later, and they felt like being in love was the 'right thing to do' because in a way it was about remembering me."

I thought instantly of Nic and Landon and wondered if they saw it that way. I wondered if they were still together. If every time they kissed, there was something in it that held a tiny piece of their memories of me.

"The dead and the living don't belong together," Theo said. "That's why you hear stories about haunted houses. Because no matter what the living do, they flaunt their life. They can't help it. And that's what I thought Ted was doing. So I got jealous. Really jealous. To the point where I couldn't control myself. And then . . ."

I tore my eyes away from my sister's window and looked at Theo.

"I tried to hurt him," he said. "I almost did—I would have— if it hadn't been for the fact that Barbara came after him. She'd been waiting in the car. It stopped me from doing something terrible. But Ted knew. He knew that I was there, and that I was angry. I never saw him again. And I've existed since then knowing that the two people I cared most about no longer had their old memories of me. Instead, I'd let myself become a monster. Ted must be dead by now, and he died thinking I was . . . bad. That I hated him. So you've got to make them leave, before the fact of their being alive gets to you, eats away at what you used to feel for them. Do you understand?"

Theo's voice was low and shaky, and I could tell by the roundedness of his shoulders how difficult it had been for him to tell me all this, to confess his misdeeds.

"I'm sorry," I said. "That must have been awful."

"It's awful every day," he said.

He seemed so abjectly miserable that I wanted to give him a big hug, but I wasn't sure what the 1940s hugging rules were.

So I lamely patted his shoulder. "Thank you for trusting me enough to tell me. But I swear that's not what's happening here. I'm *trying* to make them go."

"Well, for your own sake, as well as theirs," Theo said, standing up straight once again, "see that it doesn't take too long. All we are is energy. All we're made of is the suggestion of what we were. And the longer you've been dead, the easier it is to forget who you were. Who you wanted to be."

"I've never been who I wanted to be," I said. "Even when I was alive. I think I might actually be a better person now . . . for all that's worth."

Theo blinked at me and reached his hand out, as if he were going to touch my arm. But at the last moment he pulled it away.

"Whoever you are," he said, "whoever you were, I—I like you."

Just put your stupid hand on my arm, I thought.

His expression turned stern, and the moment was gone. "But you still need to be careful."

Then he vanished.

That night, I sat on the hallway floor between my mother's and Janie's rooms until they both clicked off their lights.

Mom called, "Good night, Jane. I love you."

After a short silence, Janie reluctantly replied, "Good night."

I closed my eyes and curled up on the floor, blurring my

thoughts and memories, trying to fool myself into thinking that I was back among them, one of the family.

It almost worked. I was lulled into a deep, soft place, and something at the back of my heart began to blossom like a shy flower. For the first time in years, I felt warm, and loved, and safe. Even if it was just an illusion.

Then I heard a noise.

I shot up, ashamed that I'd let my guard down for even a few minutes. My family's safety—not my loneliness—had to be the number one priority. I felt a wavering awareness that this might be the first sign that I needed to heed Theo's warning.

I sneaked into Janie's room and found her in bed, curled up under the covers. Her breath seemed even, and her eyes were lightly closed. I sighed with relief; she was perfectly fine. Still, no more resting for me.

I spotted the stack of Cordelia's letters on the vanity table near the window. Laid flat next to them was the newest letter. I bent down to read it.

Dear Little Namesake,

It has now been years since we were last in correspondence. I apologize for writing out of the blue, most especially because of what I must write. But it is unavoidable, as I hope you will see and understand.

First, my confession. In all the letters I ever sent you, I never told you the real truth about myself. I can't recall what I wrote, but I'm sure it must have been a lot of fluff. I was thrilled to have someone to write to, and I didn't want to scare you away. I can honestly say that our period of letter writing was one of the nicest and least lonely times of my life. Now, I don't say that to make you feel bad that we stopped . . . If you'll remember, I never wrote back to you, either. We're even on that score.

But now you are a young woman, not a child anymore, and very soon I am going to share something with you that is of a rather serious nature. It concerns me, and you, and our family history. And my home.

It is no ordinary home. It was once known as the Piven Institute for the Care and Correction of Troubled Females—or Hysteria Hall, if you were one of the local residents of Rotburg. The facility opened in 1866 with the aim of, well, caring for and correcting troubled females. It was started by my great-great-great-great grandfather, Maxwell Piven, immediately following the end of the Civil War. (I suppose a lot of women were left without husbands or suitors following all the bloodshed, and many of them may have been seen as troubled—or perhaps troublesome—to their families.)

Maxwell Piven was not, unfortunately, a tremendously nice man. He was rumored to be ruthlessly strict and abusive to the inmates here. At one point, he even institutionalized his own daughter, who up until that point had been the wardress, a female warden who oversaw the patients and their care.

That is only the background. The present situation is this: I was born here, and I have lived here all my life, and I begin to be afraid that I will die here. Because I cannot and have never seemed to be able to leave this place, no matter how I try.

But what worries me the most is that even in death I will not be free.

I will send more as soon as I can.

Okay, so she knew this place was messed up. But what did she want me to do about it? I looked back up at the date and my heart sank—she'd written this on February 25. Only a couple of weeks before her death. If things were really as bad near the end as I suspected they had been, when would she have written the rest of her message?

She probably never did. Which meant that any answers she might have shared with me had died with her.

As I sat back and prepared to mope about it for a couple of minutes, I caught movement from the corner of my eye—a shadowy form slipping along the edge of my sister's bed.

"Who's there?" I said.

It—whatever "it" was—heard me and hunched over. Moonlight touched the sloping curve of its spine and outlined its back against the window.

I stepped away.

This wasn't like the rest of the ghosts I'd seen here—not even Maria. This was something else entirely. Even if it had ever been human, it wasn't now.

Slowly, it raised its head on a slender, too-long neck, and I found myself staring into a pair of hollow, endlessly dark eyes. Eyes that didn't really seem to exist, but also seemed to look right through me.

The mere suggestion of its shape was terrifying. I could see lean, muscular arms hanging from its narrow shoulders, and the back was abnormally round, with a large hump that made the backbone more prominent. The way its legs were attached to its body was more doglike than human.

But more than that was the fact that it was . . . a shadow. It was made of mist, nothing more. Black smoke swirled inside the outline of its body.

In the moonlight, I saw the swish-swish-swishing motion of a tail.

Neither of us moved.

"*Go away*," I said, keeping my voice firm. I tried to remember how Florence had acted with Maria. The only problem was that I didn't know how to hulk out the way Florence had—not on command, anyway. For all I knew, this thing could chew me up and spit me out.

But I wasn't going to let it mess with my little sister.

I clapped my hands and stomped my feet, and the creature reared back a little, surprised. Then it opened its mouth—an enormous mouth that stretched from one side of its face to the other—and hissed at me. Its short, sharp teeth looked like a jagged row of broken black glass.

Okay. I tried to calm myself. *Reevaluate. Take things slowly.*

It hissed again, surprising me so much that I jumped backward, knocking into the dresser. Something clattered to the floor behind me.

"Hello?" Janie sat up so quickly I doubted she'd been asleep at all. When she saw her phone on the floor, she started to climb out of the bed. But something stopped her.

"What . . . ?" she said. There was a thunking, clinking noise, and she pulled the blanket away, exposing her lower legs.

One of her ankles was bound in a leather restraint.

With a frightened gasp, she looked around the room—of course not seeing anything.

"Stay calm, stay calm, stay calm," she murmured to herself,

her slender fingers working to unfasten the buckle. "The important thing is to *stay calm*."

Kicking her leg free, she slipped off the side of the bed, pausing to grab something from her nightstand, and hurried into the hallway.

The creature started to follow, and I went after them both. But just as she crossed into the hall, Janie bent down and moved her arm quickly across the doorway. The creature lunged for her, but then with a bloodcurdling howl scrambled away from the door and slinked under the bed.

I decided to use this chance to get away—except I couldn't.

When I reached the door, an invisible wall bounced me back into the room. A short *zap!* vibrated through me. I didn't even have to look down to realize what my sister had done.

Smart girl. Using the salt she took from Cordelia's office, she got herself out and locked the shadow in.

The only problem was . . . I was locked in with it.

CHAPTER 21

But I could walk through walls, right? So all I had to do was take two steps to the left and walk right out. Except when I tried, I was decisively bounced back.

By now, I knew enough about the spirit world and its weird nuances to figure that this had something to do with the salt. My sister's intention, by blocking the doorway, was to capture the evil spirit in the room—but that probably locked all supernatural beings in—not just bad guys but regular ghosts, too.

I was stuck in the room with a monster.

I heard it shift and stretch under the bed. It let out a low, sustained growl—a warning sound that, under any other circumstances, would have convinced me to put a lot of distance between us.

Of course that wasn't going to happen now.

"Stay down there," I said. "Neither of us is going anywhere, so you might as well just keep away from me."

But this thing—whatever it was—was not afraid. No amount of posturing or bluffing would make it fear me. It had teeth, claws, and an animalistic nature. Meanwhile, what was I? A defenseless ghost who was really good at . . . nothing.

And now I couldn't even run away. Super.

A louder, longer growl came from beneath the bed.

Electric energy ran through me—the afterlife version of adrenaline. There was no way to get out of this fight, so I might as well psych myself up for it.

Before long, the creature crept out and crouched on the floor, staring right at me.

It bared its teeth, and its fathomless eyes turned to acid green.

First order of business, I thought, *it's going to rip me to shreds.*

It seemed completely ridiculous to be three feet away from an open door yet totally trapped. If only there were some other way out of the room—

Well, there was the window.

Assuming I could even get out that way, there was still the fall to worry about. Ghosts could get injured. What if I broke my leg or my back or something? I shuddered at the idea of dragging myself around for the rest of eternity. I mean, last time I fell out one of these windows, I *died*.

But even that had to beat getting eaten . . . or whatever this thing was capable of doing to me.

Its whole body tensed, like it was about to attack.

You're running out of time, Delia.

I tried to remain completely still, not making any tiny moves that might telegraph my intention. Instead, I stared into the creature's horrible eyes and waited for the right moment to spring toward the window—by now, my only hope of escape.

As we stared at each other, its mouth opened to reveal its jagged teeth, and it emitted a low purring sound, almost a laugh. It enjoyed the fact that I was afraid.

Now!

In one motion, I lunged toward the window. Out of the corner of my eye, I saw the creature rear up and pounce—but I expected to be well on my way to the grass below by the time it landed.

Except, *nope.*

I slammed into the window and barely managed to shove myself away before the creature landed in the spot where I'd been standing. With a frustrated yowl, it swung to look for me.

In desperation, I ran for the door again. Maybe somehow the rules of the game had changed, and I'd find a loophole. Maybe I wanted it more now (and believe me, I did).

Or maybe the creature would leap again—and this time not miss.

Which is exactly what happened. We crashed to the floor, a tangled mess of legs and arms. Its oily flesh was warm to the touch, and despite the fact that it seemed to be made of nothing but smoke, it had pure animal strength.

It pinned me down and snapped its jaws in my face—not biting, but getting close enough for me to wonder with every snap whether this would be the one that tore into my ghostly flesh, leaving me eternally disfigured.

Its glowing eyes seemed to suck the dim light from the room, and its breath smelled of rotting death.

All I could do was flail. And wait.

With the knowledge that I was trapped, it seemed to relax slightly, to pull back and enjoy watching me writhe and fight. Its wide mouth opened in a hideous grin, and a pleased hiss emerged from the depths of its belly.

I was so close to the door. So close to escape. But I would never make it.

As my hand groped the floor helplessly, my fingers suddenly brushed against something.

A recollection of the long-forgotten texture of paper sprang up from my memory.

I got an idea. One last idea. How close was I to the doorway? Could this possibly work? It didn't matter. I had to try, because it was my only option.

Twisting my arm over my head, I shoved the piece of paper along the floor, then glanced up quickly to see if I was anywhere close to my target—

And I was—

So in one swift motion, I scooped the paper under the line of salt, and then flipped it upward over my head, aiming right for the creature's face. A good-sized spray of salt went right into its mouth, down into the depths of its darkly translucent throat.

A beat of surprise appeared in its eyes. Then the surprise turned to wrath.

But before it could bite me, it reared back with a shriek, gagging and choking, raking at its throat with its clawed fingers. I watched in horror as it actually sank its talons into the swirling smoke of its neck. Darker black smoke leaked out of the puncture wounds.

I recognized that smoke. It was the same smoke that had curled down from my ceiling, crept across the room, and enveloped my body on the night I died.

I stood over the creature. *"What are you?"* I shouted.

When I reached down to grab it, to shake it, to force it to

answer me, my fingers went right through it, as if it were made of . . . well, smoke.

The gagging stopped and it fell still onto the antique rug, at which point it occurred to me that a creature made of nothing but smoke might have no problem healing itself after being injured.

Time to go.

The hole I'd made in the salt blocking the doorway wasn't big enough to actually pass through, but it *was* a hole, and that might be enough to break the seal around the room. I ran for the wall . . . and found myself standing in the hallway, a foot away from my sister.

Janie stared at Mom's slightly opened door as if she wasn't sure she wanted to go in. She cast an apprehensive glance back at her own room . . . and did a double take when she saw the gap in the salt line.

She tiptoed back over and lowered herself to inspect it. Then she quickly looked up and down the hall, as if something might be there with her—which I suppose I was.

What I really wanted her to do was to fix the line and trap the creature back inside.

I couldn't see it, but I could hear its furious whining.

My sister sat and stared mutely at the salt. Finally, casting a questioning glance into the room, she reached down and gently spread it back into a complete line.

"Good girl," I said, letting my hand fall to her shoulder in relief. A moment later, the sensation reached my brain—the feeling of actually having touched my sister's shoulder.

She jerked away in a panic. Then she reached up and frantically rubbed her shoulder, her eyes searching the hallway again.

I looked down at my hands.

I was going to have to be more careful.

After another few seconds of looking around anxiously, Janie went to the far corner of the hall and sat down with her knees pulled into her chest. Her breaths were shaky. I didn't blame her.

"Come on," I said, sliding to the floor next to her. "Just go get Mom. Tell her what happened. Tell her you want to leave."

But my sister set her jaw, laid her head on her knees, and leaned her whole body against the wall.

"All right," I said. "Have it your way. Makes no difference to me."

But the truth is, it did make a difference. It meant everything in the world to me just to have the chance to stretch out, like a cat, on the floor in front of her—between her and anything else that might be tempted to come down the hallway. Even if she never knew I was here, a selfish part of me wanted to drink in every moment of her presence. And Mom's.

Because I knew it wouldn't last. And I knew it shouldn't.

But for one night, I could be close to them again. Couldn't I?

A crisp British voice, accompanied by the sound of jingle bells, cut through the tranquil hall. "Delia, what are you doing? Why is she sleeping out here?"

I'd been too focused on my sister's uneven breaths to hear Eliza's approach. Some bodyguard I'd make.

Pale dawn light spilled through the window. I got to my feet, feeling acutely the contrast between Eliza's flawless appearance and my chronic disheveledness. "There was something in her room."

"What kind of something?" Eliza glanced down the hall.

"Some sort of . . . shadow monster," I said. "It's blocked in with salt."

"A shadow monster?" Eliza's eyes went wide. "You saw it?"

"Yeah," I said. "It almost got me, but I threw some salt on it and escaped."

"Impossible." Eliza's eyes grew even wider.

"But I did," I said. "And by the way, I'm fine, thanks for asking."

She ignored the pointed comment and stared out the window, clearly lost in thought. "You can manipulate salt . . . It must have something to do with the fact that you can go outside."

I shrugged. "What was it, though? It's not like us."

Eliza let out a surprised snort of laughter, like I was the dumbest dead person she'd ever met. "I should say not! We're *ghosts*."

"And that thing is . . . ?"

"It's . . . a shadow," she said. "I don't really know how to define it. But it's evil."

"Okay," I said. "And no one was going to warn me about it?"

"We haven't seen one in years."

"How many years?" I asked sharply.

"Four." She cleared her throat and had the grace to look a bit sheepish. "They tend to come out when the living are here."

"Like me," I said.

"And Cordelia," she said. "There was a rather nasty one around shortly before she died. I don't know how she avoided it, honestly."

"But Nic was here. And Landon. And there were ghost hunters," I said. "They were alive. Did you see any of the—shadows then?"

"No," Eliza said, shaking her head. "But . . . it's more accurate to say they come out when they're after something."

Or some*one*. "You mean they hunt."

Her shoulders made a stiff, helpless up-and-down movement—even the way she shrugged was prim. "That's a very melodramatic way to look at it, but I suppose you could say so."

I felt the edge of my hairline grow damp with beads of phantom sweat. When I spoke, I tried to contain the frustration in my voice. "So you knew these things were here, and you never said anything?"

"What would have been the use?" She turned away and smoothed her hair uncomfortably. "You know now, don't you?"

I folded my arms in front of my chest and stared at her, put off by her evasiveness. "And you're okay with it? Living here among those things?"

"They leave us alone," she said, "and we leave them alone."

"They didn't leave me alone," I said. "Or Janie."

She dropped the attitude and regarded me with genuine concern. "What was it doing to her?"

"It was tying her to the bed. It's probably the same thing that tied her to the bed the day I died."

Eliza bit her lip. "I doubt it would have actually hurt her, though. Whereas it could have shredded *you* like a roast chicken. Do be careful if you see another one. You say you've injured it?"

"I think so. But where did it *come* from?"

"We never figured it out. I saw one in the basement once, and I've heard rumors that one lives on the third floor. Florence told me that Maria was a perfectly normal little girl—I mean, *dead*, of course, but normal—until she had a run-in with one of those."

Before I could ask anything else, a bloodcurdling, inhuman screech filled the hallway, and almost at once my nose filled with a scent like a pile of three-week-old dead fish.

We ran back to my sister's room. Eliza crouched low to the ground and peered inside. After a moment, she sat up, startled. "Well," she said. "You needn't worry about it bothering Jane. It's died. You've killed it."

I sat in stunned silence.

"Good riddance." Eliza stood and folded her arms in front of her chest. "Your sister will be safe in this room now—once the smell goes away."

I knelt and looked inside. The dark, still body seemed to be growing fainter.

"To business, then, since that's settled," Eliza said. "I think it's time you, Florence, and I talk. Form a concrete plan to get your family out of here . . . before something bad happens."

Something *bad*. Because having to fight my way out of being trapped in a tiny room with a vicious, formless creature was apparently just another day at the office.

I sighed. "Okay. Let's go talk to Florence."

   ❊   ❊   ❊

Florence and I sat on the couch in the lobby, while Eliza paced before us like a military tactician. "All right," she said. "How long do they plan to stay? Do we make an active plan to chase them away, or simply try to keep them safe until they go?"

As deeply as it pained me to think of never seeing Mom and Janie again, I was eager to get them out of the house. "Active plan," I said. "Preferably before any more shadow monsters show up."

Florence had practically swooned with dismay at the news of the creature's reappearance. Having seen her face off against Maria, I was fairly certain the delicacy was an act, but she seemed to be enjoying the drama, so I didn't bring it up.

"Have you seen any more?" she asked, looking from me to Eliza. "Did you look in the basement?"

"No," I said. "But I think it's fair to say we're on their radar." Blank looks.

"I mean, they're aware of us—maybe aware that we're aware of them," I said. "But if we're prepared, we can fight them. All it took to kill the thing was to throw salt on it. The key is not to be caught off guard."

Florence and Eliza glanced at each other. "That's just it," Eliza said. "*We* can't touch salt. I couldn't pick it up and fling it if I had a steam shovel. Your ability to move it must stem from your possessing some degree of authority here. As the former owner."

Basically meaning I was on my own. The idea of fighting the shadows by myself didn't exactly thrill me, but I was resolved to protect Mom and Janie. "Okay, then," I said. "Point me toward the salt, and I'll take care of them."

Florence looked a little faint, so Eliza gave her a bracing thump on the back.

"That would be lovely, and we'll take you up on it," Eliza said. "But you should know that the shadow creatures are only a symptom. The real core of the problem—the root—must lie somewhere else. Discovering that may prove more of a challenge."

"We don't have to discover it," Florence said, tucking her hair behind her ear. "We just need to make sure *it* doesn't discover the little Gothic girl, right?"

"It's already discovered her," I said. "That must be why *it* sent its monsters to her room."

Eliza let out a frustrated little sniff.

"Sugar, you're worrying me," Florence said to her.

Eliza fidgeted awkwardly in place, then looked pleadingly at Florence. "It wouldn't be the worst thing in the world, would it . . . ? To know what's trapped us here, and why?"

Florence's jaw dropped. "You've been happy for ninety years, and just like that you've changed all your convictions?"

"No," Eliza said stoutly. "Not *all* my convictions. But there has to be a reason for our being stuck, and I'd like to know the reason. That's all."

There was an uncharacteristically earnest note in her voice—a tiny break that hinted at years of loneliness and helplessness.

As scary as the unknown was—the idea of ceasing to exist—it was easy to appreciate the full horror of being left behind, trapped here, while everyone you love withers and dies.

Florence stared despondently at the threadbare rug beneath our feet. "Maybe it doesn't want us to know," she said. She lowered her voice as if she were about to say something scandalous. "What if you just make it *mad*?"

"We won't go poking it with sticks, I promise," Eliza said. "Anyway, that's not what's important at the moment. For now, we've got to focus our efforts on getting Delia's family off the property. Perhaps we can arrange a sewage leak or something."

Florence flopped back, her forearm over her eyes. "Lovely," she muttered.

"If we're pitching ideas," I said, "I have one that might be a little less stinky."

"I'm telling you," Eliza said, her voice straining in an effort to be patient, "this isn't going to work. I don't know why you won't believe me."

"Sorry," I said. "But I have to *try*."

After making sure I noticed her annoyed look, Eliza handed me the orange Sharpie. (We'd already been through her looking at the logo on the pen and asking me "What's a Shar-Pie?" as if it were a blueberry pie or apple pie.) "What do you plan to write?" she asked.

We were sitting on the floor on the ward side of the door, on which I was preparing to write a message to my family. Something they couldn't possibly ignore. My object-holding skills were still touch and go, so I'd persuaded Eliza to join me, just in case I needed help.

"Something powerful, but simple," I said. "Maybe . . . *Leave*? In all capital letters."

She shook her head. "Go ahead and try. *L*."

"I know how to spell, thank you." I pushed the tip of the marker against the door and paused. Then I started to make a line, the vertical part of the *L*.

Suddenly, the marker veered off course.

Eliza sat back. "See?"

I rolled my eyes, then raised the pen and tried again. Again, the pen seemed to jerk out from my control.

"I don't understand," I said. "It doesn't make sense."

"It makes perfect sense." She sat back on her heels and looked up at me, having the grace not to gloat. "If we could just send messages, everyone would be doing it. You can't cross the planes that way. It's too literal. You've got to be subtle."

Subtle. The same word Penitence had used.

"But we can control physical objects," I said. "Why can't we just draw a line?"

"You can draw a line," she said, taking the marker and drawing one.

"Great!" I said. "Draw another line, and then we'll have an *L*."

She sighed, looked at me as if I were totally hopeless, and reached over to draw another line. This one went wildly diagonal.

I was silent.

"Do you believe me now?" she asked.

"I guess I have to."

She got to her feet, leaving the marker on the floor. "We'll find a way to make them leave," she said. "I promise. But you're never going to be able to communicate this way."

I sighed. "We have to think outside the box."

"Outside of what box?" She frowned. "Have you found some sort of special box?"

"No, there's no box," I said. "Forget it."

Eliza grimaced. "I'll go look into a sewage leak."

Just then, the bathroom door opened and Mom emerged, wrapped in a towel. She walked right by the scribbled-on door.

"Janie?" Mom called. "I mean, Jane? Do you smell something? It's like . . . a dead animal. Yuck."

There was no answer.

Mom was quiet for a second. I assumed that by this point she was used to being snubbed by my sister and would just go back to her own room. But instead, she tensed and walked the length of the hall, peering inside every open door. Not finding Janie, she returned to the closed door of Room 1—my old room—took a deep, bracing breath, and opened the door.

There was a surprised shriek.

"Mom!" Janie cried.

"Janie!" Mom cried back at her. *"What are you doing in here?"*

"Sleeping," Janie said. "Trying to, anyway."

"You shouldn't be in here," Mom said, her voice firm. "You need to choose a different room. What's wrong with the one you slept in last night?"

"I didn't like that one," Janie said, and I heard the hesitation in her voice as she passed over her chance to tell Mom what had happened. "Anyway, I like it in here."

I walked over. I felt a jolt seeing Janie, her Goth-y hairstyle all mussed from sleep, in the pink bed I'd never actually slept in. The boards and broken screen had been removed from the window.

"Jane," Mom said, with a calmness that hinted at some suppressed surge of emotion, "you *cannot* stay in here."

"But—"

"I'm not debating this with you!" Mom hardly ever raised her voice, so when she went full-on angry, it was a terrible sound. "Get out of this room. And stay out."

Janie's face fell, and for a moment, she looked like a little girl again. "But I like it in here. I feel—"

"For once," Mom said, seething, "just *once*, do as I say. God, you are *so* much like your sister sometimes."

There was a heavy, painful silence.

Mom looked at the floor. "I'm sorry," she said. "I . . . I'm sorry."

Wordlessly, Janie got out from under the covers, scooped up her bag, and stalked across the hall to Room 2.

As the slam of the door echoed in the hall, my mother pressed her hands to the sides of her face, turning her head in a slow survey of the room where I'd died. Her whole body trembled almost uncontrollably. She made a low, quiet sound, a sustained hum that kept trying to break out into something fiercer. Then she fell silent, gave herself a sharp little shake, and walked away.

The trail of pain she left behind was almost tangible.

How could I have ever thought she would forget me?

CHAPTER 22

I slipped through the door to Room 2 as Janie was sitting down on the bed and pulling a thin tablet-style computer from her bag. She connected her phone to it with a short white cable, hooking it up as a wireless modem before opening the computer's web browser. I was impressed—at some point, my little sister had morphed into a tech geek.

I watched raptly over her shoulder as she pulled up a website called Paranormal Interests and logged herself in as Need2Know.

A notification window popped up. *You have 8 unread private messages.*

I watched her scroll through them. Each one was from a different sender, but they all wrote as if they knew her. *Are you there now?* someone asked. *Has anything happened, any occurrences?* someone else asked.

She clicked through them all but stopped on one from SawW. It was written with a lot more formality than the others.

Dear Jane,
    I must ask you again to reconsider. I think you are

taking an unnecessary risk. There are other ways to learn about what happened to your sister.

Janie had been talking to people on the Internet about me and my death? I was anxious to know more, but Janie was already typing a reply to SawW.

Dear Walter,

As usual, I appreciate you worrying about me—you always have great advice and that means a LOT. I printed out the pamphlet you sent, so thanks for that, too. The thing is, I can't reconsider because this is my last chance. My parents are selling the property in August, and I will never be able to come back. If I don't figure it out now, then I will never know what happened, and I will never ever be okay again. Which I guess is only fair because Delia will never get to be okay, but I still need to try. For my parents' sake as much as for mine. If I am never okay again, then they might as well have lost two daughters.

I bristled. Who was this Walter guy, and why was he messaging my sister? I had a horrified vision of some creepy mouth-breather. What kind of sleazebag would prey on an emotionally vulnerable fifteen-year-old?

She clicked *Send*, and not thirty seconds later, another little window popped up. This one said, *You have a new private message from SawW*. Next to it was a little avatar of a man who must have been Walter. To my immense relief, he looked about eighty-five years old.

Janie clicked on the window and winced when the text popped up.

IF YOU CONTINUE THIS FOOLISHNESS, THEY *WILL* LOSE TWO DAUGHTERS!

As if it could erase the ominous tone of his words, Janie quickly closed the window and sat staring at her desktop background—a photo of her and me from that perfect Halloween, the one where she was a housewife and I was a grunge rocker. In the picture, Janie was clutching my hand and laughing. I was beaming at the camera, holding her mop in my other hand.

With a sigh, Janie clicked on a folder icon on the desktop marked *Private*. It contained at least a dozen subfolders, each meticulously labeled. There was a folder called *Police Files* and one called *Historical*. She paused before selecting *Floor Plans*.

A map popped up—rather, five maps—one for each level of the building, starting with the basement and going all the way to the attic. All of the rooms were drawn out and clearly labeled.

What's more, they had some sort of notation on them—a seemingly random assortment of numbered red dots. But next my sister opened another file called *Incidents*, which was a numbered list. I scanned it quickly until I hit a familiar name:

3. Maria Gorren: died 1885, 10 yrs old, electrocuted self and Nurse Carlson

4. Harriet Carlson: died 1885, resident nurse, electrocuted by Maria Gorren

I looked at the image, searching for the red dots labeled *3* and *4*, and found them in the third-floor ward bathroom.

Perusing the rest of the list, I found Florence—

8. Florence Beauregard, 20 yrs old, died 1902, asphyxiation by hanging

I gasped. Had Florence really hanged herself? Or had she hanged herself in the same way that I'd leapt out a window—which is to say, not at all?

Farther down, I found Eliza. *19 yrs old, died 1922, unknown causes.*

I flinched at #27—*Theodore Hawkins, 19 years old, died 1940, drowning.*

The last death on the list happened in 1943. After that, nobody else died, probably because they'd shut the place down.

My heart thunked to the bottom of my chest at the sight of my own name, listed by itself farther down the page. But I was also intrigued. I was part of a pattern, an investigation . . . At least *somebody* thought there was something odd about my death. I just wished that "somebody" wasn't my little sister.

Mom, still believing my death was a simple suicide, had come here to make the final pre-sale adjustments to the property. But something told me she had no idea that Janie had a completely different goal—to actively seek out the truth about what had happened to me.

When I was alive, Janie had been sweet, flighty, and light-hearted. Now there was a spark inside her, some sizzling, simmering tension. I could see it in her eyes as they anxiously skimmed the laptop screen, in the quickness of her fingers as they tapped out words on the keyboard. In her taut, wiry posture. She was after something.

And she was determined to find it.

There was a sudden, urgent knock on the door. My sister yanked her bag over her computer just as Mom pulled the door open. The sternness of my mother's expression silenced any protests before Janie could voice them.

"I know you don't like it here," Mom said, "but that is *no reason* to deface the property, is that clear?"

Janie frowned. "Um . . . sure?"

So Mom had seen the mess Eliza and I made on the ward door . . . and she thought Janie was responsible.

They stared at each other for a long beat, until Mom said, "Okay. I'm going to town to buy some groceries and grab a few things at the hardware store. Want to come?"

"No, thanks," my sister said. "Just bring back some real food. I want Cheetos."

Mom nodded and shut the door.

Janie slipped her earbuds in her ears and flopped back on the bed with her eyes closed. But after a couple of minutes, she sat up and switched off the music.

Standing in the doorway, listening down the hall for any movement, she called, "Mom? You still here?"

No answer.

A few minutes later, Janie sat in front of the ward door with a rag and a bottle of cleaning solution, scrubbing with all her strength. When the bold orange marks had been reduced to a few pale streaks, she sat with her back against the wall and let the rag drop to the floor.

"I don't care who you are or what you do to me," she said aloud. "I'm going to find out what really happened to my sister."

"Yes, that's very brave," I said. "But you still need to be careful, you crazy dumbhead."

She obviously had some idea that this place wasn't all it seemed. She was already wary enough to protect herself using salt. But then I realized, with dread making its way down my spine like some frozen liquid, that salt might not be enough of a defense against a force that could slide through the very walls and seep into your mind.

My sister had brought a knife to a ghost fight.

And what's more, she was in terrible danger. Because my sister had become exactly what I had been, back four years earlier when the house had found me irresistible:

Janie was a troubled female.

CHAPTER 23

Operation *Just Leave, Already* was under way. Eliza had identified a rusted pipe in the bathroom, one that, with a little slamming from a wrench or sledgehammer, might shatter and flood the place.

The tools were in the basement, presumably under the watch of another shadow creature. So that's where I was headed.

The kitchen pantry was packed with salt. Standing surrounded by navy-blue cartons of the stuff, my skin thrummed and my nose and mouth filled with acrid, salty fumes. But I was able to pick up one of the cannisters and carry it out to the counter.

I needed to transfer it to a container that would make it easy to aim and throw. I found a scratched-up metal measuring cup and filled it with salt, then pushed open the kitchen door with my hip. A thrill of satisfaction went through me at the ease with which I'd been able to do it—as if I had an actual body.

I was starting to get my dead groove on. I just hoped I wouldn't be shredded into spaghetti by a shadow monster before I got to enjoy it.

Then I faced the basement door. It was locked, so I set the metal cup down and passed through the solid wood, intending to turn the lock from inside and go back for the salt.

I had to hurry—no doubt my ghostly blue glow was enough to grab the attention of any lurking shadow creature.

But just as I was struggling to get a grip on the lock, it turned from the other side. I slipped back through the door and found myself face-to-face with Janie, who stood with the keys in her hand and that Nancy Drew look in her eyes.

"Oh, come on," I said. "Don't go down there! Have you *never* seen a horror movie?"

Suddenly, there was a tremendous *thump* against the basement door.

Janie and I both jumped back.

I thought for sure that she would leave now. I know *I* would have, if I'd been in her place. But to my considerable surprise (and dismay) she took a deep breath and reached into her pocket, taking out a small paperback book—hardly more than a pamphlet. *I printed out the pamphlet you sent,* she'd written to that old Walter guy.

She unfolded it and started to read, a shade louder than a whisper. "By the authority of nature," she said, "by the forces of creation. By righteousness and through the power of good, I—"

Another huge *thud*.

My sister flinched, but her voice grew stronger. "Through the power of good, I bind you, I bind you—"

Four massive bangs, as if there was a rabid gorilla trying to get through the door.

"—*I bind you,*" she said.

Everything was silent.

And then Janie—who once spent an hour and a half on the kitchen counter because she thought she may have seen a cockroach on the floor—opened the basement door and started down the stairs into near-pitch darkness and the company of a terrifying supernatural creature.

Part of me admired her. Part of me wanted to cuff her in the back of the head.

I quickly grabbed the metal measuring cup, praying that my sister wouldn't turn and find herself being haunted by a floating container of salt. I followed her to the center of the room, where she used her cell phone as a flashlight and looked around. Aside from my faint blue glow—which she couldn't see, anyway—the LED was the only light in the room. Its small circle seemed inadequate against the looming darkness.

I stayed as close to her as I dared, scanning the room for the shadow creature, which I knew must be studying our every move. Whatever spell or incantation Janie had read seemed to have some effect—but for how long, I didn't know. I wondered if *she* even knew.

The basement was apparently the institute's long-forgotten deep storage. It was cavernous, lined with floor-to-ceiling shelves holding every possible type of domestic item: a herd of mops and brooms, teetering piles of old pots and pans and cooking utensils, decaying metal tins of soap powder, and even an entire array of old silverware and serving platters. I kept an eye out for wrenches.

As we went deeper into the blackness, I heard a sound that sent a shot of cold fear through my body. *"Delia . . ."*

I couldn't tell where it had come from.

I tensed and tried to ready myself for a fight. But a few steps later, illuminated by my pale blue glow, I saw a smoky body silently slamming against an invisible barrier. It was totally freaking out—flailing its legs, even bashing its head into whatever was holding it back. This shadow was bigger and meaner looking than the one upstairs. Its teeth were longer and more jagged in its gaping mouth, and the fog swirling within its outline seemed thicker and heavier.

Oblivious to its presence, Janie stood not two feet away, looking around. There was a wary look in her eyes, but behind it was that familiar dogged spark.

She walked a little farther into the darkness.

The shadow hurled its body against the barrier. But this time, something was different. Instead of just bouncing off, it almost seemed to catch on something. And that got its attention, big-time. It focused all its energy on that one spot, until I could see that the boundary was stretching, weakening.

My sister was still only a couple of feet ahead of me. If the monster broke free, it would go after us—first me, then her.

I would have preferred to wait until Janie had rounded the corner, so there was no chance she might turn and see what was happening. But as the creature started to make real progress toward escape, I made the call.

I drew back the measuring cup and tossed the salt onto its trapped form.

Its shriek was an otherworldly mix of agony and fury and a hint of helplessness. Shockingly, the sound gave me a healthy stab of guilt, right in the center of the heart.

This creature had been shut up in here for who knew how long—hungry, lonely, angry, and growing more so with every passing year. It hadn't chosen what it was, any more than I had.

It collapsed to the floor in a quaking heap, and I stared down at it until it went still.

I'd never killed anything bigger than an ant when I'd been alive, and now twice in a single day I'd brought down these beasts.

"I'm sorry," I said. Tears stung my eyes. I hoped that maybe now it would find some peace, even if that meant not existing. Maybe the absence of torment was its own kind of peace.

Meanwhile, my sister hadn't noticed a thing. I set the empty measuring cup down on an old wooden crate and followed her to the back of the room, where the whole wall was lined with ancient gray file cabinets.

I stood in awe for a moment. Judging by their sheer number, I guessed that these were the records from the entire history of the institute. Every girl who came in was probably notated in here—her treatments, symptoms, illnesses . . . maybe even her death.

Janie went straight for one in the middle and pulled it open, revealing olive-green file folders. She thumbed through the yellowed tabs, and, not finding what she wanted, closed that drawer and went farther left. More file folders. Still the wrong ones.

She went all the way to the leftmost cabinet and opened it.

Instead of folders, this one held large, leather-bound books whose covers were coming off in chunks and strips. Janie pulled out the top one and shone her light on it. In faded gold leaf, the cover read PIVEN INSTITUTE, 1866–1873. These were the very earliest patient records, before they moved to a more organized alphabetized system.

Flipping page after page, Janie examined the entries, each of which bore the name of a different patient, her age, and a note about her life pre-institute—*Hilda Hargreave, 29, mother of 4, housewife. Catherine Scales, 67, dressmaker, spinster.* They were handwritten logs with messily scribbled notations.

Most of them had a large note scrawled across the top: *DISCHARGED*, and a date. But a few of them didn't—the ones that were labeled *DECEASED*.

About a third of the way through the book, Janie stopped and leaned to get a closer look at the text, her interest caught.

I looked over her shoulder at the name that had grabbed her attention:

Penitence Piven, 36, mother of 1, widow, former wardress of the Piven Institute.

CHAPTER 24

*P*iven? Push-everything-off-the-table Penitence was a *Piven*? She and I were related?

I thought of Aunt Cordelia's unsent letter, where she mentioned that the institute had been founded by a man so cruel and controlling that he'd locked up his own daughter, just because he could.

Janie was making her way down the notes on Penitence's page of records. The first five, all made in different handwriting, were the same:

Remains uncooperative. Insists on seeing child.

But the sixth was different.

TREATMENT: Water therapy. 1st sign of acquiescence.

The next note made Janie draw in an indignant breath.

DIAGNOSIS: Female hysteria.

"Of course it was," Janie muttered. She turned the page again and came to the end of the notes about Penitence. The very last one read simply, in very clear handwriting, *Died, natural causes.* There wasn't even a year listed.

My sister suddenly raised her nose and sniffed the air. The

putrid scent of the dead shadow had crossed over to her plane of existence and was filling the room.

That motivated her to wrap things up. She replaced the book in the cabinet, then brushed her hands on her jeans and walked back to the stairs.

I watched her climb safely back to the first floor, but I stayed downstairs. I needed to find a wrench. And since I figured I should wait a couple of minutes before trying to sneak it upstairs, I decided to do a little research of my own.

I went to the files and flipped through the *B*s until I found *Beauregard, Florence*. But her file, and those around it, were so damaged by age and dampness that the ink was illegible. All I could make out was the typewritten *DECEASED* at the top.

Next, I looked through the *D* drawers until I came to *Duncombe, Eliza*. I pulled the file and began to read.

"How did it go?" Eliza asked eagerly, appearing in the hall. "Did you find a wrench to hit the pipe with? What about the shadow?"

"Killed it," I said, walking past her.

She began to follow me. "Wow. Great. Impressive. Next, we need to—"

"*We*," I said, turning on her, "are not going to do anything. *You* are going to stay away from me and my family. Understand?"

Eliza's face fell.

My initial plan had been to storm away, full of righteousness and cold fury, but I couldn't pass up the chance to express my anger. "You've lied to me the entire time I've known you," I said. "This *whole* time, you've pretended to be some innocent victim."

Eliza seemed practically frozen. Her voice was a whisper. "What did you find down there?"

"Everything," I said. "Your patient records, the news articles . . ."

She turned paler—her whole body became more transparent. "But . . . but those are kept in the attic. At least, they used to be."

"Well, now they're in the basement," I said. I started to walk away, then stopped to stash the wrench on an open shelf near the stairwell entrance.

She followed, hot on my heels. "Don't you dare judge me, Delia! You've no idea what really happened—"

"No idea?" I said. "Pardon me—did you or did you not kill your own brother and sister?"

She didn't answer. A shudder passed through her entire body.

"You kept hoping someone from your family would come back for you?" I asked. "Really? Is that actually what you've been telling yourself all this time? Because I have news for you. They were never going to come, Eliza. You killed *children*. And you should have been hanged for it, but your father pulled some strings—"

"No," she said, her voice dull. "I wouldn't have hanged. They'd changed over to the electric chair by then."

I didn't reply.

"How do you know all this?" she asked. "What did you find?"

"There were newspaper articles in your file," I said. "After your father arranged for you to be committed here, he and the rest of your family went back to England. That's why they never came to visit, in case no one ever told you. They weren't even in this country."

"Ah," she said faintly, biting her lip and nodding. "No, I didn't know that. No one ever told me."

"You lied to me, Eliza. You're a murderer . . . You're as bad as Maria."

Eliza's face seemed to crumple, and her mouth opened. She took a gasping breath in, and it came out as a sob. "No—*worse* than Maria," she said. "She only killed adults. I killed innocent children."

Disturbing, disturbing, disturbing. I didn't need to hear this.

"But it was an accident," Eliza said. "You have to believe me."

"You 'accidentally' set their bedroom on fire?" I asked.

"They weren't supposed to be sleeping in there!" she cried. "They always, *always* slept in the night nursery with Nanny. I only needed a small distraction so I could sneak out of the house to meet Arthur. But they—"

"Stop," I said. "Please, honestly, just stop. It makes me sick to think about it."

"How do you think it makes *me* feel?" She wept uncontrollably, from someplace deep inside herself. The way you might cry if—just for instance—you've held a horrible secret inside for almost a hundred years and it was suddenly laid out before you.

"Stay away from me," I said. "And my family. Okay?"

"You don't . . . you won't . . . are you going to tell Florence what I've done?" Eliza sobbed.

I felt a mixture of pity and frustration, and turned back to look at her. "No," I said. "If you want to go on lying to your best friend, that's your business. But you're done lying to me."

Then I walked away.

Janie was in the day room, sitting at the piano, tapping out a slow melody of flat, tired notes.

"Penitence," I said, standing over her table. "I know you're here."

But she didn't appear.

"And I know who you are," I said.

The notes from the piano slowed slightly, and I turned to check on my sister. She seemed fine, though, and when I turned back, Penitence was sitting at the table.

"You were the wardress here?" I asked.

She didn't look up from her work. "I don't talk about my life. Or my death."

"Your father built this place, didn't he?"

Her lips flattened.

"When did he die?"

She shook her head. "No one knows. He went out one night and never came back."

"But you must know if his spirit is here. Is he the one who killed me?"

"His spirit?" Her eyes went wide. "It couldn't be."

"Why not?" I asked. "He wanted to control people, didn't he? Maybe he's controlling all of us."

She looked up at me through miserable eyes. "What's here," she said, "what's in the house . . . is bigger than my father. And he was an evil man, but what's here is more than evil. What's here is . . ."

A sound caught my ear. Or, more precisely, a lack of sound. Janie had stopped playing the piano.

"It's *hungry*," Penitence said. And then she vanished.

I looked at Janie as she closed the piano and ran her finger along the top, collecting a big pile of dust and then closing her eyes and blowing it away, as if she were making a wish. After a moment, she opened her eyes, and, staring out the window at the hillside, began to hum.

I knew every note of the song. Every single note. It was "Beautiful Dreamer."

Then she started to sing, her soprano voice filling the room. *"Beautiful dreamer, wake unto me . . ."*

Something was wrong.

She walked toward the window, still singing, her eyes focused on some spot in the distance.

Something was terribly wrong.

When she reached the window, her eyes never wavered from the view, but her fingers began to claw at the metal grate that covered the glass.

"Janie!" I gasped.

Her voice descended to a rasp. *"Starlight and dewdrops are waiting for thee . . ."*

Then a movement above her caught my eye. A faint, swirling black fog had begun to seep out of the seam where the ceiling and wall met.

Oh no.

"Janie!" I said again, rushing to my sister's side. I tried to shove her, to wake her up somehow, but my hands went right through her body.

Why now? How could I fail now?

I could do this. I knew I could. I *had* to.

I kept pawing at her, trying to grab her attention . . . and I kept failing.

Her fingertips were bloody. She was making progress on the wire. She was going to open the window and leap out—or be pushed. And I was going to have to stand there and watch because I couldn't do anything. I couldn't save her.

"Janie!" I screamed at the top of my lungs. And then I screamed again. "Janie, wake up! *Wake up!*"

In a panic, I raced to the door and stuck my head through.

"Mom!" I cried, momentarily forgetting that my mother and I were on separate planes of existence. "Come quick! Mom!"

And then it hit me that my mother wasn't even there. She'd gone into town. So she would come back to find . . . No.

I raced back to my sister, who by that point had wrenched the bottom third of the screen away from the wall.

This wasn't happening. This couldn't be happening.

Except it *was* happening. And I couldn't stop it.

I circled the room, trying to move chairs and tables, desperate to get a grip on something I could use to wake my sister up . . . or knock her down.

But it wasn't working. Was this an extension of not being able to send messages? Was I really not going to be able to save Janie's life because of a technicality?

"Penitence!" I called. "Help me, please!"

But she was stuck in place. "I—I can't. I can't move. I can't leave my work."

"That's not true," I said. "Just get up. You can get up. Try. *Please.*"

Penitence's face was a mask of regret and fear, and then she vanished.

I was alone with my sister, whose glazed eyes were a searing reminder of my own past—of being overcome by the smoky haze. That dazed, disoriented feeling that directly preceded my own death.

When Janie had managed to pry half the screen out of the way, she reached through and unlatched the window. It swung open, and she set her foot on the windowsill and ducked, intending to fit her body through the smallish opening.

I couldn't stop her. I couldn't do anything.

She was going to die, right in front of me. And in a little while, Mom would come into the day room and see the open window, and—

Suddenly, there was a deep, primal yell, and someone was rushing across the room toward us.

Eliza body-slammed my sister, hurling the pair of them across the floor. Janie's head hit the carpeted ground, hard, and her eyes, which had been wide and glazed, blinked twice and then shut tightly.

She whispered, *"Ow."*

Eliza got to her feet, panting.

"Thank you," I whispered. *"Thank you."*

Eliza brushed off her hands but didn't look at me. "I tried to tell you," she said. "I'm not a killer. I spent every day of my life haunted by my brother and sister's deaths—and every day since I died, too."

I nodded.

"I wasn't crazy when I first came here. But this place . . . this place made me crazy. I started to believe I'd killed them on purpose. I was seventeen years old, Delia—a child. It was an *accident*—a terrible accident." Her eyes met mine. "Do you believe me?"

"Yes," I said. Shame welled up inside me as I remembered my cold self-importance from our earlier confrontation. Who was I to judge? I, who had nearly murdered my best friend?

With a start, I realized that Eliza had saved the lives of *two* people I loved.

I looked down at Janie, who was lying on her back, staring at the ceiling, hugging herself tightly.

"Mom?" Janie called quietly. Tears sprang from the corners of her eyes. "Mommy?"

I sat down at her side, wishing I could comfort her. But I'd have to settle for keeping watch.

"I saw the smoke, too," Eliza said softly. "When I died. I was in the infirmary, because I'd been ill. But I was getting better. I felt good, healthy, strong. Only the stronger I felt, the more I sensed that something was . . . watching me. Hovering nearby. And then one day, when the nurse left, the smoke came out of the walls and surrounded me. Everything went sort of gray, and when I woke up, they were carrying my body off to the morgue."

She gritted her teeth. "They called it a heart defect. And when they buried me out on the west lawn, no one came to my funeral, not even the nurses. There was a priest, and he read about four lines and then left."

"I'm sorry," I said.

"Do you know why, at first, I didn't want to help you find the root of evil in this house?" Eliza said.

I shook my head.

"Because," she said. "I'm afraid of what would happen if I were to move on from here. I'm afraid . . . afraid I won't make it to heaven. Because of what I've done, you see."

I looked down at my sister, who had rolled to her side and curled up in a ball, sniffling sadly.

"But it was an accident," I said.

I'd never seen Eliza look so young. She peered down at me from beneath the dark line of her bangs. "You do believe me, then?" she asked again.

Frankly, even if I didn't, it wouldn't have mattered. She'd saved Janie's life. So no matter what she'd done, I owed her forever.

But I did believe her. "Yes," I said.

She drew in a long, shaky breath. "Well, that's something, I suppose."

I turned to lean down and listen to Janie's breathing, and when I sat back up, Eliza was gone.

But Penitence was back in her seat at the table, a wretched expression on her face. "I'm sorry," she said. "I would have helped. But I've never been able to leave this spot. Not in a hundred and thirty years."

"No," I said. "You've never *chosen* to leave that spot. There's a difference."

She bowed her head.

"It's fine," I said. "Everyone has to fight their own demons. Next time I just won't bother asking for your help."

Behind me, the door to the day room opened. Mom called, "Jane? I've got your Cheetos. Will you help me—"

She stopped short at the sight of Janie lying on the floor. Dropping the grocery bags, she fell to her knees by my sister's side. "Jane? Janie? Are you okay?"

Janie opened her eyes, then reached out and grabbed Mom's hand, holding it as tightly as a little child.

"What happened?" Mom stared down at my sister's blood-covered fingers. "What happened to you?"

Janie looked at the window, where the screen was pulled away from the wall. The wall itself was streaked with fresh red blood.

Mom followed her gaze and gasped.

"There's something here, Mom," Janie said. "I don't think Delia killed herself . . . It's time to go home."

Mom helped Janie to her room and was going to help her pack, but my sister insisted she'd be all right. Mom's room was only twenty feet away, and she needed to pack up, too. My mother moved as if there were a fire burning beneath her feet, running from room to room, collecting their scattered possessions and shoving them willy-nilly into bags. Every couple of minutes, she came back and checked on Janie, who was resting comfortably, and seemed, actually, more relaxed than she had since they arrived.

Finally, Mom came into Janie's room, drenched in sweat. "Done," she said. "I'm going to start loading the car."

Janie kicked her legs off the side of the bed and stood up. "I'll help."

Mom looked torn. I could tell she wanted to keep my sister close but also wanted her to take it easy. "No, honey—you hit your head, and I'd rather you rest. It'll only be a couple of trips."

I stayed with Janie. I didn't plan to take my eyes off her until she and Mom were safely clear of the property. She sat up and tucked her phone into her purse, then got to her feet and dragged the old red suitcase out to the day room. Standing there, all of a sudden, she made a little squeaking noise, and pressed her fist to her mouth. Her body trembled, and fat tears rolled from her eyes.

"I'm sorry, Delia," she said. "I'm sorry for what I did. I hope someday you'll forgive me. But if it makes you feel better . . . I'll never forgive myself."

"You dolt!" I said. "How could that possibly make me feel better?"

She went on crying, until she leaned against the doorframe and slid to the ground. And then she cried some more. I wanted to wrap my arms around her but couldn't bear to feel her body slip through my touch.

There was nothing I could do.

Being dead really sucks sometimes.

After a couple of minutes, I realized that something was wrong. Mom should have been back by now.

Moments later, Janie reached the same conclusion. She wiped her eyes, then called, "Mom?"

No answer.

My sister got to her feet and started walking toward the day room door.

My heart began to pound.

I couldn't let her open that door.

"Stay back!" I said sharply, positive it wouldn't work.

But to my surprise, Janie stopped in her tracks. She stared at the door for another moment, then took a few backward steps.

"Stay," I said to Janie, the way you'd say it to a dog. And though she couldn't hear me, she wandered back to the piano bench and sat down.

I crossed the room toward the stairwell, a heavy, hot feeling in my chest.

"Something's wrong out there," a voice said. I turned to see Penitence sitting nervously, helplessly, in her seat.

"It's okay," I said. "Watch my sister. Call for me if something happens."

I stepped through the door.

The stairwell was completely filled with oily black smoke, so dense I couldn't see. Its bitter flavor invaded my nose and mouth.

Fear rolled through me—I was paralyzed by the memory of being trapped in this fog once before, and the horrific outcome.

Suddenly, I felt a gentle touch on my back. Then a hard shove. I stumbled and lost my balance, and felt myself falling— toward the stairs, toward a swirling black hole of fog below.

But at the last second, someone grabbed my arm and interrupted my fall.

I looked up. Penitence was standing over me. When she saw that I was steady on my feet, she disappeared.

As the smoke began to clear, I spotted a figure standing in the stairwell with me. I recognized the wavy light-brown hair. The open-knit gray cardigan.

It was my mother.

And she was looking right at me.

Only it wasn't really my mother. Her eyes were completely black. And when she spoke, wisps of black smoke escaped from her mouth.

"Pardon me, Delia," she said, with an exaggerated, grotesque air of courtesy. "I was expecting someone else."

I froze, terrified.

Then, as if it had been sucked out into a vacuum, the smoke left her body and the blackness disappeared from her eyes. My mother stood at the top of the stairs, looking around in alarmed confusion.

"How did I get here?" she asked.

"Mom?" I said.

But she didn't answer. She couldn't see me anymore, of course. Whatever controlled the smoke had the power to bridge the living and dead worlds. When it was inside her, she had been its portal. Now the smoke was gone, and my mother was herself again.

I wish I could say that made me feel better.

CHAPTER 25

I ran back to the day room, where my sister was on her phone, leaving someone a message.

"Dad?" I heard her say. "It's Janie. Listen, Mom and I are at the Piven Institute and there's something weird going on. I know you're busy in New York, but we need you—"

The door from the stairwell creaked as it opened a few inches.

"Jane?" Mom called, her voice faint.

Janie hung up without saying good-bye and dropped the phone on the piano bench. Then she walked warily in the direction of the stairwell. "Mom?"

When there was no answer, she pushed the door open another couple of inches.

My mother was on the floor, holding her head in her hands.

"Did you . . ." Mom's voice trailed off in confusion. She looked shaky and ill. "I don't remember. I don't . . . I don't feel very well. I think I might need to lie down. It must be a migraine or something."

"Yeah, you don't look good," Janie said. "Let me drive you into town, okay? There's an urgent-care place."

Mom looked up and squinted, as if the dim stairway was painfully bright. "But you can't drive."

"Of course I can," Janie said, doing her best to be cheerful. "I'm just not supposed to. Totally different."

Mom didn't look up, and Janie went rigid.

"Hey," she said, leaning down. "Let's just get you into bed for a few minutes."

Mom groaned as she stood up, and then my sister shepherded her back to the ward and into the room where she'd slept the night before. Janie helped Mom lie down on the bed. Then she pulled over the stool and sat down, studying Mom's face anxiously.

I stood in the doorway and sighed. So much for progress.

Eliza appeared next to me, holding the wrench I'd left downstairs. "Delia, something's wrong with your mother," she said. "I saw her in the main hall, and she was acting terribly odd."

"She got possessed or something," I said, my voice shaking. "The smoke, it was, like . . . inside her. She could see me." I glanced at Mom, who was lying in the bed, her complexion a distinctly grayish hue. "And now she looks terrible."

"I think I know what happened." Eliza set the wrench down outside the door and went over to the bed, inspecting my mother from a few inches away. "She's not in danger, but she probably feels awful."

"What was it?"

"The house," Eliza said. "Toying with her. Probably using her to get to your sister."

I was expecting someone else, Mom had said.

She'd been expecting Janie—planning to push her down the stairs.

Instead, she'd pushed me. And I would have fallen, too, if it hadn't been for Penitence.

Twice now, in a *single hour*, the house had tried to kill my sister. I was beginning to think there was no way to stop it from getting what it wanted. I thought all we had to do was get them out the door, but even that was beginning to seem impossible.

"We need to buy some time," I said. "How did Cordelia survive here for so long?"

"Carefully," Eliza said. "She used quite a bit of salt."

It was unlikely that my mom and sister wouldn't notice an invisible hand pouring copious amounts of salt around the house. "What else did she do?" I asked.

"I don't know," Eliza said. "We weren't exactly bosom friends."

I stared at my mother's sallow skin and the exhausted way she drew her breaths—almost in two stages, an inhale interrupted by a stutter.

"Well, *somebody* here was friends with her," I said, suddenly recalling something I'd read long ago. "She mentioned in her letter that there was someone I could go to for help."

Eliza seemed flummoxed. "I have no idea who that would have been."

"Maybe Florence?" I said.

"If it was, she never mentioned it to me," Eliza said. "And I never saw Cordelia around the lobby or the parlor."

"No, you wouldn't have," I said. "She spent most of her time on the third floor."

"Then . . . that's where you should look, I suppose," Eliza said, sounding less than thrilled on my behalf.

We both turned to glance at Mom and Janie. My sister leaned forward as my mom struggled to sit.

"We need to leave," my mother said, her teeth gritting against the pain.

Janie patted Mom's arm. "We can wait a couple of minutes. Just till you feel better. You know what? Actually, maybe I'll just call the police. Where's your phone?"

"It's in my purse," Mom said.

"Where's your purse?"

Mom barely managed to shake her head. "I don't know."

"No problem," Janie said. The forced nonchalance of her words did not match the rigidity of her shoulders as I followed her back to the day room.

She went right to the piano bench, looking for something.

She'd left her phone here.

"Oh, come on," she muttered, bending to look at the floor.

"Penitence," I said, and she appeared. "Did you move a cell phone off the piano bench?"

She cocked her head. "A what?"

"A little box," I said. "A flat, shiny box."

"Oh, the one she carries around," Penitence said. "No. But . . . you said it was shiny?"

Um. "Have you seen a *non*-shiny box?"

She sighed. "No, but the girls love shiny things. I'd imagine they've added it to their collection."

"Which girls?" I asked.

"The pair," she said. "The ones in their nightgowns. Died

in ninety-six. Tuberculosis. Rosie and Posie, or whatever their names are. If something goes missing, it's a fair bet they took it."

The nosy girls. "Where do they live?" I asked. "The lobby?"

"I'm not sure," she said. "But I doubt it. I believe the grand Southern lady rules the lobby. I'd try the third floor. That's where they lived when they were here."

Janie pushed the hair away from her face, wearing a defeated expression as she went back to Mom's room.

Mom was asleep, but her face still looked drawn and tense.

"She's okay," Eliza told me.

"Someone took Janie's phone," I said. "She can't even call for help. I need to go to the third floor. But . . ." I glanced at Mom and Janie. They were sitting ducks.

"I'll help," Eliza said. "I can provide a distraction. Draw attention to myself."

"How?" I asked.

She shrugged. "I'll think outside the ball."

"Box," I said.

Her eyes glittered. "Perhaps I'll take a little stroll about the grounds."

"Are you sure that's a good idea?" I asked.

The usually stoic line of her mouth quirked up on one side. "No. But you must admit it's an interesting one."

"Be careful."

She nodded. "I'll have Florence help me. We'll be fine."

As I reached the third-floor landing, I saw Maria standing a short distance away from the top step.

"Back off," I said. "I've poured salt on uglier monsters than you."

She shrank away.

There was a peculiar, agitated feeling among the ten or so ghosts lined up against the hallway walls. I didn't see the two giggling girls among them, though. One, a girl about my own age wearing a straitjacket, growled and lunged as I went by. Another, a woman in her thirties, stood in the center of the hall with her mouth open and eyes shut, her fists clenched and her body jittering around in a silent scream.

Something had rattled them.

The enormity of the house hit me all at once—the thieving girls could literally be anywhere, and the things they took could have been in any of a million hiding spots. I paused in the hallway, awash in despair. It wasn't going to work. How could you find something small in a place this big?

I was outside Cordelia's office, and as I cast a glance inside, I had a sudden flash of memory: *Whenever I need something, I seem to be able to find it here.* Could she have meant that literally? That things went missing and turned up in her office? It didn't seem possible, but at the same time it felt like the most obvious thing in the world.

There wasn't time to agonize over it. I went inside, using one of Cordelia's books to break the line of salt and then immediately repair it behind me.

I walked to the desk and started looking through the drawers. The top ones were packed full of a lifetime's worth of paper clips, rubber bands, entire rolls of unused postage stamps, and a motley collection of pens and pencils. Plenty of implements for letter writing but no sign of my sister's cell phone—or any other stolen shiny objects.

So what was here? Where were the answers I'd been so confident I would find, back when I was alive? What did I think would be waiting for me? Because there had to be *something*.

Aunt Cordelia had left me her house for a reason. She wanted me to do what she hadn't been able to do. She would have found a way to tell me . . . But how?

Of course. She would have written me a letter.

I remembered the letter Janie had pulled from the desk blotter. What had it said?

And I have something to share with you . . .

Maybe the "something" didn't mean facts or an idea. Maybe she meant she had an actual *thing* to share—another letter. What if the one Janie had found was just an introduction, and the real information was someplace else?

I opened each desk drawer, pushing the trinkets and office supplies out of the way. I was sure I would find something. Aunt Cordelia had planned for this. Something may have gone wrong at the end, but she'd been planning it for a long time. No way would she have left the most important element to chance.

"What are you looking for?"

The voice, low and garbled, practically gave me a heart attack. I turned to see Maria standing just on the other side of the salt line.

"How long have you been there?" I snapped.

"Long enough to know that you're looking for something," she growled.

"I'm looking for something my aunt wanted me to have," I said. I wasn't about to give her any specifics, for fear that she knew where the letter was and might go back and destroy it.

Maria's eyes traveled over the newspaper-covered walls. It was almost physically painful to look at her disfigured face and ruined body. Instead of focusing on her monstrous flaws, I forced myself to look beneath them for the shape that used to be a little girl.

"She came in here every day," she said.

"I know," I said.

"But then she stopped."

"She died," I said.

"Yes, I know." Maria looked me straight in the eye. "I helped her."

I blinked. "You *what*?"

Her beady eyes were fixed on me, fearless. "She was sick and hurt and getting worse. She was frightened of what she might do."

"What did she think she might do?"

"She didn't know," Maria said. "The house nearly got her, in the end. There were smoke beasts everywhere. She was scared and sad. So I helped."

"But she killed herself," I said. "Do you mean you helped her kill herself?"

Maria tilted her head. "Not exactly. I told her that if she left, she could die and be free."

I was only a foot away from Maria now, with the wall of salt between us. Anger and disbelief throbbed inside me as I stared down at her oozing skin, her thick-scarred eyelids. But behind the horror show of her face, something in her eyes was surprisingly intelligent and human.

"That's impossible. How could you have *told* her? We can't tell living people anything," I said, a razor edge in my voice.

My intensity caused Maria to take a step back. Her eyes darted around the room, refusing to meet mine. "She was nice to me," she said. "She knew I came in here. She called me her little friend. She had pretty pictures for me to look at. She would set them down on the floor in the morning, and I would sit and look at them. And at the end of every day, she would cut one out so I could take it with me. I still have them all. I'm very careful with them. They're my favorite things. And she gave me a blanket, because it's so cold here. I—I'm still cold, but I like the blanket very much."

I pictured Aunt Cordelia leaving small offerings for this poor, destroyed creature, speaking to her kindly, as if she were a normal little girl and not a beast.

And then I remembered something I'd seen years earlier—a cut-out picture of a box of cat food.

Was it possible I'd been wrong about Maria? That we were *all* wrong about Maria?

I lowered my voice and crouched down to her eye level. "How did you tell her what to do?"

Maria didn't answer. She looked like she was afraid she'd be in trouble.

"If you did help her, then . . . thank you," I said. "She didn't want to die here."

"I know!" Maria's rotting chin jutted up toward me, hurt

and defiant. "No one should die here. If you die here, you can never go home."

"Do you want to go home?" I asked.

Our eyes met. Hers were disconcertingly honest, like any child's. She nodded.

"Then maybe you can help me. I'm looking for something—my aunt used to write me letters. I think she wrote one, but never mailed it. I think it's here somewhere."

Maria's ruined hands wrung the front of her dress. "I found her one day, when she was sick. I was a little scared of her, because that was when she was very bad. The smoke had gotten her, so she yelled and chased me . . . but I knew that wasn't really her. Later, I heard her crying, so I came back. She was very weak, and she fell on the floor. The salt was broken, so I stayed here to chase the bad ghosts away from her, and then I went up to her, and I . . ." She lowered her hand, as if placing it across an imaginary forehead. "I told her, *Shhh, don't cry, it's Maria, I will help you.* I told her she had to leave, and not come back. Otherwise it would get her—the black fire."

"What's the black fire?" I asked.

Maria's uneven eyebrows rose in surprise. "It's the bad thing," she said. "It lives here, and it holds on to us. It won't let us go. If you try to leave, it will send something after you."

Like . . . smoke?

The room was totally quiet. "All right, Maria," I said. "Thank you for helping Cordelia. I'll bet she really thought you were a nice girl."

"She did," Maria said. "That's why she gave me her most important letter to hide, even from herself. Because when she was a bad lady, she wanted to throw it away."

I felt like the room was closing in on me. Words swam in and out of my mind's grasp. "You *have* the letter?"

She nodded. "Do you want to see it?"

"Yes, I do," I said, my heart beating so hard I could feel it in my chest. "In fact, I think she may have meant for you to give it to me."

Maria's rotting jaw pulled back, and her mouth formed a grotesque grimace.

It took me a minute to realize she was smiling.

"Come out," she said, looking down at the salt.

I hesitated. Could this be a setup? Was she luring me to some dark, remote corner so she could attack me, out of the reach of my friends? Should I really believe her . . . ?

What choice did I have?

I knelt down and started to use the book to push the salt out of the way. To my amazement, Maria knelt, too, and began brushing it away with her fingers. A sickening smell, like burning flesh, faintly entered the air.

"No, stop," I said, stopping myself just short of touching her charred-looking arm. "You'll hurt yourself."

She went on moving the salt around. "It doesn't matter if I get hurt."

"Most of the others can't do that," I said.

"Yes, they can," she said. "Only they're scared. I don't get scared. I won't cry. I never cried, not even when I was a baby. I only cry now because . . . I miss my mother sometimes."

After we'd moved enough salt for me to pass through, Maria carefully filled in the line. The almost imperceptible searing sound made my chest ache.

"I need to keep them away from her nice things," she said, by way of an explanation. "The bad ghosts, I mean."

She stood up. And then she reached over and took my hand.

I cringed at the feeling of her paper-dry skin against my fingers, even as I braced myself for an attack. But she didn't seem intent on hurting me. She led me out into the hallway.

It was deserted. The screaming woman, the straitjacketed girl—they had disappeared. All the ghosts had disappeared. I had an unpleasant thought of rats jumping off a sinking ship.

But before I had time to wonder where they'd gone, Maria led me through the wall, into a lavatory. It was a surprisingly spacious room, lit pale blue by sunshine that streamed through the high, mesh-encased window. A tiled shower area took up most of the floor space. There were restraints on the walls, and a splintered wood chair bolted to the floor with more restraints on it. The shower controls were on the wall near the door.

"Nurse brought me in here once," Maria said. "But the water was too cold. I told her I wanted a bath instead."

And a toaster, I thought.

Then Maria pointed behind me, and I turned around, expecting to see a toilet and sink.

But the floor was completely covered with images cut from magazines and children's books—hundreds, maybe thousands, of puppies, kittens, bouquets of flowers, letters of the alphabet, numbers, cheerful-looking houses, and babies and children and families . . . so many families. And tucked way back in the corner was a picture I recognized—the Christmas tree drawing I'd sent with my letter so long ago.

It looked like some surrealist art installation. If Aunt Cordelia had given her one picture every day, this must have been five years' worth of pictures.

In the corner, tucked between a filthy, broken toilet and the wall, was a small flannel blanket, the kind tiny babies get in the hospital, with ducklings and baby rattles on it. It was soiled and limp with age.

Maria walked across the pictures without disturbing them at all. "These are my pictures, and this is my bed," she said, carefully stretching the blanket out and sitting down on it. "Cordelia gave it to me."

I pictured her huddled on a rag in the corner of a dark, creepy bathroom, waiting the way a lost child waits for her parents. Except Maria had been here for more than a century, and no one was ever coming back for her.

"I . . . like your pictures," I said, reaching down to touch a picture of a collie.

"I love puppies. I had a dog once, named Buttons. He liked me. Nobody likes me now." Her gravelly voice sank to weariness. "Not since Cordelia died. But I'm not angry that she left. I know why she had to do it."

I was trying to figure out how to ask for the letter, but before I had a chance, she reached under her blanket and pulled out a stained, yellowing envelope. She handed it up to me.

The writing on the outside read *DELIA*.

"Look," I said, showing Maria. "That's my name. You did great. That's just what Cordelia wanted."

She gave me a chilling grin. "I like helping. Are you going to read it? You can read it in here, if you want."

I didn't quite know what to say.

"I won't snoop," she said. "I can't read, anyway."

"Um . . . okay." It seemed like as good a place as any. There was relative privacy and decent light.

"Here," she said, spreading the edges of the blanket for me. I sat down next to her. "Can I help open the envelope?"

"How long have you had this letter?" I asked, handing it over.

"I don't know . . . How long ago did she die?"

"Four years ago," I said.

"Four years, then," she answered, opening the seal and handing the sheets of folded paper to me.

"You're a good girl, Maria," I said.

I began to read.

CHAPTER 26

My dear Namesake,

There is no easy way to say what I must now say, so I will simply begin, with the hope that you will give an old woman (who cares very much for you) credit for not being completely out of her mind.

My home is haunted. I will now do my best to explain.

What You Must Know:

Actual haunted houses (or institutes) are quite rare. Most hauntings are explained away by scientific means. Unfortunately, the Piven Institute is, as they say, "the real deal."

I chose to share this with you, Delia, because I believe you are both young enough to believe me and strong enough to continue my mission, which I adopted as my life's work: to destroy the evil that lives beneath my feet.

I pray you will never have to read this letter, that you will simply inherit an old piece of land that once held a house whose distressing history will never be known to you. But if you are reading it, then the house has found a way to get to me.

What Knowledge I Have Gathered of the Evil Spirit:

There is more than one kind of spirit. This building is home to quite a few paranormal residents, women who died during their stays here. Most of them are harmless (with one or two notable exceptions).

But why are there so many ghosts here to begin with? I believe that the underlying "cause" is a spirit or energy that is most definitely not harmless. Rather, it is a malicious force that has trapped the others here.

You have heard, I suppose, of cursed objects. I believe that, due to great tragedy or trauma that occurred here, the very land and structure were transformed and came to possess some spiritual power. I do not think that what drives that power is any single ghost but rather a sort of accumulation of malicious energy. The house hungers for loneliness and pain. I don't know how else to explain it.

This force seems intent on controlling not only my ghostly cohabitants but myself as well. This is why I do not receive visitors, and why I live alone. I have groceries delivered from town once a week, but I never so much as invite the delivery boy inside.

In my research, I have come to believe that problem likely originated with the disappearance of the founder, our ancestor Maxwell Piven. He signed out in the logbook one day, but then was never seen again. My conviction is that he died on the property and was likely not given a proper burial. This would create within the house and property an immense sense of having been wronged. Perhaps on some level, Maxwell's spirit seeks revenge.

I don't know. What I do know is that, after he died, women who had formerly been helped and healed within these walls began to die here. Up until that time, this had been a very progressive home with an excellent record. Something changed, drastically, in the mid-1880s. The staff did their best to cover up and explain away the deaths, but over time it became obvious that something was very wrong. Only in the 1940s, after a terrible tragedy involving the death of a county surveyor on the property, did the state do a proper investigation, which led the medical board to finally close it down for good.

My father passed away soon after, when I was quite young, and he left the property to me. For most of my life, I lived here by myself. I was never happy. When I began receiving your letters, it was as though a veil lifted, and I looked back on those wasted years and began to wonder what had compelled me to stay here. Upon reflection, I reached the conclusion that it was not simply out of my own personal lack of ambition—which is what all the town gossips would say about me, that I was too lazy and selfish to have a family!—but due to the intervention of something very powerful in the house.

How did I know this? I don't know. But have you ever had someone believe something about you that you know to be untrue? And your sense of inner justice won't let you simply surrender to the opinions of others? It was that way for me. I knew that I had not been lazy or selfish. In spite of my many unhappy years, I have always managed a decent amount of self-respect. So I gave myself credit that others did not extend. In the end, we must always be the judges of our own consciences.

I closed my eyes, resting them for a moment. Yes, I knew that feeling.

I began to investigate, to look for a way to cleanse the house. The older such a force gets, the more powerful it becomes. I considered, at one point, simply burning down the building, but I believe that demolishing the house will not rob it of its power—rather, it would simply cease to confine the spirits that dwell here any longer. The damage a force so wicked could do as a "free agent" is a terrifying thought to me. Not to mention that the unfortunate souls who call this place their home would be displaced and left to wander. A ghost needs a home or it becomes a wraith, a hopeless, pathetic creature living in eternal misery.

This is why you must find whatever is the center of the house's power. And you must destroy it. I have never been able to find it, though I have devoted the past several years of my life to looking. Now, the house is fighting back. It is hoping to catch me off guard. I imagine that one day it will succeed, and that will be the end of me—on this plane, at least.

The task I've given you is unfair. I understand that. I'm expecting you to succeed where I have failed. But trust me when I say that if I didn't believe you would be able to do this, I wouldn't ask you to. We Pivens are made of stern stuff.

Our ancestor, by creating such a place, has caused much death and destruction. And so I believe that, as Pivens, it is our duty to clear the evil from the earthly realm.

So you see, Little Namesake, this is why I have decided that you must have the house. I rely on you, in the event of my failure, to see this mission through. Once the evil is removed, and the poor spirits who are trapped here have been freed to move on as well, then you may do whatever you like with the property.

You can probably sell it for quite a bit of money, enough to make you comfortable and reward you for a noble task well carried out. Your only stipulation in selling it should be that the building will be destroyed. A building with a history such as this one has does not deserve to stand. It has committed its own crimes, and it must pay its own price.

I think that before I mail this letter, I will send you a bit of history about the house, which I have yet to write. I am sorry for going out of order, but I feared my bouts of forgetfulness would grow worse before I had a chance to put this down clearly for you.

In spite of the years and distance, I remain,
Your fond aunt,
Cordelia Jane Piven

PS—If you ever need assistance, go to the third floor. Bring some nice pictures cut from a magazine. I have a little visitor of whom I am very fond. Be clear in asking her for help and I am confident that she will do her best for you.

CHAPTER 27

I set the letter down.

"Was it a nice letter?" Maria asked.

"No," I said. "But she said something very nice about you."

Her eyes lit up. I was growing used to looking at her. My mind played along, reconstructing how she once might have looked, molding the distortedness of her features into the face of a little girl.

"So why did you try to attack me that day?" I asked. "Right after I died?"

She blinked and stared up in surprise. "Attack you?"

"When you had the sheet on. You were coming closer."

"I only wanted to see you," she said. "I wanted to meet you."

"You weren't going to hurt me?"

"Oh no." She shook her head. "I had the sheet on because I didn't want you to be afraid of me."

Was everything I'd heard about Maria a lie? I recalled what Florence had told me—that the little girl had tried to kill her own father.

"Did you ever hurt someone?" I asked. "A man?"

Her shoulders slumped and her chin sank to meet her chest.

"Maria, it's okay. You can tell me. I almost killed a person once."

She glanced up at me. "You did? Were you naughty?"

"Very." I nodded. "I lost my temper."

"I was naughty," she said. Then she raised her head and looked at me, a burning intensity in her gaze and a hint of rebellion in her voice. "I used to imagine hurting him. He wasn't nice. He was very, very unkind to all the ladies. He told me he would take me away from my mother. And then . . . one day . . . he did. Up to the third floor."

"Who was the bad man?" I asked. "Was it Maxwell?"

She buried her face in her hands and didn't answer.

"Did you hurt him, Maria?"

"No!" She shrank away, as if I might roughly grab her and demand an answer. "It wasn't me. I'm not the one who hurt him. But I'm glad he got hurt."

"Who did it?" I asked. "Please tell me."

She pressed her lips together. A tear glistened at the corner of her eye.

"Okay, it's okay," I said. "You don't have to tell me who it was. But do you know what she did to him?"

"Of course I do," she said. "She made a cake. But it wasn't her fault—the other part."

"What other part?"

"We found it," Maria said. "Nurse Carlson and me. We were good friends. We liked cake, and we liked to explore sometimes when no one was watching. We found it in the kitchen one night, and it already had a piece cut out of it, so we thought we could have some, too. Only . . . it wasn't a good cake. It was a very bad cake."

"It was . . . poisoned?" I asked.

She nodded. Her sorrow seemed to fill the room, and she wilted like a flower petal. "We died. Nurse died first. She told me to run and get help for myself, but I loved her, so I couldn't leave her there, cold and lonely. Then we both woke up, and we were . . . what we are. When the wardress found our bodies, she made them take us upstairs and make it look like we died in the bathroom—like I hurt Nurse. But I didn't die in the bath. And I would *never* hurt Nurse. She was so good. She was my especial friend even when I was a baby. I don't know why they did that."

Probably because an insane inmate killing herself and a nurse was a lot better than two innocent people being inexplicably poisoned.

"I have hurt someone," Maria was saying quietly. "I begged Nurse to eat the cake. It was my fault she died."

"No, Maria," I said. "It wasn't. Did you ever find out who made the cake?"

She shook her head.

"All right," I said. "That's okay."

I sat back, reflecting on what I'd learned about Maria's life and death. And still trying to process the fact that Great-Aunt Cordelia, who was, like, a billion years old, had basically lived a Buffy the Vampire Slayer life, and we never had a clue.

"Wait," I said. "The wardress that made them move the bodies—was her name Penitence?"

Maria blinked. "No."

No, she couldn't have been, because Maxwell was the one who committed Penitence. So it must have been someone new by that point. "Is she here—is she a ghost? The wardress?"

"No," she said. "I don't think so. She was here for a very long time, but they sent her away, after the other thing happened."

"What happened?" Fresh hope bloomed in my heart. Maria obviously knew something important. I just had to coax it out of her. "Did someone get hurt? Was it the black fire?"

Maria's eyes went wide, and then she ducked away, trying to make herself small in the corner.

"It's okay, Maria," I said. "You can tell me what happened. I won't be angry."

"But *she'll* be angry," she said. "If you try to put out the fire, she'll know I told."

"Who?" I said.

She shot me a sharp glance out of the corner of her eye. "You *know* who."

In my shock, I dropped my coaxing voice. "No, I don't know who it is. I really don't."

She turned to face me, exasperated to the point of being offended. "The one I tried to save you from!"

"In the hallway?" I asked. "When the walls were closing in?"

"No, that was just the house being naughty." Her expression was wounded now, as if I'd misunderstood her on purpose. "The one in the lobby. She smells like flowers."

"Do you mean Florence?" My blood went icy in my veins. "Are you saying Florence isn't nice?"

Maria's voice rose to an agonized cry. "How do you think I got like this? I used to be pretty, like you!"

"Maria, what do you mean?"

"She wanted me to bring her things," Maria said, turning away. "Because she can't go to the basement, and I can. She wanted the fire. I tried to get it for her, but I couldn't. Then she was angry because I failed. She said I was a bad girl, and she only likes good girls."

Wait. *Florence* had done this to Maria? But that was impossible. Florence had always been sweet to me, since the day she protected me from Maria . . .

But then, Maria wasn't actually a threat. So why had Florence been nice to me?

She only likes good girls.

Because I hadn't tested the limits. She was fine, as long as I behaved. I remembered how she'd sat up waiting for me the night I'd been outside with Theo. Like she'd been keeping tabs on me. So what would she do to someone who *did* test the limits?

"Eliza!" I said, leaping to my feet. "Eliza doesn't know!"

The reason Florence and Eliza had gotten along perfectly well since 1922 was that Eliza had never tried to leave the house. But as of a few minutes ago, that had changed.

Suddenly, a scream cut through the silence. *"DELIA!"*

It was Penitence.

"Let's go!" I said. Maria grabbed my hand, and we ran down the hall toward the stairs. I started to descend, but Maria stayed on the landing above me, shaking her head with tiny movements.

"I can't go down there," she said. "I can't go onto the second floor."

"It's okay!" I said, halfway to the second-floor landing. "Go back to your room and stay there! I'll come get you when it's safe to come out."

She ran away, carried on noiseless feet.

In the day room, I found Penitence wringing her hands in a panic. "She was here! She never comes to the second floor. But she came, and she attacked them, and she . . ."

I didn't need to ask who. I pushed past her. "Where?"

"In Room 2," Penitence said. "But—"

"Are they okay?" I asked.

Penitence stared at me without answering.

I raced through the day room, trying to assure myself that everything would be fine. If Florence had kept her secret this long, she was probably waiting for some big moment to reveal herself, right?

I swung into the ward hall and froze. All was quiet.

They're fine, I told myself. *Everything is fine.*

Then I heard a whimper from my sister's room.

I ran in. The first thing I saw was my mother, stretched out on the bed, half-asleep.

But no Janie.

A faint ringing sound broke the silence—followed by a voice so wretched and weak that I hardly recognized it. "Delia?"

I rushed to the other side of the bed, where Eliza lay on the floor. Her left arm rested limply on her side, hideously bruised and broken looking. Both of her legs looked similarly abused, and her hair seemed to be coming out in large clumps.

"Florence did this," Eliza whispered. She shivered violently. "When I tried to leave, she attacked me. Then she came up here. She was going to hurt your mother, but Janie and I stopped her just in time."

"Where is she now?" I asked. "My sister, where is she?"

Eliza lifted her head, and when I saw her face, I nearly recoiled. A blistered, blackened line stretched diagonally from her hairline, across a ruined eye and nose, through the corner of her discolored lips, and ended in a gaping, dark wound at the tip of her chin.

"The smoke," she said. "The smoke took over your sister, and mesmerized her. They left together."

I went limp. Janie could be dead by now.

"I think your sister is alive," Eliza said. "Florence is probably using her . . . as bait. To catch you."

That gave me a hint of hope. "I have to go," I said. "I have to find Janie. But I'll be back."

"Go," Eliza urged. "But be careful."

"Penitence!" I called, running out. "I'm going downstairs. Keep Eliza and my mother safe."

"What are you going to do?" she asked, following me to the door. "You can't fight her! You have no idea how strong she is. She's tapped into some kind of dangerous power."

"Yeah, well, too bad," I said, shoving the door open and starting down the stairs. "So have I."

Florence was evil. She wasn't the evil force in the house, but she was tapped into it—maybe obsessed with it, or she wouldn't have sent Maria to bring her the black fire.

She only likes good girls.

She bullied and assaulted the ghosts who tested the limits or failed to abide by her standards. How long had she been watching me, waiting for me to make a mistake so she could punish me?

And now she had my sister.

I stopped in the kitchen, grabbed a container of salt from the pantry, and pushed open the door to the lobby.

Florence was posed on the couch, as lovely as a painting, wearing her brightest, most glittering smile.

"Well, hello there, sugar," she said. "Lookin' for me?"

CHAPTER 28

I started to take a step toward her, but she held up a hand.

"Halt," she said. "Just wait right there, if you please. There's another guest coming to this party, and I'd hate for you to miss her."

The door opened behind me. "Delia . . . ?"

I spun around and found myself looking into my sister's eyes. I'd tried to brace myself, but nothing could have prepared me for the sight.

They were wide, amazed.

Don't fall for it, I told myself. *It's a trick.*

But there wasn't a glimmer of evil in Janie's expression.

"Delia, is it really you? Can you hear me?"

I tried to block out the sound of her voice saying my name— it cut too deeply, right to my core, and brought back too many memories, too much pain.

"I can't believe it," Janie said. "You're *here*. There's so much I need to tell you."

I took a step back. "No," I said. "You're not my sister."

"But, Deedee, you know I am. Of course I am."

She spoke like my sister. She reasoned like my sister. I began to feel that I'd be willing to let the house do whatever it wanted, if only I could see and talk to my sister. Maybe there was some kind of deal we could strike.

No. No. That was exactly what the house was trying to do to me—use my sister to break down my defenses.

"What did Mom used to say to us?" I felt like I was going to choke on my own sadness. "Every night before bed, when we were young?"

She smiled tenderly. "You tell me."

"Just say it, Janie," I said. "And then I'll know it's you."

Her smile faltered.

"You don't know," I whispered. "Because you're not her. You're just a monster."

She shook her head. "This makes me so sad . . ."

"'And though she be but little, she is fierce,'" I said. "I'm sorry. I'm sorry."

I pulled the salt from behind my back and threw it at my sister's face.

She gasped and tried to block it with her hands, but it was too late. She began to choke, to make sounds as if she couldn't breathe, and a look of pure rage came into her eyes. She began to stalk toward me, but she was quickly growing weak. Halfway across the room, the life seemed to drain out of her, and she collapsed to the floor.

I watched her for a few beats, until I saw her chest rise and sink with a breath.

Florence broke the silence with a low chuckle. "Well, sugar, looks like it's just you and me. I suppose you saw what I did to your friend upstairs."

"I did," I said. "And she was your friend, too."

"*'Nature teaches beasts to know their friends.'*" She grinned, pleased with herself. "You're not the only one who knows a little Shakespeare."

"What are you after?" I snapped. "What do you think you're going to accomplish? What good is it keeping people trapped here?"

"Well, honey, on that line of thinking, what good is anything?" she asked, delicately twisting the ends of her hair around a slender finger. "Why question the *why* of things that simply *are*?"

"Just answer my question," I said.

She patted the sofa next to her. "You come sit down, and we'll have a nice little talk."

I walked across the room and perched on the edge of the cushion. We both knew I'd listen, that I couldn't just attack her, because I needed more information about the house if I was going to stop whatever was in it.

"I suppose you know Penitence," Florence drawled. "Everybody knows Penitence. Penitence was in charge of the institute—I mean, under her old daddy, Maxwell. She did her best to run the place, but she was never good enough for him. She tried to be nice to the patients, be their friend. He just thought they oughtta be taught to behave. One day she ran off and got herself married without his permission. And then there was going to be a baby. But her husband fell off a horse and died, and she had to come back. Well, her daddy promised he would welcome her, and he did—but not as the wardress. Oh, no. He thought she needed to learn a lesson, so he admitted her as a patient. And when that baby was old enough to walk and talk, he took it away. He kept Penitence on the second floor and sent her baby to the third floor."

I reeled.

Maria.

"How do you know all this?" I asked.

"I was friends with the wardress who took over when Penitence was committed. She told me all the gossip. She said Maxwell got worse, treating the patients more strictly with every passing year. But Penitence turned as meek as a little mouse, and eventually he trusted her a little. And do you know what I think happened? I think she took that trust and killed him with it. And it just happened to be on the same night that the little brat took a thousand-volt swim with a third-floor nurse."

I nodded.

Florence leaned forward, an eager spark in her eyes. "I believe a great power was born here that night. The very ground beneath us was defiled, and it began to drink in the misery, loneliness, and confusion of its inhabitants. It *craved* the sadness that seeped through the walls of the house like blood."

The way she spoke reminded me of the way my sister used to talk about the boy bands she liked. Florence was totally fan-girling the evil spirit.

"Things changed. Women who came here—not all of them, but some of them—stopped getting better. Girls who should have gone home after a month or two showed no improvement at all. Some went mad. Some died. Some tried their best to get out, and had to be made to stay, if you know what I mean. What am I saying? Of course you do.

"It was the truly troubled girls who had it the worst—not us third-floor girls, but anyone with a secret. Something buried, that was eating away at them. Like our little friend, Eliza, for example. The house latched on to girls like that, girls who carried the scent of pain when they passed through the halls. It took hold and decided not to let them go."

"Were you one of those girls?" I asked.

She smiled warmly. "Yes, I was, thank you for asking."

"Why were you locked up, Florence?"

"I suppose I was just tired," she said airily. "In need of a little rest."

"What did you do?" I pressed. "Getting sent to the third floor is a pretty big deal."

"What do you think I did?" she asked. "A pretty little Southern belle . . . I couldn't hurt a fly, could I? Gentle as a kitten, wasn't I?"

As gentle as a kitten, and with the razor-sharp claws of a kitten, too. "Is that what people thought?"

"It's what they all thought." Her eyes flashed. "Do you know that my mother had the nerve to be ashamed of me? After everything she'd sacrificed, I still couldn't make it work, she said. I was scaring the men away, she said. I was too obvious— too *desperate* for love. She said once a man smelled a hint of desperation, nothing could keep him around. Not even my looks . . . which were fading, she said."

The bitterness saturated her voice like dye seeping into a cloth.

"What did you do?" I asked.

"I killed her," Florence said simply. "The day after my fiancé changed his mind, I felt awful for letting her down—I really did. I went out walking and brought her back a bouquet of flowers . . . buttercups. I took them to her room, where she was laid up with a headache, because of me. I held them out to her, and she said—I'll never forget—*Why would you bring me a pack of weeds, Florence? God knows I've got enough reminders that you've been unable to bloom where you were planted.*"

Her eyes clouded over with something like nostalgia—a gentle sadness.

"Terrible last words, don't you think? So what I did was, I told her to sit up and I would fluff up her pillow for her. I even got out her favorite music box—I thought the song was more than fitting."

"'Beautiful Dreamer'?" I asked.

"Oh, you know it? Then I took the pillow, and I smothered her with it. Oh, it was a struggle. She was strong. But I was stronger. And do you know, I think I just *wanted* it more."

The self-satisfied glint in her eyes turned my stomach.

"So they sent me here, along with my music box, and it was the making of me. I found something precious and important. Something worth protecting. I found the house's *soul*," she said, savoring the word. "I spent time with it, shared my pain with it. You see, I was used to being taken care of, told what to do, petted, admired—I didn't like looking after myself. All my life, I'd had my mama, and suddenly she was gone. So I found some-thing new: The *house* became my mama. It took care of me. It protected me. I sat for many happy hours playing that music box and just soaking in the love.

"The problem is, I was so happy and well-behaved that they moved me down to the second floor. But my new room wasn't the same at all. They didn't let me take my music box. I could no longer feel the house's spirit. My friend the wardress said it was time I learned to be like the other girls. But you know, I never was like other girls. I begged to go back upstairs, but she wouldn't let me—said there wasn't room. So I stole her keys and did something very brave."

"You killed yourself," I said.

She brightened and pointed toward the ceiling. "I swung from that very chandelier, honey."

I looked up at the light fixture, which dripped with grimy teardrop-shaped crystals. And as I stared at it, an apparition faded into view—a beautiful girl's body hanging limply, eyes closed, hair falling in rippling waves down over her shoulders, fingers slightly splayed as if she'd been caught by surprise.

Then the hanging girl's lips curled into a smile, and her eyes opened. They were filled with black smoke, which slinked in narrow, grasping tendrils toward us. Florence walked over to the vision, letting one of the fingers of smoke travel gently across her cheek with the softness of a mother's touch.

The girl's body vanished, and Florence's lips curled into an ugly, triumphant smile. "You can imagine how I felt when I woke up and found that I was part of the house at last. I could live here forever—in my home, where I belong. This house loves me, and I it. What the house wants, I want. And really, how much is it to ask for? A little obedience in exchange for a comfortable home . . . It's our duty, if you think about it."

Outside, the summer sun was high overhead, leaving the yard oddly shadowless.

"Anyway, that's the long way round of telling you that I'm afraid you aren't going to be allowed to leave us, honey," she said. "Nor your sister, nor your mama."

"That doesn't work for me," I said. "Sorry."

She carefully smoothed her skirts, like a warrior adjusting her armor before the battle. "Oh, I'm sorry, too."

I stood. We were the same height, standing eye to eye. "Florence."

"Yes?"

"Let's be clear," I said. "I'm not afraid of some pathetic old control freak of a ghost."

"You're braver than you are smart," she said, sneering. "If you haven't sense enough to be afraid of me, I'll just have to teach you to be. And it looks like you're out of salt, sweet pea."

"Doesn't matter," I said.

Her eyes widened, mocking me. "I can't wait to remind you of all these valiant words when you're a crushed and broken smear of bones and blood on the floor."

"I'm a ghost," I said, letting my arms relax by my sides. "I don't bleed."

She was trying to seem lighthearted, but I could tell she was a little unnerved by my confidence. "You got some trick up your sleeve?"

"I don't need tricks," I said. "I'm stronger than you."

She stepped toward me.

I *didn't* need a trick. I really wasn't afraid of her. I knew what she was fighting with, and what I was fighting with.

I called up the thoughts I usually fought to suppress—being trapped in the room with the smoke—watching my family drive away—Aunt Cordelia dragging herself down the driveway in the frigid morning air—Maria being hurt—Nic, pale and bleeding—my mother's unfathomable pain—my sister sobbing with guilt, bearing the weight of my death—

The world began to vibrate around me.

Power filled my body as if I was summoning it out of thin air.

At the same time, Florence exploded with light. I heard a high-pitched wail as her strength grew.

And then we slammed into each other.

Our arms came together, our hands clasped, and we pushed against each other—not just with our physical forms, but with the strength of our innermost souls, our deepest feelings.

And that was how I knew I was going to win. Because I was fighting with love—to defend the people I cared about. To earn their safety and freedom.

Florence was fighting with fear. If she lost, she had nothing. Not even the memory of having been truly loved.

It was like arm wrestling, only with my entire being. The struggle was somehow about the right to occupy the space we were both in. To extinguish the other's energy would leave the loser helpless against whatever revenge the winner chose to exact.

And Florence's vengeance would be vicious, if she should win.

But she wasn't going to win.

"The house doesn't love you, Florence," I whispered. "It's incapable of love. It's only using you because you'll do as it says. Because it can control you, like your mother controlled you . . . but some dark part of you knows that, doesn't it?"

She fought back with a burst of rage, and for a moment I was rocked backward as she almost got the better of me.

But then she began to fade.

"You know it won't have any use for you if you don't win this," I said. "If you're not perfect."

Then I made the most dangerous choice I've ever made—in life or death.

I pulled my right hand out of her left hand, momentarily breaking the cycle of energy between us.

And I reached up and dug my nails across her perfect face.

She screamed in a way I'd never heard anyone scream, living or dead—fury and terror in a desperate mix. In the chaos of the moment, I scratched her again. Her once-flawless beauty-queen complexion was permanently raked with the marks of my fingernails.

She reached up with both hands to feel the deep lines cutting across her face.

I put my hands on her shoulders, completing the circuit once again, and let a final blast of energy pulse through me.

Florence went down in a heap on the floor. She was unconscious . . . but maybe not for long.

I didn't waste a single moment. I dragged her motionless form toward the back hall, then down the basement stairs. I laid her down in a corner and ran back up to the kitchen, where I grabbed as many cartons of salt as I could carry.

Back in the basement, I poured a thick circle of salt around her, in a tight outline surrounding her body. She began to stir as I finished emptying the third canister.

"What have you done?" Her eyes popped open, and her hands reached up toward her damaged face. She let out an enraged howl. *"What have you done to me?"*

"Sorry, sugar," I said, dropping the empty salt container. "Looks like you're not the prettiest dead girl here anymore."

She moved to get up, but the barrier slammed her back. She tried moving in every direction, but she was penned in. She had hardly enough room to get to her feet, and when she finally did, she only had an area about the length and width of a coffin to move around in.

"What now?" she wheezed. "You're just going to leave me here forever?"

"Nobody's staying forever," I said. "I'll be back to deal with you later."

Her infuriated screams echoed behind me as I went upstairs.

Janie was still passed out on the floor of the lobby.

I reached down and rested my palm against her cheek.

"Janie," I said. "I'm sorry I was such a jerk to you when I was alive. I know you loved me anyway. You may never understand what happened to me, but that doesn't matter. All you need to understand is that it's not your fault—it was never your fault."

A faint rose tint began to return to my sister's cheeks.

I waited until her eyes fluttered weakly open, until I saw the haziest flash of recognition in them. Then I bent down and kissed her on the forehead.

"I love you," I said. "So unbelievably much."

Her eyes went wide, but she could no longer see or sense my presence.

I sat back and watched her carefully for signs of injuries or lingering aftereffects from her brief possession. She seemed fine—a little dazed, but that was understandable.

She got to her feet and moved with purpose to the back stairs, stopping to look at and then pick up Mom's purse from the bottom step. Upstairs, she crossed through the day room into the ward.

"Mom?" she called. "Where are you?"

A weak voice, heavy with relief, answered her from Room 2. "Here, Janie."

When Janie walked in, Mom struggled to act normal, pushing herself up to a sitting position.

I glanced at the floor. Eliza was gone.

But in this moment, I had to stay with my family.

"What happened?" Mom asked. Her voice sounded like someone had taken sandpaper to it.

Janie didn't even sit down. "I want to go," she said. "Right now. If I have to carry you down the stairs, I will."

"That won't be necessary," Mom said. "I think I can make it. Leave the bags, leave everything. We only need the car keys. They're in my purse."

Janie dug through Mom's purse for a minute and then looked up, dismay etched on her features. "No, they're not," she said. "Where could they have gone? Who would have taken them?"

"I'm sure no one took them." But my mother's voice didn't match the confidence level of her words. "I could have left them downstairs, I guess. Maybe they're in the car. But I don't think so."

My sister's eyes flashed. "What about your phone?"

"In my purse," Mom said.

Janie's lips parted, and after a deep inhale, she said, "No, it isn't."

"Well, they must be somewhere," Mom said.

But as my sister looked around the room, I could tell she had zero expectation of finding the missing items.

She knew the house too well by now.

CHAPTER 29

When I emerged into the hall, Penitence came up to me. She was studiously calm, her eyes wide and concerned.

"I moved Eliza into Room 4," she said, and in her voice I heard the rhythm and inflection of not just a helpless bystander but of a woman of authority—a wardress. "I thought she'd be more comfortable. Go see her, and I'll keep watch here."

Eliza was lying on top of the covers, her eyes open but unfocused—so unlike her that a chill went through me.

Someone's walking on my grave.

"Never thought I'd end up back on the ward," she said, trying to smile but managing only a grimace of pain.

I knelt beside her. "You're going to be all right."

"Delia, honestly." She made a cross face at me, and her mood actually seemed to lift. "Your optimism is truly colonial."

"I'm so grateful for what you did," I said, reaching down to smooth what remained of her hair. "You saved my sister and my mother."

"I told you I would," Eliza said, a hint defiantly. "I seem to have a thing for playing the hero, don't I? If only I were a more competent fighter."

A seizure-like convulsion shook her body. But after a few seconds, she opened her eyes. "Don't look at me like that. Ghosts don't die from injuries like this. I'm not going anywhere . . . anywhere at all, I suppose. Ever again."

I leaned over, meaning to take her hands, but they were wrecked and limp, as if all the bones had been crushed. "I'm so sorry," I said.

"Oh, don't be maudlin," Eliza said. "Now my outsides match my insides. Damaged soul, damaged body."

"You're wrong," I said. "Your soul is perfect."

She slumped against the pillow, staring out the window at the sinking sun.

"I don't think I've watched the sunset in seventy-five years," she said quietly.

"I imagine it gets old after a while," I said, pulling up a chair and sitting next to her.

"It shouldn't, though, should it? How could something so incredible get old?" She sighed weakly. "Shouldn't you go look after your family?"

"In a minute," I said. "Penitence is with them."

Eliza tried and failed to stretch, then gave up and settled uncomfortably back against the bed. "So what happened with Florence? You won?"

"She's been neutralized," I said.

"You *do* keep astounding me, Delia." She sighed and looked back out the window. "How terribly sad, though. I thought she was my friend."

"She's been very lost for a very long time," I said.

Eliza clucked quietly. "Haven't we all?"

"Maybe," I said. "But I'm going to fix things, if I can."

She nodded, and then there was a long pause. When she spoke again, her tone was soft and sad. "I know it's foolish, but . . . I'd sort of hoped this would have redeemed me. I thought perhaps my business was to help you, and then I could drift off into the ether to the sound of angelic trumpets or something. But . . . I suppose not. There must be more work to do."

In spite of her attempt to sound breezy, there was palpable, painful disappointment in her voice.

"I think I know what the work is," I said. "There's a black fire somewhere. I have to find it and put it out."

"Black fire . . ." Eliza repeated. Then, staring out the window, she offhandedly recited, *"'Black flames of evil burning bright, darkening the darkest night . . . extinguish'd by the blood of light, day is born from endless night.'"*

"What?" I said, sitting up. "What's that?"

"It's just a poem," she said. "A little thing I had to recite in school. You've never heard of it? Lord Lindley. Some pompous old marquess from the seventeen hundreds."

Lindley. Where had I heard that name before?

"'Blood of light'?" I echoed.

"Oh, you know," she said. "It's quite simplistic—innocence vanquishing evil and all that. It's designed to scare children into piety. It goes on and on. *Men's sons, mindless of evil's blight, awaken blind to their perilous plight,* et cetera et cetera . . . *fight, white, knight . . .* It's amazing he found so many rhyming words. You find Lindley in a lot of stodgy old books."

Books. That was it. I remembered the books on the parlor

shelves, with the authors' names in gold and silver on the spines. And among those names: *Lindley*.

"If it's an actual fire," I said, thinking out loud, "it could be the source of the black smoke."

"But it's not an actual fire," she protested. "It's just a poem."

"Nothing's 'just' an anything here," I said. "I think there's an actual black fire somewhere. It can't be a coincidence. Maxwell liked that poet well enough to keep his collected works. Maybe there's some connection—something to do with Maxwell's death."

"If you say so," Eliza said. "I remain skeptical."

"Yeah, surprise," I said. "So . . . it can be extinguished by blood of light. That might mean that someone innocent can put it out."

"Who around here could possibly pass as innocent?" Eliza asked. "Except maybe—"

She waited for me to say it.

"Janie," I said. "She was never committed here. She was never locked in. She doesn't belong to the house. She's innocent."

"She's a very bright girl," Eliza said. "You've *got* to save her, you know. It wouldn't do to have her die here."

"I know," I said. "What do you think it means, though, the blood of light? Her actual blood?"

"I hope not," Eliza said. "How ghastly."

The sun grew smaller and thinner, until it was just a sliver dipping below the distant hillside—and then it suddenly seemed to expand in a moment of brightness.

And then it disappeared.

"Oh," Eliza said in surprise, as though the answer to some riddle had just occurred to her. The bells on her wrist jingled faintly. "Delia—I think you may be right. I think maybe . . ."

I turned to see why she'd stopped speaking.

She was gone.

All that remained of her were the ghostly bells resting on the bedspread.

CHAPTER 30

I told myself not to cry. I had to believe that Eliza was in a better place now.

What's more, her last, unfinished words only convinced me more thoroughly that there was something to my theory about the poem.

When I reached Room 2, Mom and Janie had given up on finding their phones or the car keys. With my mother's arm draped over my sister's shoulder, they slowly progressed in the direction of the downstairs hallway.

But what would they do once they were outside? As badly as Mom wanted to be okay, she was unsteady on her feet. No way would she make it down the driveway. Janie might have to leave her behind and go to the highway to flag down a passing car. And it wasn't safe for either of them to be anywhere on the property for much longer.

As they were coming down the main hall, there was a banging noise from the lobby.

My sister froze, "What was that?"

"Probably nothing," Mom said, putting her hand on Janie's arm.

"Hang on," Janie said. "Let me go see . . ."

"Janie, no!" Mom said, and the spike of fear in her voice was sharp enough to stop my sister before she could walk away.

I moved past them to investigate, keeping my eyes on the walls and ceiling to look for tendrils of black smoke. What if this was a trap? A distraction? What if—

There was more horrible banging on the door.

"Lisa? Jane?" someone shouted. *Bang! Bang!* "Are you in there? What's going on?"

It was Dad.

Mom rushed forward and unlocked the door. "Brad, what are you doing here?"

My father's hair was thinning. He was skinnier than I'd ever seen him but still wearing his old clothes. It was like my death had turned him into an old man—practically a stranger.

Then his face twisted in frustration and anger, and I thought with relief, *There's Dad.*

"I get out of a seminar, and I have half an incoherent voice mail from Jane saying you're here—why would you *ever* come back here?—and then I couldn't reach either of you on your cell phones. I paid six hundred bucks for the next flight from New York, rented a car in Harrisburg, and—"

He was so busy working himself up that he didn't notice my sister until she'd thrown her arms around him.

"Daddy, you came!" Janie cried, tears streaming down her cheeks. "You came . . ."

My father was utterly disarmed by her reaction. His tone, when he spoke next, was significantly subdued. He glanced at Mom. "Lisa . . . what's going on?"

"Nothing good," Mom said grimly. "You said you rented a car?"

"Yes," Dad said.

"Great. We'll explain on the way."

"On the way where? Where are your things?"

"Forget our things," Mom said. "Let's go."

Dad nodded, bewildered, but the way Janie clung to him silenced his questions. "I'm parked right out front," he said. "Are you all right, Lisa?"

"She's sick," Janie said. "She can't really walk."

"Here," Dad said, and he and Janie wrapped their arms under Mom's arms to help support her weight. The three of them went quickly through the lobby to the main doors.

Only, by the time they got there . . . the doors were gone.

I don't know how to explain it, except that it was as if the walls had simply stretched over the space where the door had been.

Dad basically turned white. "What's going on?"

"Oh no," Mom said. "Oh no—the window! Hurry! Get out! Get Janie out!"

They all ran toward the window.

But before they could reach it, the walls had swallowed the window, too.

Dad was on the verge of freaking out. "I don't understand," he said. "What's happening?"

What was happening was that the house *really* didn't want them to go.

"The superintendent's apartment!" Janie said, running for the main hall.

"Jane, wait—" Dad said.

But she'd already run through the door.

Dad raced to grab it before it closed . . . but before he could reach it, the place where the door had been was transformed into a smooth expanse of red wallpaper.

"No!" Dad shouted. "No! Jane, come back!"

Mom joined him, banging on the wall with her fists. *"Janie!"*

I had the advantage of being able to move through walls, so I slipped into the hall, where my sister stood staring at the spot that, until about ten seconds earlier, had been a door. Then she leapt into action, pounding on the wall.

"Mom? Dad?" Her voice rose. "Mom! Dad! Help me! I'm stuck!"

In the lobby, my parents were shouting themselves hoarse. I slipped back out to see them.

Finally, Mom stepped away from the wall. "Brad," she said, "stop. We need to think. We need to be smart about this."

"Smart?!" he yelled. "This house just trapped our daughter! Janie's locked in there, just like—"

Suddenly, he froze and just looked at Mom, stared at her with an expression so horrified that you would have thought he'd just seen death itself.

"Just like Delia was," he whispered. "Delia was right. She was right. There's something here. She knew that, and she wanted to leave, but we didn't let her. My God, Lisa, she was right."

Mom didn't answer. Her mouth a hard line, she turned and surveyed the room. "Come on," she said. "We're going to get Janie out if it kills us."

In the hallway, Janie sat with her back to the wall, sobbing. I hated to leave her, but I had to get a better look at the situation. So I dashed outside.

When I got about fifteen feet from the house, I turned and looked up at the side of the building. It was just as I feared— there wasn't a single window or exterior door left in the entire structure. Only solid stone walls.

"What's going on?" Theo appeared beside me, staring up at the house.

"My family's in there," I said. "I need to get them out."

He stared at the bizarrely solid sweep of stone and shook his head. "How?"

"Not sure," I said. "I guess I'll tear the place to pieces by hand if I have to. Want to help?"

"But aren't you afraid?" he asked. "Of what it could do to you?"

"Actually," I said, "that's the least of my concerns."

I don't know if he tried to say anything else. I was already back inside. In the lobby, Dad was trying to make a call, but he couldn't get a signal. Finally, he chucked the phone across the room in frustration.

"Brad, we have to stay calm," Mom admonished. "We have to make a plan."

"Tell me what happened today," Dad said.

"I don't know, exactly," Mom said. "Something went after Janie, and then . . . the day has been a blur for me."

"What does that mean?" he demanded.

"I mean, I was coming down the stairs and everything after that is a blur," Mom said, a note of irritation underlying her words. "I'm not being purposefully obtuse."

It turns out that watching your parents bicker is just as annoying when you're dead as when you're alive. Anyway, I didn't have time to stand around and pout about their behavior.

I had a packed schedule.

Penitence was bent over and focused on her invisible blanket as if nothing had happened. She didn't even seem to notice that the walls had devoured the day room windows.

"What did you do with his body?" I asked. "Did you bury it?"

She looked up, startled, but didn't even have to ask who I was talking about. "No. I—I burned it. In the incinerator."

Black fire. Of course.

"And where's the incinerator?" I asked.

Penitence looked pained by the memory. "In the basement. Why? They've since built a new one away from the main building. They had to stop using the old one because the chimney wasn't properly sealed."

"Let me guess—too much smoke seeped out?"

She nodded.

"All right, come on," I said. "I have to show you something."

"Show me what?" she shot back. "Haven't I done enough for today?"

This was no time to be coy. "Your daughter's been living alone on the third floor since she died, and I'm taking you to meet her."

Penitence gasped, and I felt a little guilty for not cushioning the blow at all.

"No," she finally said, shaking her head. "She went crazy. She killed herself and murdered a nurse. It was terrible."

"Wrong," I said. "That's not what happened at all. It was a cover-up."

She looked at me disbelievingly. "What would you know about it?"

"I know what Maria and Florence told me," I said. "You made a cake for your father. Maria and the nurse found it in the kitchen."

Penitence raised her hand to her mouth. "Oh no," she said. "No . . ."

"They ate it and died, but the staff covered it up. You were hiding out in the basement after burning your father's body, so you didn't know any of this. It was a pretty grim night here."

Grim enough to curse the very land.

"It can't be." She shook her head and pressed her hands over her ears. "It can't be true."

"They posed the dead bodies to look like they'd died in the bathroom, but they were poisoned by the same cake that killed Maxwell."

Now she began to choke on her sobs. "No! I don't believe you!"

"Believe it or not," I said. "It's what happened. And now she's upstairs, and she's lonely and scared, and she needs her mother. And I'm not trying to rush you, but I don't have a lot of extra time."

"But if what you say is true, then I can't," Penitence said, her voice hollow. "She must hate me."

"She doesn't hate anyone, but for a hundred and fifty years, she's been hiding in a bathroom on the third floor. Alone. Tortured by other ghosts. The only person who was ever kind to her was my aunt Cordelia."

Penitence pressed both hands to her chest, scrunched her eyes closed, and made a terrible keening sound. "I'm a bad mother," she whispered.

"If you don't go to her now, you *are* a bad mother. She needs you." I was running out of patience. I reached over and grabbed her firmly by the arm. "Come on, we're going upstairs."

I stuck my head inside the bathroom. "Maria?"

She was nestled on her greasy blanket, rearranging the assortment of pictures on the floor. After a moment, she blinked and looked up at me. Then the spark lit up in her eyes. "You came back!"

"Yes," I said, stepping almost all the way inside. "I did. I beat Florence."

Her eyes widened.

"Maria, I have someone I want you to talk to."

"No, thank you," she said, turning away. "No one likes me."

"This person likes you," I said. "I promise."

Then I pulled Penitence in behind me. I'd warned her that Maria had been through a lot, but actually seeing the little girl's ruined face and body must have been like being punched in the gut. Penitence was silent, staring.

I crouched down, still holding Penitence's hand. "Maria, this is your mother," I said. "Do you remember her?"

Maria nodded but shrank away.

"She's not going to hurt you. She's come to take care of you."

They gazed at each other for a long time—long enough that I began to worry that this wasn't going to work, that too much time had passed, and too many things had gone wrong.

Then Maria reached out and wrapped her clawlike fingers around her mother's hand. "Would you like to see my pictures?"

Penitence looked down at the floor and nodded.

Maria shuffled her feet. "You can have one, if you like. Any picture at all."

"You choose for me."

Maria bent down and picked up a picture of a mother with a small baby, and handed it to her mother.

"I'm sorry I'm not a pretty girl anymore, Mother," she said. "I understand if you don't want to be around me. Nobody likes to be around me."

"I do," I said.

Penitence stood to her full height, which I'd never actually seen—she'd always been hunched over like an old woman, but she was half a head taller than me. "Maria, we'll never be apart again. I'll always be here with you. Is . . . is that all right?"

Maria nodded.

"Then let's go," Penitence said. "We must go downstairs."

And then, with Maria clutching her mother's skirts like a security blanket, we made our way back to the second floor.

"What will you do now?" Penitence asked, as Maria ran happy circles around the day room. "I—I can't help but feel that I owe you."

"You don't owe me anything," I said. "Stay here with Maria. If I do what I hope I'm about to do, I want you two to be together when it all goes down."

CHAPTER 31

Mom and Dad had dragged the sofa to the center of the room and flipped it like an animal carcass. They seemed to be trying to disassemble it, with Dad's car keys as their only tools.

In the main hall, Janie had calmed herself enough to walk around, testing the walls and looking for a way out. She'd peeled away huge sections of the wallpaper, to no avail. She tried the remaining doors that lined the hall, but they were all locked.

Suddenly, she cut short her inspection and turned around.

"I know someone's here," she whispered. "You're trying to help me, aren't you?"

I nearly fell through the wall.

"Who are you?" she asked.

Collecting myself, I walked past her to the far side of the rug, and in one quick motion, I pulled the corner up—just enough to reveal my name scratched into the floor.

DELIA.

The rug flumped back down disapprovingly.

My sister was quiet for a long time.

"I knew it was you," she said at last. "Can you help me get out of here?"

I could, actually. In fact, I needed her to come with me—it was part of the plan. Passing through the wall, I unlocked the door that would lead her to the service hallway and down to the basement.

Janie heard the click and pushed the door open, wonder and wariness in her eyes.

She followed me through, trailing a few feet behind, waiting as I unlocked and carefully opened each subsequent door. We passed Rosie and Posie, staring as always, and I paused.

"Thanks for stealing all their stuff, guys," I said. "Really helpful."

The one on the right blushed, and the one on the left scowled.

"Have you ever thought of maybe using your powers for good instead of annoyingness?" I asked. "Never mind. I have to go."

Then I opened the one that led down into the basement.

"What are you doing down there?" the girl who had blushed asked.

"Trying to save us all," I said. "You can thank me later."

The girls vanished.

Janie hesitated at the top of the steps, and I didn't blame her. The basement smelled like a dead skunk had been rotting in there for a year. The dead shadow creature, its smoky form significantly paler than before, was piled near the center of the room. And then there was Florence, still trapped.

Not much of a welcome wagon.

"You!" Florence struck at the barrier between us, but she was helpless to escape. "I'll kill her! I'll tear you both to shreds!"

"Yeah, yeah, go ahead and try," I said.

She snarled and filled up with light, but she was powerless against the six-inch-wide pile of salt. Still, her manic, evil energy added a heavy feeling to the air, and I could tell by the way Janie's shoulders hunched closer to her ears that it was having an effect on her.

Careful not to draw my sister's attention in Florence's direction, I knocked over a few small objects on my way to the back of the room, to indicate that she should follow me.

Janie stopped, considering a scratched-up metal box attached to the pillar at the bottom of the stairs. Finally, she popped it open and flipped a switch inside. Dim light spilled from the old bulbs hanging from the ceiling at random intervals.

"Probably should have looked for that last time," she said.

Then she followed me.

The old incinerator room, walled-off with bricks and guarded by a barred metal door, was off to the right, positioned perfectly so that its leaking chimneys would permit the evil fog to penetrate the rooms at the front of the house. I took a few steps toward it before noticing that my sister wasn't behind me. I turned to look for her, and saw that she was frozen in place.

There was something wrong with this room, and she sensed it.

But I couldn't afford to lose her trust now.

"Delia, is it really you?" she asked into the air. "Can you find some way to tell me it's you? Knock twice?"

I reached for the nearest hard object, an old crate, and

tried to knock on it. But my knuckles passed silently through the wood.

Janie was asking for a specific message. I couldn't do that.

I had no way to tell her it was me.

"I'm sorry. It's just, I . . . I don't know if I can do this," Janie said. "It kind of feels like those slasher movies you and Nic used to let me watch with you. What if you're not even Delia? What if you're something evil pretending to be her? And you're luring me to my doom? Give me a sign. Any sign."

She wanted a signal, but what if I couldn't send her one?

Of course, she was completely right—I could be any ghost, misleading her, tricking her.

We were so close, and the situation was so frustrating that, without thinking, I turned and knocked over the nearest knock-overable object.

It happened to be a mop.

Janie gasped.

Yes! *A mop.* I remembered her housewife costume from Halloween and searched the surrounding shelves for the other objects I needed.

Almost giddily, I knocked a stocky-looking metal teapot off the shelf. It hit the ground and bounced heavily one time, then rolled onto its side.

My sister held her breath.

Next, I swept an entire stack of frying pans to the floor with a deafening *crash!*

Then there was silence.

Janie swallowed hard and balled her hands into determined fists. "All right, Delia," she said. "What now?"

I felt a swell of joy and had to remind myself that this wasn't the time for celebrating. I walked across the room and opened the door to the incinerator room.

Janie came and stood in the doorway. We were practically shoulder to shoulder, not that she'd know it.

The incinerator itself hulked in the corner, a six-foot-tall, eight-foot-long, and six-foot-wide fortified box of iron and brick. The air smelled stale and faintly burnt—a sweet blend of toast and smoke.

I stepped inside, flipped up the lever on the incinerator's two-by-two-foot-square metal hatch, and pulled it open.

Janie's eyes went wide. "No way, Delia! I'm not going in there."

There was a petulance in her voice that made me feel like we were just two normal sisters trying to figure out how to glue together a broken vase before our parents came home.

"I never said you had to," I said. "Nobody's going inside the incinerator."

But when I opened the door and peered down into the belly of the structure, I could see nothing but pitch darkness. Which meant that one of us *was* going in, and since I was the only one of us who could produce her own light, it was probably going to be me. Better me than my sister—but still.

"Delia?" Janie asked, stepping close. "Are you going in? Be careful. Are you sure it's safe?"

Nope. Not sure at all.

What, Delia, you're going to give up now?

Of course not. There was no fire in the incinerator. It wasn't even hot. It was just dark.

298

I repeated those facts to myself—*not hot, just dark*—as I moved through the thick brick wall.

"Are you okay?" Janie asked.

I looked around, a very bad feeling rising in my stomach.

I was not, in fact, okay.

I was surrounded by fire.

The flames reached as high as my head. They looked like normal fire in the way they jumped and leapt, but instead of being bright orange, they were the fathomless, velvety black you'd expect to find in a black hole. And, like a black hole, they devoured the light that radiated off of my ghostly form, until parts of myself were missing and I started to get pretty worried that I was being burned alive by the dark flames without even knowing it.

But no. If I moved my arm, the invisible parts became visible again—even if only for a moment. And I didn't feel any burning—not from heat, anyway. They were actually quite cold, like on a frosty night, when the wind goes right through your clothes.

Any relief I felt was only temporary, though. Because immediately I was faced with the reality of being surrounded by dark flames and having no way to put them out except apparently spilling the blood of my little sister, which—call me crazy—I had a feeling she wouldn't be totally cool with.

And then disaster struck.

"Delia, I'm coming in!" Before I could stop her, Janie climbed up and propelled herself through the incinerator hatch, landing clumsily inside with me. "What . . . What's happening in here? What's . . . Is this *fire*?"

299

Her voice faded out as she held her hand in the light that spilled in through the hatch, studying the way the flames made it vanish.

"Am I dead now?" she asked. "Am I a ghost?"

To be honest, I wasn't sure. I stepped between her and the opening. "Can you see me? Can you hear me?"

She looked around wildly. "Delia? Are you still here?"

I practically crumpled with relief. If she were dead, she'd have been able to hear me. And the oily smoke didn't seem to be gathering around us—yet. At least there was that.

"Okay, this was a bad idea," she said. "I'm willing to admit that."

Janie stepped toward the hatch and tried to climb back out.

Then she grunted in confusion and looked down toward her feet.

I knelt closer, using my glow to see what was happening.

The flames had begun to wrap themselves around Janie's legs, like a mummy's bandages. What's more, they'd begun to wind up my legs, too—trapping me just as effectively as my sister.

My sister let out a scream and tried to slap the tendrils away, but it didn't work.

"Delia?" she cried. "Are you still here?"

"Of course I am," I said.

From the darkness came a succession of pitiful sniffles. Then one big sniffle. "Don't panic," Janie whispered to herself, a hint of steel in her voice. "Just don't panic."

I was overcome with love and admiration for my brave little warrior of a sister. Maybe I'd have been nicer to her, all those years ago, if I'd known that a fighter's spirit resided inside her. I should have encouraged her, nurtured her, tried to bring out her hidden strength—instead of looking down on her for being different from the rest of us.

But she'd become this person on her own—and maybe, in some weird way, it had been my death that brought those qualities to life.

"Wait!" Janie said, her voice alive with hope. "Maybe I can . . . how did it go? By the authority of nature . . . by the forces of—um, creation. By righteousness and . . . and . . . Aw, *shoot*."

I held my breath.

"The power of good!" she burst out. "Through the power of good, I bind you, I bind you, I—*mmph*."

Before she could finish speaking the incantation, the flames had wound all the way up to her mouth, high enough to gag her, holding her words in.

She struggled and grunted, but it was impossible. She couldn't speak. I wondered for how long she'd even be able to breathe.

Could *I* do it?

I squeezed my eyes shut and tried to remember the words. The supple fingers of flame reached my waist, and I knew I was almost out of time.

I had to go for it.

"*By-the-authority-of-nature-by-the-forces-of-creation-by-righteousness-and-through-the-power-of-good—*" The flames raced up my body now, trying to reach my mouth, so I spat the words out as fast as I could—"*IbindyouIbindyouIbindyou!*"

It worked.

Janie gulped in a huge breath of air as the flames fell away from her mouth. "I bind you!" she yelled.

"It's cool," I said. "I took care of it."

Reaching down, I found I could peel the flames off my body as if they were strips of pantyhose. Then I reached over and pulled off the ones from Janie's legs, too. She realized what was happening and started to help.

"You're still here," she said softly. "I knew you'd stay."

"Like I'd leave you," I said. "Come on, let's get out of here."

She was already climbing out. I followed her, and then we both stood staring back into the yawning darkness. The dark fire was subdued for the moment, but it still burned—and I was positive it was struggling and fighting to break free of the spell, just as the shadow creature had.

"We totally failed," I said. "Awesome."

"We're going to figure it out," Janie said.

Suddenly, the silence of the room was interrupted by a *thwack thwack thwack* sound coming from the stairs.

My sister took a few tentative steps closer, to see if someone was there. I hurried ahead of her, in case we'd been joined by someone unpleasant.

But there was no one—just a book, lying haphazardly on the floor after apparently being bowled down the steps.

As I walked over and looked at its shiny silver spine, I heard a pair of high-pitched giggles from the hallway.

It was *The Selected Works of Lord Percival Lindley 1757–1789.*

Unbelievable. They'd actually helped for once.

"Thank you, Rosie and Posie!" I called.

Janie reached carefully for the book and flipped it over in one swift motion, her eyes already searching the page.

It had fallen open to the black fire poem.

"Read it," I said. "Please, read this page."

But my sister made a move to turn the page. Summoning all my strength, I reached down and pinned the paper in place so she couldn't do it.

For a confused moment, she tried again. Then she understood.

She leaned over the page and began to silently read. A moment later, she inhaled a little "ah!" sound, and I knew she'd found the poem. After reading it over, she sat up. "I get the dark fire, but the 'blood of light'? What's the 'blood of light'?"

She reread the poem.

"It's about innocence," she said out loud. "It's supposed to be the blood of an innocent person. And you thought I could be the innocent person . . ."

"Yes, yes, yes," I said. "Smart girl. So, so smart."

But Janie slumped over, pressing her hand over her eyes. Then she swallowed hard and looked up.

"I'm sorry, Delia," she said. "I would do it, but it wouldn't work. I'm not—innocent."

If I could have grabbed her by the shoulders and shaken her, I would have. "Stop. Just stop it. You had nothing to do with my death—"

"I did it myself!" she burst out. "I did it; I put the straps on my own legs and said it was you because I was trying to get you in trouble . . . I was such a bad person."

She was talking about the day I died—when she'd been

strapped into the bed. I tried to recall the details of the incident. She'd been asleep, and some evil spirit from the house had trapped her in the bed.

"I did it." She was wretched, her voice empty. "I did my ankles and then I slipped my hands through the wrist ones and . . . and then I blamed you. That's why they locked the door to your room. Then you *died*."

This logic probably made sense to her fifteen-year-old brain. Probably when one pulls a stupid prank, and gets one's sister in trouble for it, and something tragic happens to one's sister, it's natural for one to blame oneself. I could understand how, to a living human, with—no offense—a somewhat limited perspective on reality and existence, this might make sense.

But to me, it was utter nonsense.

"That's not why I died," I said. "Are you kidding me? This house was never going to let me leave."

She hunched over, sobbing. "I'm sorry, Delia. I'm sorry."

My impatience was close to bubbling over, and in the mash-up of emotions, some distant big-sister part of my brain took over.

I grabbed her by the shoulders, and she gasped.

"Now, listen up," I said. "I wasn't the best big sister. I didn't look out for you the way I should have. But if you think I'm going to let you sit here and throw yourself a pity party while an evil force tries to murder you, you're deluded. You weren't a bad person. You were a twerp. There is a *world* of difference."

Her eyes bored straight into mine. "Delia?" she whispered.

"Now, I'm really sorry about this, because you're going to have to get a tetanus shot," I said. Then I dragged her toward the incinerator, grabbed her hand, wrestled one of her fingers away from the others, and scraped it on a sharp piece of metal sticking out from the door.

"Ouch!" she squealed. But she didn't try to get away.

Apparently, all those times I wrestled her into submission were in preparation for this, the day she would need to recognize my particular headlock style and not struggle out of it.

"Okay," she said, grabbing her arm away and swatting at me. "Fine."

A spot of blood was beginning to pool on the tip of her wounded finger.

"I need to just drop it in there, right?" She reached her hand just inside the incinerator, pressed her thumb against the cut finger, and squeezed.

As the drop of blood began to fall, time slowed down.

The blood hovered in the air, and my sister's face was an unmoving mask of determination.

Shivers traveled over me like a cloak, and I knew we were no longer alone.

I turned around.

The basement behind me was filled with smoke, swirling and churning at a barely perceptible speed.

And out of the smoke came a voice: *"Delia . . ."*

I moved myself to block my sister—as if anything I did could prevent the fog from invading her body and soul.

I expected a shadow creature to leap out at me like a monstrous predator, ready to tear me to pieces.

But instead of a vicious attack, what came next was the slow, simple sound of footsteps.

A silver-haired man walked out of the mist, wearing a plain black suit with a crisp white collar and a red silk necktie. He was clean-shaven, and something about his easy confidence made me think of an old-fashioned movie star. On his hands were white gloves. With one hand he easily removed the rounded black hat from his head, and a moment later it disappeared into thin air.

Then he gave me a little bow and a polite smile.

"Delia," he said warmly. "What a pleasure to meet you at last, my dear."

And there it was. The voice I'd been hearing since the day I died.

I tensed as he came closer. Noticing this, he stopped and held his hands up as if to show me he was unarmed.

"I am your great-great-great-great—oh, I don't know. Let's just say grandfather. I'm your grandfather, Maxwell Piven." His voice was deep and welcoming. Trustworthy. A home-for-the-holidays kind of voice. It was hard to believe he was the father of Penitence, whose gritty plainness was the stark opposite of this effortless self-assurance.

He appeared to be charming and courteous. His eyes showed no hint of the psychotic control freak I would have expected, and he (unlike me) didn't seem poised to strike at any moment.

"May we have a little talk?" he asked.

"Be my guest," I said, crossing my arms in front of my chest. His easy, casual manner made me uncomfortable and self-conscious. I would have preferred a harsh taskmaster or a vicious bully—someone I could fight. But he didn't seem interested in fighting.

"Ah, but *you* are *my* guest." He leaned casually against one of the tall shelves and proceeded to start pulling off his gloves, one finger at a time. "And that is why we need to speak. I confess that I am . . . troubled. While I do feel quite a bit of admiration for what you're doing—what you *think* you're doing—I'm concerned that it may have unintended consequences. And I see that you're concerned, as well."

I didn't understand what he meant, and my expression must have telegraphed my cluelessness. He gestured around the basement.

"*You* control your own sense of time," he said. "Judging by the fact that you've created a distortion in this moment, I can only guess that you were apprehensive about your course of action. It's understandable that you must be dreading the choice ahead of you."

"What choice?" I asked.

"You face a terrible decision, Delia," he said, frowning. "It was very clever, employing the blood of an innocent to quench the dark fire. I'm gratified that you show an appreciation for Lord Lindley, a truly fine man and poet. But the time has come now to choose, dear child . . . Who will survive?"

"What do you mean?" I asked.

He sighed, as if he was regretful to have to deliver difficult news. "When Jane's blood touches the dark fire, it will ignite a fuel that has been accruing for nearly one hundred and fifty years. This old incinerator simply won't be capable of containing the explosion. Therefore, you have two options, the first being to pull your sister away and seal the hatch closed. It will hold, sending the bulk of the force upward through the chimneys, which as you and I both know are already compromised. These particular chimneys go through the wall bordering the lobby—and unfortunately, their weakest point is located just on the other side of the room in which your dear mother and father are, at this very moment, desperately trying to reach your sister. The faulty chimney will no doubt fail at that exact point, effectively destroying the lobby and everything contained within it, including your parents." He paused. "Your other choice is simply to leave the hatch open, thereby sacrificing your sister in the resultant blast, but saving your parents."

There was a long silence during which I tried to figure out whether he was lying and came to the conclusion that he wasn't.

His voice became gentler. "I don't mean to offer advice, but in your place, I would save your sister. Your parents would most certainly prefer to perish in order to spare her life."

"I can just get my sister to safety," I said. "I'll take her out of the basement—how hard is that?"

"Ah," he said softly. "But you see, you are at a crossroads—as you always are when you distort time. One must *choose* at a crossroads; one cannot simply plunge forward, off the path. Simply put, your subconscious would return time to its normal state before you were able to get your sister to safety. Of course, you're more than welcome to try. But even if you do, I would still close the hatch. As I said, I believe your parents would much rather your sister survive than themselves."

"Shut up!" I said, gritting my teeth. "You're evil—of course you're going to come here and torment me—"

"Torment?" he repeated, a sympathetic lilt in his voice. "Oh no. Delia, I've come to help you. I bring an alternative to both of those tragic outcomes."

The room seemed to be growing warmer, as if the supernatural smoke was already being transformed into blisteringly hot *real* smoke.

"I don't believe you," I said. "Why would you help me?"

"You're smart," he said. "And you show initiative, which I appreciate very much. My own daughter never quite did; her passivity gave her a lifetime of unhappiness. Therefore, I'm here to offer a compromise. One I think you'll agree is exceedingly fair."

"What?" I asked.

"All you must do is reach over and intercept that drop of blood before it makes contact with the fire," he said, delicately demonstrating in pantomime. "Catch it in your hand and drop it anywhere *outside* of the incinerator."

"Why should I do that?" I asked.

"Because if you do, I'll let your family live. I'll release them from captivity here . . . and I'll release you as well." He stepped closer, hand pressed to his heart. "I know that your fondest wish is to return to your home and live among them. To belong. To be loved. This way, your wish will be a reality."

"Like you'd let me go," I said. "After you *murdered* me to make me stay."

He laughed then, a genteel little laugh, and touched his lips with the spotless white handkerchief from his jacket pocket. "My dear, you must believe me when I tell you that, had I known the extent of your inquisitive nature, I would have reconsidered that decision. You're quite a match for me, and I don't mind admitting it. It does reflect well on the family, after all."

I felt a creeping sense of disgust, watching him stand there like he was posing for a magazine ad for ascots or whatever, all while he spoke so casually of life and death and destruction.

And yet, his offer—if it was genuine—did seem shockingly fair. All he wanted was me out of his hair. For that, he was willing to let my entire family escape unharmed. Not to mention that Janie knew I existed now. Who was to say she and I wouldn't find some way to communicate? I could live with her, be her friend. Like some oddball sitcom: *My Sister, the Ghost.*

All for the price of . . . what? Of *not* causing an explosion that would be the death of my sister or parents—or possibly all of them? Because even if I closed the hatch, Janie would still have to find her way out of a giant burning building.

I could take the deal, get my parents and Janie out of the house, and go. Leave with them. Never come back.

It seemed ridiculously clear. What was I going to do, let them die?

Take the deal.

I looked at Maxwell, who didn't seem overeager to hear my response; he stood with perfect patience, rocking back slightly on his heels.

"Are you *really* Maxwell?" I asked.

The question surprised him, though he tried to hide it. "Who else would I be?"

I shrugged. "You tell me."

He narrowed his eyes and shook his head.

"Because I don't think you're Maxwell," I said. "You're too friendly."

He laughed. "Well . . . thank you? Though I don't suppose that's a compliment."

"I don't think Maxwell would have negotiated with me," I said. "I think he would have tried to move the blood himself. But you can't do that, can you . . .? Because you're just smoke and mirrors."

A shock of darkness passed through his eyes, and the corner of his mouth twitched.

"You're only pretending to be confident," I said. "The real Maxwell wouldn't have been afraid of me."

He didn't answer, but his body shimmered helplessly for a split second.

"You're not even a real ghost," I said. "You're only something horrible, pretending to be a ghost. Without your shadows and smoke, you're weak. You're not even strong enough to touch me. You can't stop the blood, and you can't stop me . . . no matter what I decide to do."

The expression on his face shifted, but as it did, his whole face loosened, like melting wax, as if he were unable to control the mask he hid behind. He tried to snap it back, but it was a clumsy effort. The face I was looking at no longer resembled Maxwell's.

"If you could stop me," I said, stepping toward him, "you'd grab my arm before I could slap you."

Then I drew back my hand and smacked him. Part of me had expected a strong grip on my wrist, a brutal counterblow.

But my hand went right through the smoke that formed his face and sent little eddies spinning through it.

"See? I'm stronger than you," I said. "I'm a pretty powerful ghost, actually."

He didn't reply—he couldn't, because his face had lost its form. It was like the signal was scrambled.

That was fine. I didn't need to talk anymore. I knew what I was going to do.

But it had to be done quickly.

My parents and sister weren't going to die today. But I also wasn't going to run away and abandon the other souls who'd been trapped here for a century or more. I wasn't going to leave this contaminated building standing, hungry, while more innocent victims were delivered to it like a takeout meal.

For every member of my own family I saved, how many others would die? If I took Maxwell's deal, how many more best friends, sisters, brothers, mothers, and fathers would suffer for my choice?

No. It was time to fix this. I had to.

Because this was my business.

This was *my* house.

"Go," I said, turning away. "Your time here is done."

The sound behind me was like a cross between a tornado and a scream, and when I looked back over my shoulder, the fog in the room had begun to take form. Maxwell was dissolving, and other bodies were forming from the smoke—an army of shadow creatures, twenty of them at least.

But they weren't on my time line, so I didn't concern myself with that fight.

I gently took hold of my sister and pulled her away from the incinerator, positioning her behind a brick-lined pillar near the door. Mindful of Maxwell's warning, I was unwilling to chance a time speed-up by carrying her to the hall. I'd felt the truth in his speech about decisions and crossroads.

The shadow monsters were almost fully developed.

I closed the incinerator hatch, pulling the lever upright into its locked position, and walked through the brick wall. Inside, I used my own blue light to find the droplet of blood hovering in midair. I scooped it into the palm of my hand, cradling it to my chest as if it were something tiny and precious—which, of course, it was.

Time was going to ramp back up at any millisecond, and I needed to be ready.

I fell to my knees.

I was going to use my own body to contain the explosion. I'd probably be blasted into bits of ectoplasm, but that wasn't enough to scare me. What could I possibly be afraid of—pain? Oblivion? Even my old pet fear of being forgotten shrank to inconsequentiality in the face of the alternative, which was letting the house have everything it wanted. Letting its ruthless power grow, unchecked, while I stood by and did nothing.

I crouched lower. The fire, still bound by my incantation, strained helplessly to climb up my legs. I held my breath and leaned over. If the blood hit the fire before I had a chance to cover it with my body, the result would be catastrophic. The blood had to touch the fire at the exact moment at which I threw myself on top of it.

I'm strong. I can do this.

I let myself fall.

As gravity pulled me down, I gently turned my hand so that the blood would make contact first.

Time sped up again, and the black flames filled my view. I crashed down into them, noticing for the briefest fraction of a moment that they were as soft as a feather bed.

There was a spark in my chest—the spark of the fire and the blood making contact.

It felt exactly like a heartbeat.

And then I didn't feel anything.

It was so simple, so quick, so natural . . .

Almost as if my whole life had been leading up to this moment.

CHAPTER 32

What followed could have taken a thousandth of a second or a hundred years. I didn't have any way to gauge the passage of time. There was no pain, no fear, no actual sensation at all except the feeling of being . . . changed.

"Come on, then. Are you planning to lie about all day?"

The voice was British, annoyingly full of itself, and maybe the most wonderful sound I'd ever heard.

"Eliza?" I asked without moving.

Someone lifted me and set me upright, and I found, to my surprise, that I could see.

And that I was still in the incinerator.

In front of me was Eliza's semi-ghostly figure—ghostly in the sense that she clearly wasn't a living, corporeal being, but also distinctly *not* a ghost—not in the way I knew ghosts, at least (and I knew a thing or two about ghosts by then).

Instead of a pale blue glow, Eliza emitted white light, bright enough to fill the small metal chamber and illuminate its sooty walls and floor, as well as the few charred scraps of trash that had survived its last run.

"Cheerio," said Eliza, grinning. "Didn't think you'd see me again so soon, did you?"

"Did it work?" I asked.

"Seems to have done," Eliza said.

"Did I blow up my family?"

"Not even one little bit."

"Oh, that's really good news," I said. I felt raw and slightly stiff, like I'd just woken from a very long sleep.

Then it sank in: Eliza was here. All of her. Perfectly unharmed.

"What's going on?" I asked. "What happened to me? Am I still a ghost? Am I still dead?"

"No, you've been magically returned to life," Eliza said. "Of course you're still dead. Don't get overexcited."

"But what are you doing here?" I asked. "You . . . moved on, didn't you?"

Her smile, though small, was highly pleased—like she had a happy secret. "I did," she said. "As have you. Which means that we're free."

"To go?" I asked.

"Or stay," Eliza said, frowning. "But I don't see why you would. I waited for you, but now we've no one left to wait for."

"How did you know to wait for me?" I asked.

She raised her eyebrows. "Your ability to get into trouble left me with no doubt that you'd be blowing yourself to smithereens before too long. And I was right, wasn't I?"

"But my family—" I passed through the incinerator wall

and found the basement bathed in blinding white light. After a moment, I realized that it was *my* white light.

"Your family—any of the living—are no longer your concern," Eliza said. "That's one big difference. Actually, you have no concerns at all. If you take a moment to rest, you'll feel it— the calm. I know I'm a bit of a cynic, but even I can say it's very lovely."

"But I need to find them," I said.

"Delia . . ." Eliza said as I walked to the stairs.

Except, *walked* would be the wrong word. Unlike when I was a regular ghost, I felt no connection to the physical world. No breeze went through me, no reverberations of my human life remained—no fluttering, nervous stomach, burning eyes, or aching head. I simply looked where I wanted to go, and then I was there. So I found myself at the bottom of the steps.

First I saw Janie, crawling up the stairs, the sleeve of her shirt over her face like a mask.

Then I noticed something I hadn't seen when I'd first looked around the room and been blinded by my own vivid glare.

Smoke. Billowing clouds of thick, sooty smoke.

The room was on fire.

I had kept the incinerator from exploding, but the house was still going to burn to the ground. And I could only presume that at that very moment the faulty chimney was leaking toxic fumes into the room where my parents had been, not to mention the halls and back passages they would most definitely navigate in their search for my sister.

"Eliza!" I called. "Come help!"

I went to Janie's side, intending to help her, but when I reached her, no matter how I tried, there was nothing I could do. I couldn't lift her or drag her upstairs. I couldn't touch the door or unlock it or open it.

"What's going on?!" I cried. "What's the point of this if I can't help her? What's the point of any of it?"

"You're not meant to help her," Eliza said, her voice low and firm. "I'm sorry, Delia, but this is outside of your influence."

I stared at her in horror. How could she be so *calm*? "But my sister's going to die!"

"Well, if she does," she replied, "you've ensured that she won't be stuck here, in the house. And that's enough."

"That's not enough!" I shouted. "I'm not going to float around here and watch my sister die! That was the whole *point*!"

Eliza stood in front of me and took hold of my arms. It didn't feel like being held by another person but rather like being locked into place by an immovable force. "If it were your business to save your sister's life, you wouldn't be here," she said. "Do you understand? There's a plan, Delia. Everyone has a place in it. And you've done your part. There's nothing else you can do."

"Impossible," I said. "I'll go get my parents—"

"They can't see you," she said. "Or hear you. I'm telling you. Everything you were intended to accomplish has been done."

The absolute nonnegotiability of what she was saying rang too true for me to bother debating.

Her mouth turned down in a frown. "I'm very sorry, truly. I know you like to change things, but you won't change this. You've got to accept it."

"You don't know that," I said. "How could you know that?"

"I know it," she said. "If you'd stand still for a minute, you'd know it, too."

But I couldn't stand still and let some mythical veil of knowledge slowly descend over me. Not while my family was in danger.

Being at one with the universe would just have to wait.

Janie coughed as she reached the top of the stairs, then stretched up toward the doorknob and tried to turn it—but it wouldn't turn. The bolt was locked. She started to get to her feet but had to duck down to take another huge gasp of air.

I reached for the bolt, but even as I did so, I knew it was pointless.

My sister gagged and doubled over, trying desperately to get another breath, enough air to sustain herself.

It didn't work.

She went limp, slumping unconsciously against the door.

"Oh my God," I said.

"You needn't worry," Eliza said. "She won't suffer."

So was this really how it was supposed to be? After everything that had happened—was my sister really supposed to die?

And yet, standing there with my heart slowly breaking, I did feel the beginning of the peace Eliza had hinted at—a feeling that what would happen now must happen.

Suddenly, a figure appeared through the door, interrupting my reverie—Penitence.

I'd never been so glad to see a ghost before.

She unlocked the bolt and pulled the door open.

"Come on!" she called into the hallway.

Maria appeared behind her mother. "Where is she? Where's Delia?"

"Child, we haven't time to think about that. Help me."

Then a nurse appeared at the doorway, the grouchy one I'd encountered in the kitchen so long ago—she was the Nurse Carlson who'd been kind to Maria.

Now she looked gentle and industrious as she, Penitence, and Maria surrounded my sister, trying to lift her. They were able to get her up and into the hall—but just barely. And each of them was significantly paler for the effort.

"You're too weak," said a voice from below.

Penitence turned to look down at Florence, who remained trapped in her circle of salt.

"You're not strong ghosts, any of you," Florence said. "You won't be able to carry her. But I could help you."

"No, thank you!" Penitence snapped.

They bent once again to try to lift my sister. This time, they failed to get her off the ground.

"I'm tellin' you," Florence said. "I'll help."

"You've already tried to kill her," Penitence said. "Why should we trust you?"

"Because what choice do you have? And what could I possibly do now?" Florence's voice shrank. "Maybe this is my last chance to do something good. I'd like the chance to do *something* good."

There was a pause, and then Maria scampered down the stairs and over to Florence's enclosure. She reached down and, with one grand swipe of her arm, made a break in the salt line.

Together they ran back to Janie's unconscious body, and with Florence's help, picked my sister up off the floor.

"Come on," Nurse Carlson said. "Through the kitchen."

But as they started down the hall, Rosie and Posie, in their matching nightgowns, came running from that direction. "The kitchen's burning!" one of them cried.

"We'll go through the lobby," Penitence said. "It's farther, but perhaps it's not on fire yet."

I followed close behind as the ghosts carried my sister through the main hall. Smoke had begun to seep through the doors and swell in dark clouds near the ceiling. The air was warm.

"Hurry, ladies," Nurse Carlson urged. "Don't lag. Almost there now."

The door between the lobby and hall had been restored—probably when the black flames had been extinguished—and my parents were on the other side, struggling to break the lock.

"Set her down, quickly!" Nurse Carlson ordered. Gently, the four ghosts lowered Janie to the floor. Penitence turned the bolt and my parents rushed through. Mom knelt by Janie and felt for a pulse.

"She's breathing!" Mom shouted.

Without wasting a moment, Dad scooped Janie into his arms, and he and Mom raced out the front doors.

"Let's go," Penitence said. "We've got to get out of here."

She, the nurse, and Florence started to follow my parents, but Maria stayed put.

"Maria!" Penitence called. "Come on!"

"But there are more ghosts," Maria said. "Lots more. On

the third floor. They're trapped. Or they think they are. We need to go help them."

Penitence came and crouched in front of her. "My dear, they'll be all right. We're all going to be all right. But we might as well not be inside the house. We might as well save ourselves the pain."

Maria's stubborn chin jutted up toward her mother. "I'm not afraid of pain," she said. "I think being scared is worse than being hurt. I'm sorry, Mother. I'm going back. You can come if you like."

Penitence hesitated, then nodded and took hold of the little hand. And as they headed back into the hallway, Nurse Carlson turned and followed them as well.

Florence stood in the doorway, her hair flowing wildly behind her, looking strangely lost. She was a ghost without a cause, dazed by her sudden freedom. Even her hatred was useless to her at this point.

With a start, I noticed a person running from outside into the lobby. Theo. He stopped in front of Florence.

"Does anyone inside need help?" he asked.

She stared at him, still dazed, and then suddenly woke up. "I think so," she said. "On the third floor."

"Then come on," he said to her. And they both went after the others.

"You all right?" Eliza's voice startled me. She hadn't left my side the whole time, but I'd been too focused on Janie to notice. "Of course you are. Now, let's go see your family."

We walked outside, the building smoking behind us.

My parents were loading Janie into the backseat of Dad's car. Mom climbed in with her, while Dad got into the driver's seat.

Without thinking, I sprinted over and hurled myself into the car.

To be honest, I didn't expect it to work. But I landed neatly on the front passenger seat.

As we drove down the driveway, I was in shock.

The force that had bound me to the house was gone, so I was free. I could go anywhere I wanted. A dream I hadn't even dared to dream was coming true.

I was going to go home with my family.

I turned and looked back at the house, where Penitence, Maria, Florence, Theo, and Nurse Carlson were shepherding out small groups of ghosts, most of them in gray Piven Institute nightgowns. Eliza stood next to them, watching me go.

I waved good-bye to her.

Then I turned to look over at my family. Janie coughed, Mom stroked my sister's face, and Dad drove like he was in a police chase. We were fifty feet from the gate.

Time slowed down.

In the wind from the open window, Mom's hair moved through the air in slow motion, like a beautiful jellyfish. My father leaned back in his seat and began to reach back to pat Janie's hand. I ached with love for them.

Finally, I could be happy again. I could live out my days at home. They would never forget me.

Janie knew I existed now. She would talk to me, and . . .

And try to look for me. Try to reach me.

Every day of her life, she would spend in constant longing, trying to communicate with someone who would always be just out of her reach. She would sense me, dream about me . . . It would consume her, an ever-present reminder of the worst thing that had ever happened to her.

She wouldn't go to college, because she would feel too guilty that I never had a chance to go. She would spend her whole life trying not to do anything that would make me envious or sad. Everything would be about me and the chance that she might find a way to make me just a shade more real, to bring me back to her, even if it was only an illusion.

But I wasn't real, was I? And I wasn't coming back.

We were nearing the edge of the property.

This was my final crossroads.

I knew that if I wanted to, I could leave with my family.

But I also knew . . . I couldn't.

"I want you to know," I said to them, "that you are the best family a girl could have ever asked for. Dad, you were always there for me. You answered every question I ever asked you honestly, even if you didn't want to. Mom, you were my rock. You loved me even when I was awful to you. You took care of me every minute of my life. You were my first love."

I turned to my sister. "And, Janie . . . Janie, my bright, fierce, amazing baby sister. You're so ridiculously smart. And strong. And loyal. You're a hero. You're going to change the world."

Time sped up. Inexplicably, Dad slammed his foot on the brake, and the car stopped.

They were all silent.

"Just wait a second," Dad said, his voice gruff with wonder. "Listen . . ."

They listened.

"I love you all," I said. "I love you so much."

They all looked at one another, their eyes wide, in a triangle of *did you hear something?*

"It's time for me to go now," I said.

And then I climbed out of the car.

I watched them drive away.

CHAPTER 33

As I walked back up the driveway, I could see the hungry flames through the faraway windows, devouring everything inside. In the distance, sirens blared, but I knew they'd never save the building. Rotburg was too small a town to fight a fire of this scale on short notice, and besides that, the fire was tearing through the house as if it had been waiting a hundred and fifty years for the chance.

More ghosts were outside now, standing in clumps and staring up at our former home. There were women of every age—teens and old ladies, wearing everything from drab hospital-issue nightgowns to elaborate velvet robes. There was also Theo, standing among them.

And they were all . . . changing.

Each one of them seemed to glow around their edges with a silvery outline. The ones who were hunched had begun to stand straighter. The ones who'd worn haunted, faraway looks seemed to be returning to awareness.

The edges of my vision were beginning to blur.

"Delia!"

Theo could see me? He left the crowd and came walking over—unhurried as usual.

He was glowing, too.

"What did you do?" he asked, a broad smile on his face. "It was you, wasn't it? It had to be you."

"I guess," I said. "I thought it was time somebody took care of the problem."

He looked at me, and there was a gentleness, an openness, in his eyes. As if some great weight had been lifted from his shoulders. "Do you . . . Can I do something I've been wanting to do for a long time?"

"Okay," I said.

He moved closer, wrapped his arms around me, and kissed me sweetly.

It was the kiss from the end of an amazing first date. A good-bye with a hello attached to it. An *I hope we meet again* kiss. A *had circumstances been different this would have been only the first of many kisses* kiss.

It was brief, but it ignited some new sense of joy in me, some moment of letting go, of realizing that Landon was never the love of my life, and that was okay—maybe I didn't have one yet. Maybe I never would.

But if I had, a kiss like this one might have been how it started.

Theo pulled away and cocked his head. "On to a new adventure. Perhaps we'll meet somewhere else along the path."

"I hope so," I said.

He took a few backward steps and started to disappear.

Right before he vanished, he smiled at me and waved. I waved back. Then I kept making my way toward the house.

A lovely little girl about ten years old, with thick dark-brown hair flowing over her shoulders, came running up to me.

"You came back!" she said. "She *said* you'd come back."

"Oh my—*Maria*?" I asked.

Maria beamed. "I'm pretty again, aren't I? Don't say it. I don't mind being pretty, but I don't want to turn vain."

Her face was perfect and her skin was smooth. Her body was whole and healthy.

"You've always been pretty," I said.

The fog was pushing in farther, giving everything an ethereal glow.

She glanced over at Penitence with the affectionate possessiveness only a child can have. "Mother says we're going someplace. All of us."

"I suppose we are," I said.

"Look," Maria said, pointing behind me.

Each of the ghosts around us was starting to fade—her subtle white glow gradually taking over her body and then dissolving into thin air. Every one of them wore a serene expression. The wretched women from the third floor, Nurse Carlson, Rosie and Posie . . . One by one, they disappeared.

"Where are we going?" Maria asked. "Will it be nice?"

Penitence came over and reached for Maria's hand. "It's a place where mothers and daughters are never apart."

"And sisters?" Maria asked, looking at me.

"Sisters and brothers, as well," Eliza said.

"And every little girl gets her own warm bed," I said. "And a soft blanket made just for her."

Maria clutched her mother's hand and nestled happily against her long, black skirt. Penitence reached out her other hand and took hold of mine. And I reached for Eliza's.

Eliza turned around, looking for someone.

"Florence," she called.

Florence, whose glow was subtler than ours, stood off to the side, studying her own hands in amazement. She looked up at Eliza, her cheeks streaked with tears.

"Come on, then," Eliza said. "Don't just stand there like a statue."

Florence came over and hovered just outside the circle for a moment, until Eliza grabbed her and pulled her in among us.

"But I've been so terrible," Florence said softly.

"Be that as it may," Eliza said. "It's done now, so you might as well be here with us. No need to leave anyone out."

The whole world seemed to be made of softly lustrous white light.

"What now?" Maria asked.

"Now we are here, together," said Penitence in a hushed voice. "We are all together."

The warm white light grew and expanded around us.

Maybe there was a kind of happily ever after, after all.

A feeling of exquisite contentment filled my heart and quieted the questions in my soul.

Peace, I thought, turning my face toward the sky. *Rest in peace.*

ACKNOWLEDGMENTS

With heaps and heaps of gratitude, I would like to acknowledge the existence and assistance of the following folks:

Christopher, my sweetest girl, G, Matthew Elblonk, Ashley Collom, Adam Shear, and everyone at DeFiore and Co., Aimee Friedman, David Levithan, Jennifer Ung, Emily Cullings, Yaffa Jaskoll, Charisse Meloto, Stephanie Smith, Jeremy West, Bess Braswell, Emily Morrow, Larry Decker, and the rest of the brilliant Scholastic team. Marisol, Mom, Helen, Dad, Ann, Jeff, Vicky, Juli, Kevin, Jillian, Rebekah, Zack, Robert, George, Duygu, Onur, Ali, Micah, Bethany, Terry, frousins, fraunts, fruncles, and other less neatly categorizable family members, long-suffering and oft-neglected friends, Soapboxies, H Club, lads, buns, my awesome UPS man, author buddies, bookseller buddies, librarian buddies, teacher buddies, amazing readers, their parents, and everyone who cares about the written word and acts on that impulse . . .

You are all seriously super great.

ABOUT THE AUTHOR

Katie Alender is the acclaimed author of several novels for young adults, including *Bad Girls Don't Die*; *From Bad to Cursed*; *As Dead as It Gets*; *Marie Antoinette, Serial Killer*; and *Famous Last Words*. A graduate of the Florida State University College of Motion Picture Arts, Katie now lives in Los Angeles with her husband, daughter, and dogs. She enjoys reading, sewing, gardening, and preparing and eating delicious high-calorie foods. To find out more about Katie, visit katiealender.com.